WEDDING DAY

The lines at the marriage license window in the Municipal Building had been too long. While they waited, he suggested they go up to the roof—"We can see for miles."

Fourteen stories above the street, they sat on the parapet edging the roof. He eased himself down, swung in front of her. His hands moved to her knees, cupped them.

"We'd better be going, hadn't we, darling?" she said.

"In a minute, baby. We still have time."

His hands moved down over the silken swell of her calves—then, with cobra speed, he ducked, hands streaking down to catch her heels—stepped back and straightened up, lifting her legs high.

For one frozen instant, their eyes met. . . .

A Kiss Before Dying

IRA LEVIN

PYRAMID BOOKS • NEW YORK

A KISS BEFORE DYING

A PYRAMID BOOK
Published by arrangement with Simon and Schuster

Simon and Schuster edition published February 1953
Pyramid edition published September 1964
   Sixth printing, November 1972

ISBN 0-515-02843-6

Printed in the United States of America

Pyramid Books are published by Pyramid Communications, Inc.
Its trademarks, consisting of the word "Pyramid" and the
portrayal of a pyramid, are registered in the
United States Patent Office.

Pyramid Communications, Inc., 919 Third Avenue,
New York, New York 10022

HIS PLANS HAD BEEN RUNNING SO BEAUTIFULLY, so goddamned beautifully, and now *she* was going to smash them all. Hate erupted and flooded through him, gripping his face with jaw-aching pressure. That was all right though; the lights were out.

And she, she kept on sobbing weakly in the dark, her cheek pressed against his bare chest, her tears and her breath burning hot. He wanted to push her away.

Finally his face relaxed. He put his arm around her and stroked her back. It was warm, or rather his hand was cold; all of him was cold, he discovered; his armpits were creeping with sweat and his legs were quivering the way they always did when things took a crazy turn and caught him helpless and unprepared. He lay still for a moment, waiting for the trembling to subside. With his free hand he drew the blanket up around her shoulders. "Crying isn't going to do any good," he told her gently.

Obediently, she tried to stop, catching her breath in long choking gasps. She rubbed her eyes with the worn binding of the blanket. "It's just . . . the holding it in for so long. I've known for days . . . weeks. I didn't want to say anything until I was sure . . ."

His hand on her back was warmer. "No mistake possible?" He spoke in a whisper, even though the house was empty. "No."

"How far?"

"Two months almost." She lifted her cheek from his chest, and in the dark he could sense her eyes on him. "What are we going to do?" she asked.

"You didn't give the doctor your right name, did you?"

"No. He knew I was lying though. It was awful . . ."

"If your father ever finds out . . ."

She lowered her head again and repeated the question, speaking against his chest. "What are we going to do?" She waited for his answer.

He shifted his position a bit, partially to give emphasis to what he was about to say, and partially in the hope that it would encourage her to move, for her weight on his chest had become uncomfortable.

"Listen, Dorrie," he said, "I know you want me to say we'll get married right away—tomorrow. And I want to marry you. More than anything else in the world. I swear to God I do." He paused, planning his words with care. Her body, curled against his, was motionless, listening. "But if we marry this way, me not even meeting your father first, and then a baby comes seven months later . . . You know what he'd do."

"He couldn't *do* anything," she protested. "I'm over eighteen. Eighteen's all you have to be out here. What could he do?"

"I'm not talking about an annulment or anything like that."

"Then what? What do you mean?" she appealed.

"The money," he said. "Dorrie, what kind of man is he? What did you tell me about him—him and his holy morals? Your mother makes a single slip; he finds out about it eight years later and divorces her, divorces her not caring about you and your sisters, not caring about her bad health. Well what do you think he would do to you? He'd forget you ever existed. You wouldn't see a penny."

"I don't *care,*" she said earnestly. "Do you think I care?"

"But I do, Dorrie." His hand began moving gently on her back again. "Not for me. I swear to God not for me. But for you. What will happen to us? We'll both have to quit school; you for the baby, me to work. And what will I do?—another guy with two years' college and no degree. What will I be? A clerk? Or an oiler in some textile mill or something?"

"It doesn't matter . . ."

"It does! You don't know how much it does. You're only nineteen and you've had money all your life. You don't know what it means not to have it. I do. We'd be at each other's throats in a year."

"No . . . no . . . we wouldn't!"

"All right, we love each other so much we never argue. So where are we? In a furnished room with—with paper drapes? Eating spaghetti seven nights a week? If I saw you living that way and I knew it was my fault . . ."—he paused for an instant, then finished very softly—". . . I'd take out insurance and jump in front of a car."

She began sobbing again.

He closed his eyes and spoke dreamily, intoning the words in a sedative chant. "I had it planned so beautifully. I would have come to New York this summer and you would have introduced me to him. I could have gotten him to like me. You would have told me what he's interested in, what he likes, what he dislikes—" He stopepd short, then continued. "And after graduation we would have been married. Or even this summer. We could have come back here in September for our last two years. A little apartment of our own, right near the campus . . ."

She lifted her head from his chest. "What are you trying to do?" she begged. "Why are you saying these things?"

"I want you to see how beautiful, how wonderful, it could have been."

"I see. Do you think I don't see?" The sobs twisted her voice. "But I'm pregnant. I'm two months pregnant." There was silence, as though unnoticed motors had suddenly stopped. "Are

8

. . . are you trying to get out of it? To get away? Is that what you're trying to do?"

"No! God no, Dorrie!" He grabbed her by the shoulders and pulled her up until her face was next to his. "No!"

"Then what are you doing to me? We *have* to get married now! We don't have any choice!"

"We *do* have a choice, Dorrie," he said.

He felt her body stiffen against his.

She gave a small terrified whisper—"No!"—and began shaking her head violently from side to side.

"Listen, Dorrie!" he pleaded, hands gripping her shoulders, "No operation. Nothing like that." He caught her jaw in one hand, fingers pressing into her cheeks, holding her head rigid. "Listen!" He waited until the wildness of her breathing subsided. "There's a guy on campus, Hermy Godsen. His uncle owns the drugstore on University and Thirty-Fourth. Hermy sells things. He could get some pills."

He let go of her jaw. She was silent.

"Don't you see, baby? We've got to try! It means so much!"

"Pills . . ." she said gropingly, as though it were a new word.

"We've got to try. It could be so wonderful."

She shook her head in desperate confusion. "Oh God, I don't know . . ."

He puts his arms around her, "Baby, I *love* you. I wouldn't let you take anything that might hurt you."

She collapsed against him, the side of her head striking his shoulder. "I don't know . . . I don't know . . ."

He said, "It would be so wonderful . . ."—his hand caressing—"A little apartment of our own . . . no waiting for a damn landlady to go to the movies . . ."

Finally she said, "How . . . how do you know they would work? What if they didn't work?"

He took a deep breath. "If they don't work,"—he kissed her forehead, and her cheek, and the corner of her mouth—"If they don't work we'll get married right away and to hell with your father and Kingship Copper Incorporated. I swear we will, baby."

He had discovered that she liked to be called 'baby.' When he called her 'baby' and held her in his arms he could get her to do practically anything. He had thought about it, and decided it had something to do with the coldness she felt towards her father.

He kept kissing her gently, talking to her with warm low words, and in a while she was calm and easy.

They shared a cigarette, Dorothy holding it first to his lips and then to hers, where the pink glow of each puff would

9

momentarily touch the feathery blonde hair and the wide brown eyes.

She turned the burning end of the cigarette towards them and moved it around and around, back and forth, painting circles and lines of vivid orange in the darkness. "I bet you could hypnotize someone this way," she said. Then she swung the cigarette slowly before his eyes. In its wan light her slim-fingered hand moved sinuously. "You are my slave," she whispered, lips close to his ear. "You are my slave and completely in my power! You must obey my every bidding!" She was so cute he couldn't help smiling.

When they finished the cigarette he looked at the luminous dial of his watch. Waving his hand before her, he intoned, "You must get dressed. You must get dressed because it is twenty past ten and you must be back at the dorm by eleven."

2

HE WAS BORN IN MENASSET, on the outskirts of Fall River, Massachusetts; the only child of a father who was an oiler in one of the Fall River textile mills and a mother who sometimes had to take in sewing when the money ran low. They were of English extraction with some French intermixed along the way, and they lived in a neighborhood populated largely by Portuguese. His father found no reason to be bothered by this, but his mother did. She was a bitter and unhappy woman who had married young, expecting her husband to make more of himself than a mere oiler.

At an early age he became conscious of his good looks. On Sundays guests would come and exclaim over him—the blond-ness of his hair, the clear blue of his eyes—but his father was always there, shaking his head admonishingly at the guests. His parents argued a great deal, usually over the time and money his mother devoted to dressing him.

Because his mother had never encouraged him to play with the children of the neighborhood, his first few days at school were an agony of insecurity. He was suddenly an anonymous member of a large group of boys, some of whom made fun of the perfection of his clothes and the obvious care he took to avoid the puddles in the schoolyard. One day, when he could bear it no longer, he went up to the ringleader of the hazers and spat on his shoes. The ensuing fight was brief but wild, and at the end of it he had the ringleader flat on his back and was kneeling on his chest, banging his head against the ground again and again. A teacher came running and broke up the fight. After that, everything was all right. Eventually he accepted the ringleader as one of his friends.

10

His marks in school were good, which made his mother glow and even won reluctant praise from his father. His marks became still better when he started sitting next to an unattractive but brilliant girl who was so beholden to him for some awkward cloakroom kisses that she neglected to cover her paper during examinations.

His school-days were the happiest of his life; the girls liked him for his looks and his charm; the teachers liked him because he was polite and attentive, nodding when they stated important facts, smiling when they attempted feeble jokes; and to the boys he showed his dislike of both girls and teachers just enough so that they liked him too. At home, he was a god. His father finally gave in and joined his mother in deferent admiration.

When he started dating, it was with girls from the better part of town. His parents argued again, over his allowance and the amount of money spent on his clothes. The arguments were short though, his father only sparring halfheartedly. His mother began to talk about his marrying a rich man's daughter. She said it jokingly, of course, but she said it more than once.

He was president of his senior class in high school and was graduated with the third highest average and honors in mathematics and science. In the school yearbook he was named The Best Dancer, The Most Popular, and The Most Likely to Succeed. His parents gave a party for him, which was attended by many young people from the better part of town.

Two weeks later, he was drafted.

For the first few days of Basic Training, he coasted along on the glory he had left behind. But then reality rubbed off the insulation, and he found the impersonal authority of the Army to be a thousand times more degrading than his early schooldays had been. And here, if he went up to the sergeant and spat on his shoes, he'd probably spend the rest of his life in the stockade. He cursed the blind system which had dropped him into the infantry, where he was surrounded by coarse, comic-book-reading idiots. After a while he read comic-books too, but only because it was impossible to concentrate on the copy of *Anna Karenina* he had brought with him. He made friends with some of the men, buying them beers in the PX, and inventing obscene and fantastically funny biographies of all the officers. He was contemptuous of everything that had to be learned and everything that had to be done.

When he was shipped out of San Francisco, he vomited all the way across the Pacific, and he knew it was only partly from the lift and drop of the ship. He was sure he was going to be killed.

On an island still partially occupied by the Japanese, he became separated from the other members of his company and

11

stood terrified in the midst of a silent jungle, desperately shifting this way and that, not knowing in which direction safety lay. A rifle slapped, sent a bullet keening past his ear. Jagged bird screams split the air. He dropped to his stomach and rolled under a bush, sick with the certainty that this was the moment of his death.

The bird sounds fluttered down into silence. He saw a gleam in a tree up ahead, and knew that that was where the sniper waited. He found himself inching forward under the bushes, dragging his rifle with one hand. His body was clammy cold and alive with sweat; his legs were trembling so badly that he was sure the Jap would hear the leaves rustling under them. The rifle weighed a ton.

Finally he was only twenty feet from the tree, and looking up, he could discern the figure crouched in it. He lifted his rifle; he aimed, and fired. The bird chorus shrieked. The tree remained motionless. Then suddenly a rifle dropped from it, and he saw the sniper slide clumsily down a vine and drop to the ground with his hands high in the air; a little yellow man grotesquely festooned with leaves and branches, his lips emitting a terrified sing-song chatter.

Keeping the rifle trained on the Jap, he stood up. The Jap was as scared as he was; the yellow face twitched wildly and the knees shivered; more scared, in fact, for the front of the Jap's pants was dark with a spreading stain.

He watched the wretched figure with contempt. His own legs steadied. His sweating stopped. The rifle was weightless, like an extension of his arms, immobile, aimed at the trembling caricature of a man that confronted him. The Jap's chatter had slowed to a tone of entreaty. The yellow-brown fingers made little begging motions in the air.

Quite slowly, he squeezed the trigger. He did not move with the recoil. Insensate to the kick of the butt in his shoulder, he watched attentively as a black-red hole blossomed and swelled in the chest of the Jap. The little man slid clawing to the jungle floor. Bird screams were like a handful of colored cards thrown into the air.

After looking at the slain enemy for a minute or so, he turned and walked away. His step was as easy and certain as when he had crossed the stage of the auditorium after accepting his diploma.

He received an honorable discharge in January of 1947, and left the Army with the Bronze Star and the Purple Heart, and the record of a shell fragment traced in a vein of thin scar tissue over his dextral ribs. Returning home, he found that his father had been killed in an automobile accident while he was overseas.

He was offered several jobs in Menasett, but rejected them as being of too little promise. His father's insurance money was

12

sufficient to support his mother and she was taking in sewing again besides, so after two months of drawing admiration from the townspeople and twenty dollars a week from the federal government, he decided to go to New York. His mother argued, but he was over twenty-one, if only by a few months, so he had his way. Some of the neighbors expressed surprise that he did not intend to go to college, especially when the government would pay for it. He felt, however, that college would only be an unnecessary stopover on the road to the success he was certain awaited him.

His first job in New York was in a publishing house, where the personnel manager assured him there was a fine future for the right man. Two weeks, however, was all he could take of the shipping room.

His next job was with a department store, where he was a salesclerk in the men's wear department. The only reason he remained there an entire month was that he was able to buy his clothes on a twenty per cent discount.

By the end of August, when he had been in New York five months and had had six jobs, he was again prey to the awful insecurity of being one among many rather than one alone; unadmired and with no tangible sign of success. He sat in his furnished room and devoted some time to serious self-analysis. If he had not found what he wanted in these six jobs, he decided, it was unlikely that he would find it in the next six. He took out his fountain pen and made what he considered to be a completely objective list of his qualities, abilities and talents.

In September, he enrolled in a dramatic school under the G.I. Bill. The instructors expressed great hopes for him at first; he was handsome, intelligent, and had a fine speaking voice, although the New England accent would have to be eliminated. He had great hopes too, at first. Then he discovered how much work and study were involved in becoming an actor. The exercises the instructors gave—"Look at this photograph and act out the emotions it brings to mind"— struck him as ridiculous, although the other students seemed to take them seriously. The only study to which he applied himself was diction; he had been dismayed to hear the word 'accent' used in relation to himself, having always thought of it as something someone else had.

In December, on his twenty-second birthday, he met a fairly attractive widow. She was in her forties and she had a good deal of money. They met on the corner of Fifth Avenue and Fifty-Fifth Street,—quite romantically, they later agreed. Stepping back onto the curb to avoid a bus, she tripped and fell into his arms. She was embarrassed and terribly shaken. He made some humorous comments on the ability and thoughtfulness of Fifth Avenue bus drivers, and then they went down the

13

street to a dignified bar where they had two Martinis each, for which he paid the check. In the weeks that followed they attended small East Side art movies and dined in restaurants where there were three or four people to be tipped at the end of the meal. He paid many more checks, although not again with his own money.

Their attachment lasted for several months, during which time he weaned himself away from the dramatic school—no painful process—and devoted his afternoons to squiring her on shopping tours, some of which were for him. At first he was somewhat embarrassed at being seen with her because of the obvious discrepancy in their ages, but he soon found himself getting over that. He was, however, dissatisfied with the relationship on two accounts; firstly, while her face was fairly attractive, her body, unfortunately, was not; secondly, and of greater importance, he learned from the elevator operator in her apartment house that he was only one of a series of young men, each of whom had been replaced with equinoctial regularity at the end of six months. It seemed, he reflected humorlessly, that this was another position with no future. At the end of five months, when she began to exhibit less curiosity about how he spent the nights he was not with her, he anticipated her move and told her that he had to return home because his mother was deathly ill.

He did return home, after reluctantly excising the custom tailor's labels from his suits and pawning a Patek Philippe wristwatch. He spent the early part of June lounging around the house, silently lamenting the fact that the widow had not been younger, prettier, and open to a more permanent sort of alliance.

That was when he began to make his plans. He decided he would go to college after all. He took a summer job in a local dry goods store because, while the G.I. Bill would cover his tuition, his living expenses would be quite high; he was going to attend a good school.

He finally chose Stoddard University in Blue River, Iowa, which was supposed to be something of a country club for the children of the Midwestern wealthy. There was no difficulty in his gaining admission. He had such a fine high school record.

In his first year he met a lovely girl, a senior, the daughter of the vice-president of an internationally organized farm equipment concern. They took walks together, cut classes together, and slept together. In May she told him that she was engaged to a boy back home and she hoped he hadn't taken it too seriously.

In his sophomore year, he met Dorothy Kingship.

3

HE GOT THE PILLS, two grayish-white capsules, from Hermy Godsen. They cost him five dollars.

At eight o'clock he met Dorothy at their regular meeting place, a tree-shrouded bench in the center of the wide stretch of lawn between the Fine Arts and Pharmacy buildings. When he left the white concrete path and cut across the darkness of the lawn he saw that Dorothy was already there, sitting stiffly with her fingers locked in her lap, a dark coat cloaking her shoulders against the April coolness. A streetlamp off to the side cast leaf shadows on her face.

He sat down beside her and kissed her cheek. She greeted him softly. From the rectangle of lighted windows in the Fine Arts Building drifted the conflicting themes of a dozen pianos. After a moment he said, "I got them."

A couple crossed the lawn towards them and, seeing the bench occupied, turned back to the white path. The girl's voice said, "My God, they're all taken."

He took the envelope from his pocket and put it into Dorothy's hand. Her fingers felt the capsules through the paper. "You're to take both of them together," he said. "You're liable to get a little fever, and you'll probably feel nauseous."

She put the envelope in her coat pocket. "What's in them?" she asked.

"Quinine, some other things. I'm not sure." He paused. "They can't hurt you."

He looked at her face and saw that she was staring off at something beyond the Fine Arts Building. He turned and followed her gaze to a winking red light miles away. It marked the local radio station's transmitting tower, which stood atop Blue River's tallest structure, the Municipal Building,—where the Marriage License Bureau was. He wondered if she were staring at the light because of that, or only because it was a winking red light in a sky of darkness. He touched her hands and found them cold. "Don't worry, Dorrie. Everything will be all right."

They sat in silence for a few minutes, and then she said, "I'd like to go to a movie tonight. There's a Joan Fontaine picture at the Uptown."

"I'm sorry," he said, "but I've got a ton of Spanish homework."

"Let's go over to the Student Union. I'll help you with it."

"What are you trying to do, corrupt me?"

He walked her back across the campus. Opposite the low

15

modern shape of the Girls' Dormitory, they kissed goodnight. "See you in class tomorrow," he said. She nodded, and kissed him again. She was trembling. "Look, baby, there's nothing to worry about. If they don't work we get married. Haven't you heard?—love conquers all." She was waiting for him to say more. "And I love you very much," he said, and kissed her. When their lips parted, hers were pressed into an unsteady smile.

"Good night, baby," he said.

He returned to his room, but he couldn't do his Spanish. He sat with his elbows planted on the bridge table, his head in his hands, thinking about the pills. Oh God, they must work! They *will* work!

But Hermy Godsen had said: "I can't give you no written guarantee. If this girlfriend of yours is two months gone already . . ."

He tried not to think about it. He got up and went to the bureau and opened the bottom drawer. From under the neatly folded pajamas he took two pamphlets whose supple covers gleamed with a copper finish.

On first meeting Dorothy and discovering, through one of the student-secretaries in the Registrar's office, that she was not merely one of the 'Kingship Copper' Kingships but actually a daughter of the corporation's president, he had written a businesslike letter to the organization's New York office. In it he represented himself as contemplating an investment in Kingship Copper (which was not entirely an untruth), and requested descriptive brochures of its holdings.

Two weeks later, when he was reading *Rebecca* and pretending to love it because it was Dorothy's favorite book, and when she was doggedly knitting him bulky argyle socks because a previous boyfriend had liked them and so the knitting of them had become the badge of her devotion, the pamphlets arrived. He opened their envelope with ceremonial care. They proved wonderful—*Technical Information on Kingship Copper and Copper Alloys* and *Kingship Copper, Pioneer in Peace and War* they were called, and they were crammed with photographs: mines and furnaces, concentrators and converters, reversing mills, rolling mills, rod mills and tube mills. He read them a hundred times and knew every caption by heart. He returned to them at odd moments, a musing smile on his lips, like a woman with a love letter.

Tonight they were no good. "Open-cut mine in Landers, Michigan. From this single mine, a yearly output . . ."

What angered him most was that in a sense the responsibility for the entire situation rested with Dorothy. He had wanted to take her to his room only once—a down-payment guaranteeing the fulfillment of a contract. It was Dorothy, with her gently closed eyes and her passive, orphan hunger, who had wished

16

for further visits. He struck the table. It really was her fault! Damn her!

He dragged his mind back to the pamphlets, but it was no use; after a minute he pushed them away and rested his head in his hands again. If the pills didn't work . . . Leave school? Ditch her? It would be futile; she knew his Menasset address. Even if she should be reluctant to seek him out, her father would hasten to do so. Of course there could be no legal action (or could there?), but Kingship could still cause him plenty of trouble. He imagined the wealthy as a closely knit, mutually protective clan, and he could hear Leo Kingship: "Watch out for this young man. He's no good. I feel it my duty as a parent to warn you . . ." And what would be left for him then? Some shipping room?

Or if he married her. Then she would have the baby and they'd never get a cent out of Kingship. Again the shipping room, only this time saddled with a wife and child. Oh God!

The pills *had* to work. That was all there was to it. If they failed, he didn't know what he'd do.

The book of matches was white, with *Dorothy Kingship* stamped on it in copper leaf. Every Christmas Kingship Copper gave personalized matches to its executives, customers and friends. It took her four strokes to light the match, and when she held it to her cigarette the flame trembled as though in a breeze. She sat back, trying to relax, but she couldn't tear her eyes from the open bathroom door, the white envelope waiting on the edge of the sink, the glass of water . . .

She closed her eyes. If only she could speak to Ellen about it. A letter had come that morning—"The weather has been beautiful . . . president of the refreshment committee for the Junior Prom . . . have you read Marquand's new novel? . . ."—another of the meaningless mechanical notes that had been drifting between them since Christmas and the argument. If only she could get Ellen's advice, talk to her the way they used to talk . . .

Dorothy had been five and Ellen six when Leo Kingship divorced his wife. A third sister, Marion, was ten. When the three girls lost their mother, first through the divorce and then through her death a year later, Marion felt the loss most deeply of all. Recalling clearly the accusations and denunciations which had preceded the divorce, she recounted them in bitter detail to her sisters as they grew up. She exaggerated Kingship's cruelty to some degree. As the years passed she grew apart, solitary and withdrawn.

Dorothy and Ellen, however, turned to each other for the affection which they received neither from their father, who met their coldness with coldness, nor from the series of odorless and precise governesses to whom he transferred the custody the courts had granted him. The two sisters went to the same schools and camps, joined the same clubs and attended the same dances (taking care to return home at the hour designated by their father). Where Ellen led, Dorothy followed.

But when Ellen entered Caldwell College, in Caldwell, Wisconsin, and Dorothy made plans to follow her there the next year, Ellen said no; Dorothy should grow up and become self-reliant. Their father agreed, self-reliance being a trait he valued in himself and in others. A measure of compromise was allowed, and Dorothy was sent to Stoddard, slightly more than a hundred miles from Caldwell, with the understanding that the sisters would visit one another on weekends. A few visits were made, the length of time between them increasing progressively, until Dorothy austerely announced that her first year of college had made her completely self-reliant, and the visits stopped altogether. Finally, this past Christmas, there had been an argument. It had started on nothing—"If you wanted to borrow my blouse you might at least have asked me!"—and had swollen because Dorothy had been in a depressed mood all during her vacation. When the girls returned to school, the letters between them faded to brief, infrequent notes . . .

There was still the telephone. Dorothy found herself staring at it. She could get Ellen on the line in an instant . . . But no; why should she be the one to give in first and chance a rebuff? She squashed her cigarette in an ashtray. Besides, now that she had calmed down, what was there to hesitate about? She would take the pills; if they worked, all well and good. If not; marriage. She thought about how wonderful that would be, even if her father did have a fit. She didn't want any of *his* money anyway.

She went to the hall door and locked it, feeling a slight thrill in the unaccustomed and somewhat melodramatic act.

In the bathroom, she took the envelope from the edge of the sink and tilted the capsules into her palm. They were gray-white, their gelatin coating lustrous, like elongated pearls. Then, as she dropped the envelope into the wastebasket, the thought flashed into her mind—"What if I don't take them?"

They would be married tomorrow! Instead of waiting until the summer, or more likely until graduation—over two years —they'd be married by tomorrow night!

But it wouldn't be fair. She had promised she would try. Still, tomorrow . . .

She lifted the glass, clapped the pills into her mouth, and drained the water in a single draught.

4

THE CLASSROOM, in one of Stoddard's new buildings, was a clean rectangle with one wall of aluminum-framed glass. Eight rows of seats faced the lecturer's platform. There were ten gray metal seats to a row, each with a right arm that curved in and fanned to form a writing surface.

He sat in the back of the room, in the second seat from the window. The seat on his left, the window seat, the empty seat, was hers. It was the first class of the morning, a daily Social Science lecture, and their only class together this semester. The speaker's voice droned in the sun-filled air.

Today of all days she could have made an effort to be on time. Didn't she know he'd be frozen in an agony of suspense? Heaven or hell. Complete happiness, or the awful mess he didn't even want to think about. He looked at his watch; 9:08. Damn her.

He shifted in his seat, fingering his keychain nervously. He stared at the back of the girl in front of him and started to count the polka dots in her blouse.

The door at the side of the room opened quietly. His head jerked around.

She looked awful. Her face was pasty white so that the rouge was like paint. There were gray arcs under her eyes. She was looking at him the instant the door opened, and with a barely perceptible motion, she shook her head.

Oh God! He turned back to the keychain in his fingers and stared at it, numb. He heard her coming around behind him, slipping into the seat on his left. He heard her books being put on the floor in the aisle between them, and then the scratching of a pen on paper, and finally the sound of a page being torn from a spiral-bound pad.

He turned. Her hand was extended towards him, holding a folded piece of blue-lined paper. She was watching him, her wide eyes anxious.

He took the paper and opened it in his lap:

> *I had a terrible fever and I*
> *threw up. But nothing happened.*

He closed his eyes for a moment, then opened them again and turned to her, his face expressionless. Her lips made a tight nervous smile. He tried to make himself return the smile, but he couldn't. His eyes went back to the note in his hand. He folded the paper in half, then folded it again and again, until it was a tight wad, which he placed in his pocket. Then

19

he sat with his fingers locked firmly together, watching the lecturer.

After a few minutes, he was able to turn to Dorothy, give her a reassuring smile, and form the words "Don't worry" with silent lips.

When the bell sounded at 9:55, they left the room with the other students who were laughing and pushing and complaining about coming exams and overdue papers and broken dates. Outside, they moved from the crowded path and stood in the shadow of the concrete-walled building.

The color was beginning to return to Dorothy's cheeks. She spoke quickly. "It'll be all right. I know it will. You won't have to quit school. You'll get more money from the government, won't you? With a wife?"

"A hundred and five a month." He couldn't keep the sourness out of his voice.

"Others get along on it . . . the ones in the trailer camp. We'll manage."

He put his books down on the grass. The important thing was to get time, time to think. He was afraid his knees were going to start shaking. He took her by the shoulders, smiling. "That's the spirit. You just don't worry about anything." He took a breath. "Friday afternoon we'll go down to the Municipal—"

"Friday?"

"Baby, it's Tuesday. Three days won't make any difference now."

"I thought we'd go today."

He fingered the collar of her coat. "Dorrie, we can't. Be practical. There are so many things to be taken care of. I think I have to take a blood test first. I'll have to check on that. And then, if we get married Friday we can have the weekend for a honeymoon. I'm going to get us a reservation at the New Washington House . . ."

She frowned indecisively.

"What difference will three days make?"

"I guess you're right," she sighed.

"That's my baby."

She touched his hand. "I . . . I know it isn't the way we wanted it, but . . . you're happy, aren't you?"

"Well what do you think? Listen, the money isn't that important. I just thought that for your sake . . ."

Her eyes were warm, reaching.

He looked at his watch. "You have a ten o'clock, don't you?"

"*Solamente el Español.* I can cut it."

"Don't. We'll have better reasons to cut our morning classes." She squeezed his hand. "I'll see you at eight," he said. "At the bench." Reluctantly, she turned to go. "Oh, Dorrie . . ."

20

"Yes?"

"You haven't said anything to your sister, have you?"

"Ellen? No."

"Well you better not. Not until after we're married."

"I thought I'd tell her before. We've been so close. I'd hate to do it without telling her."

"If she's been so rotten to you the past two years . . ."

"Not rotten."

"That was the word you used. Anyhow, she's liable to tell your father. He might do something to stop us."

"What could he do?"

"I don't know. He would try anyway, wouldn't he?"

"All right. Whatever you say."

"Afterwards you'll call her up right away. We'll tell everybody."

"All right." A final smile, and then she was walking to the sun-bright path, her hair glinting gold. He watched her until she disappeared behind the corner of a building. Then he picked up his books and walked away in the opposite direction. A braking car screeched somewhere, making him start. It sounded like a bird in a jungle.

Without forming a conscious decision he was cutting the rest of the day's classes. He walked all the way through town and down to the river, which was not blue but a dull muddy brown. Leaning on the rail of the black-girded Morton Street Bridge, he looked into the water and smoked a cigarette.

Here it was. The dilemma had finally caught up with him and engulfed him like the filthy water that pounded the abutments of the bridge. Marry her or leave her. A wife and a child and no money, or be hounded and blackmailed by her father. "You don't know me, sir. My name is Leo Kingship. I'd like to speak to you about the young man you have just employed . . . The young man your daughter is going with. . . I think you should know. . ." Then what? There would be no place to go to but home. He thought of his mother. Years of complacent pride, patronizing sneers for the neighbors' children, and then she sees him clerking in a dry goods store, not just for the summer, but permanently. Or even some lousy mill! His father had failed to live up to her expectations, and he'd seen what love she'd had for the old man burn itself into bitterness and contempt. Was that in store for him too? People talking behind his back. Oh Jesus! Why hadn't the goddamned pills killed the girl?

If only he could get her to undergo an operation. But no, she was determined to get married, and even if he pleaded and argued and called her "baby" from now till doomsday, she'd still want to consult Ellen before taking such a drastic measure. And anyway, where would they get the money? And suppose something happened, suppose she died. He would be involved

21

because he would have been the one who arranged for the operation. He'd be right where he started—with her father out to get him. Her death wouldn't do him a bit of good.

Not if she died that way.

There was a heart scratched into the black paint of the railing, with initials on either side of the arrow that pierced it. He concentrated on the design, picking at it with his fingernail, trying to blank his mind of what had finally welled to the surface. The scratches had exposed cross-sections of paint layers; black, orange, black, orange, black, orange. It reminded him of the pictures of rock strata in a geology text. Records of dead ages.

Dead.

After a while he picked up his books and slowly walked from the bridge. Cars flew towards him and passed with a rushing sound.

He went into a dingy riverside restaurant and ordered a ham sandwich and coffee. He ate the sandwich at a little corner table. While sipping the coffee, he took out his memorandum book and fountain pen.

The first thing that had entered his mind was the Colt .45 he had taken on leaving the Army. Bullets could be obtained with little difficulty. But assuming he wanted to do it, a gun would be no good. It would have to look like an accident, or suicide. The gun would complicate matters too much.

He thought of poison. But where would he get it? Hermy Godsen? No. Maybe the Pharmacy Building. The supply room there shouldn't be too hard to get into. He would have to do some research at the library, to see which poison . . .

It would have to look like an accident or suicide, because if it looked like anything else, he would be the first one the police would suspect.

There were so many details—assuming he wanted to do it. Today was Tuesday; the marriage could be postponed no later than Friday or she might get worried and call Ellen. Friday would be the deadline. It would require a great deal of fast, careful planning.

He looked at the notes he had printed:

    1. *Gun* (n.g.)
    2. *Poison*
        a) Selection
        b) Obtaining
        c) Administering
        d) Appearance of (1) accident
                or (2) suicide

Assuming, of course, that he wanted to do it. At present it was all purely speculative; he would explore the details a little. A mental exercise.

22

But his stride, when he left the restaurant and headed back through town, was relaxed and sure and steady.

5

HE REACHED THE CAMPUS AT THREE O'CLOCK and went directly to the library. In the card catalogue he found listed six books likely to contain the information he wanted; four of them were general works on toxicology; the other two, manuals of criminal investigation whose file cards indexed chapters on poisons. Rather than have a librarian get the books for him, he registered at the desk and went into the stacks himself.

He had never been in the stacks before. There were three floors filled with bookshelves, a metal staircase spiraling up through them. One of the books on his list was out. He found the other five without difficulty on the shelves on the third floor. Seating himself at one of the small study tables that flanked a wall of the room, he turned on the lamp, arranged his pen and memorandum book in readiness, and began to read.

At the end of an hour, he had a list of five toxic chemicals likely to be found in the Pharmacy supply room, any one of which, by virtue of its reaction time and the symptoms it produced prior to death, would be suitable for the plan whose rudimentary outline he had already formulated during the walk from the river.

He left the library and the campus, and walked in the direction of the house where he roomed. When he had gone two blocks he came upon a dress shop whose windows were plastered with big-lettered sale signs. One of the signs had a sketch of an hourglass with the legend *Last Days of Sale*.

He looked at the hourglass for a moment. Then he turned around and walked back towards the campus.

He went to the University Bookstore. After consulting the mimeographed booklist tacked to the bulletin board, he asked the clerk for a copy of *Pharmaceutical Techniques,* the laboratory manual used by the advanced pharmacy students. "Pretty late in the semester," the clerk commented, returning from the rear of the store with the manual in his hand. It was a large thin book with a distinctive green paper cover. "Lose yours?"

"No. It was stolen."

"Oh. Anything else?"

"Yes. I'd like some envelopes, please."

"What size?"

"Regular envelopes. For letters."

The clerk put a pack of white envelopes on the book. "That's

23

a dollar-fifty and twenty-five. Plus tax—a dollar seventy-nine."

The College of Pharmacy was housed in one of Stoddard's old buildings, three stories of ivy-masked brick. Its front had broad stone steps that led up the main entrance. At either side of the building were steps leading down to a long corridor which cut straight through the basement, where the supply room was located. There was a Yale lock on the supply room door. Keys to this lock were in the possession of the usual university functionaries, the entire faculty of the College of Pharmacy, and those advanced students who had received permission to work without supervision. This was the regular arrangement followed in all departments of the university which used enough equipment to necessitate the maintenance of a supply room. It was an arrangement familiar to almost everyone on campus.

He came in at the main entrance and crossed the hall to the lounge. Two bridge games were in session and some other students sat around, reading and talking. A few of them glanced up when he entered. He went directly to the long clothes rack in the corner and put his books on the shelf above it. Removing his corduroy jacket, he hung it on one of the hooks. He took the pack of envelopes from among his books, removed three of them and folded them into his hip pocket. He put the rest of the envelopes back with the books, took the lab manual, and left the room.

He went downstairs to the basement corridor. There was a men's room to the right of the stairwell. He entered it and after looking under the doors to make sure the booths were empty, dropped the manual on the floor. He stepped on it a few times and then kicked it all the way across the tiled floor. When he picked it up it had lost its blatant newness. He put it on the ledge of a sink. Watching himself in the mirror, he unbuttoned the cuffs of his shirt and rolled the sleeves halfway up his arms. He unfastened his collar and lowered the knot of his tie. Tucking the manual under his arm, he stepped out into the corridor.

The door to the supply room was midway between the central stairwell and one end of the corridor. On the wall a few feet beyond it was a bulletin board. He walked down to the board and stood before it, looking at the notices tacked there. He stood with his back turned slightly towards the end of the corridor, so that from the corner of his eye he could see the stairwell. He held the manual under his left arm. His right arm was at his side, fingers by his keychain.

A girl came out of the supply room, closing the door behind her. She carried one of the green manuals and a beaker half full of a milky fluid. He watched her as she went down the corridor and turned to climb the stairs.

Some people entered from the door behind him. They

24

walked past, talking. Three men. They went straight down the corridor and out the door at the other end. He kept looking at the bulletin board.

At five o'clock bells rang, and for a few minutes there was a great deal of activity in the hallway. It subsided quickly though, and he was alone again. One of the notices on the board was an illustrated folder about summer sessions at the University of Zurich. He began to read it.

A bald-headed man emerged from the stairwell. He had no manual, but it was apparent from the angle at which he approached and the movement of his hand towards his keychain that he was coming to the supply room. There was, however, the look of an instructor. . . . Putting his back toward the approaching man, he turned a page of the Zurich pamphlet. He heard the sound of a key in the door, and then the door opening and closing. A minute later, it opened and closed again, and the sound of the man's footsteps diminished and then changed to a stair-climbing rhythm.

He resumed his former position and lighted a cigarette. After one puff he dropped it and ground it under his foot; a girl had appeared, coming towards him. There was a lab manual in her hand. She had lanky brown hair and horn-rimmed glasses. She was taking a brass key from the pocket of her smock.

He lessened the pressure on the manual under his arm, letting it drop down into his left hand, conspicuous with its green cover. With a last casual finger-flick at the Zurich folder, he moved to the supply room door, not looking at the approaching girl. He fumbled with his keychain as though the keys had caught in the pocket's lining. When he finally brought out the bunch of keys the girl was already at the door. His attention was on the keys, shuffling through them, apparently looking for a certain one. It seemed as though he didn't become conscious of the girl's presence until she had inserted her key in the lock, turned it and pushed the door partially open, smiling up at him. "Oh . . . thanks," he said, reaching over her to push the door wide, his other hand tucking the keys back in his pocket. He followed the girl in and closed the door behind them.

It was a small room with counters and shelves filled with labeled bottles and boxes and odd-looking apparatuses. The girl touched a wall switch, making fluorescent tubes wink to life, incongruous among the room's old-fashioned fittings. She went to the side of the room and opened her manual on a counter there. "Are you in Aberson's class?" she asked.

He went to the opposite side. He stood with his back to the girl, facing a wall of bottles. "Yes," he said.

Faint clinkings of glass and metal sounded in the room. "How's his arm?"

"About the same, I guess," he said. He touched the bottles,

25

pushing them against each other, so that the girl's curiosity should not be aroused.

"Isn't that the craziest thing?" she said. "I hear he's practically blind without his glasses." She lapsed into silence.

Each bottle had a white label with black lettering. A few bore an additional label that glared POISON in red. He scanned the rows of bottles quickly, his mind registering only the red-labeled ones. The list was in his pocket, but the names he had written on it shimmered in the air before him as though printed on a gauze screen.

He found one. The bottle was a bit above eye level, not two feet from where he stood. *White Arsenic*—As_4O_6—POISON. It was half filled with white powder. His hand moved towards it, stopped.

He turned slowly until he could see the girl from the corner of his eye. She was pouring some yellow powder from the tray of a balance into a glass cup. He turned back to the wall and opened his manual on the counter. He looked at meaningless pages of diagrams and instructions.

At last the girl's movements took on sounds of finality; the balance being put away, a drawer closing. He leaned more closely over the manual, following the lines of print with a careful finger. Her footsteps moved to the door. "So long," she said.

"So long."

The door opened and closed. He looked around. He was alone.

He took his handkerchief and the envelopes from his pocket. With the handkerchief draped over his right hand, he lifted the arsenic bottle from the shelf, put it on the counter and removed the stopper. The powder was like flour. He poured about a tablespoonful into the envelope; it fell in whispering puffs. He folded the envelope into a tight pack, folded that into a second envelope and pocketed it. After he had stoppered and replaced the bottle, he moved slowly around the room, reading the labels on drawers and boxes, the third envelope held open in his hand.

He found what he wanted within several minutes: a box filled with empty gelatin capsules, glittering like oval bubbles. He took six of them, to be on the safe side. He put them in the third envelope and slipped it gently into his pocket, so as not to crush the capsules. Then, when everything appeared as he had found it, he took the manual from the counter, turned out the lights, and left the room.

After retrieving his books and his jacket, he left the campus again. He felt wonderfully secure; he had devised a course of action and had executed its initial steps with speed and precision. Of course it was still only a tentative plan and he was in no way committed to carry it through to its goal. He would see how the next steps worked out. The police would never believe that Dorrie had taken a lethal dose of arsenic by accident. It would have to look like suicide, like obvious, indisputable suicide. There would have to be a note or something equally convincing. Because if they ever suspected that it wasn't suicide and started an investigation, the girl who had let him into the supply room would always be able to identify him.

He walked slowly, conscious of the fragile capsules in the left-hand pocket of his trousers.

He met Dorothy at eight o'clock. They went to the Uptown, where the Joan Fontaine picture was still playing.

The night before, Dorothy had been anxious to go; her world had been as gray as the pills he had given her. But tonight—tonight everything was radiant. The promise of immediate marriage had swirled away her problems the way a fresh wind swirls away dead leaves; not only the looming problem of her pregnancy, but all the problems she had ever had; the loneliness, the insecurity. The only hint of gray remaining was the inevitable day when her father, having already been appalled by a hasty unquestioning marriage, would learn the truth about its cause. But even that seemed of trifling importance tonight. She had always hated his unyielding morality and had defied it only in secrecy and guilt. Now she would be able to display her defiance openly, from the security of a husband's arms. Her father would make an ugly scene of it, but in her heart she looked forward to it a little.

She envisioned a warm and happy life in the trailer camp, still warmer and happier when the baby came. She was impatient with the motion picture, which distracted her from a reality more beautiful than any movie could ever be.

He, on the other hand, had not wanted to see the picture on the previous night. He was not fond of movies, and he especially disliked pictures that were founded on exaggerated emotions. Tonight, however, in comfort and darkness, with his arm about Dorothy and his hand resting lightly on the upper slope of her breast, he relished the first moments of relaxation he had known since Sunday night, when she had told him she was pregnant.

He surrendered all his attention to the picture, as though answers to eternal mysteries were hidden in the windings of its plot. He enjoyed it immensely.

Afterwards he went home and made up the capsules.

He funneled the white powder from a folded sheet of paper into the tiny gelatin cups, and then fitting the slightly larger cups that were the other halves of the capsules over them. It took him almost an hour, since he ruined two capsules, one squashed and the other softened by the moisture of his fingers, before he was able to complete two good ones.

When he was finished, he took the damaged capsules and

27

the remaining capsules and powder into the bathroom and flushed them down the toilet. He did the same with the paper from which he had poured the arsenic and the envelopes in which he had carried it, first tearing them into small pieces. Then he put the two arsenic capsules into a fresh envelope and hid them in the bottom drawer of his bureau, under the pajamas and the Kingship Copper pamphlets, the sight of which brought a wry smile to his face.

One of the books he had read that afternoon had listed the lethal dose of arsenic as varying from one tenth to one half of a gram. By rough computation, he estimated that the two capsules contained a total of five grams.

6

HE FOLLOWED HIS REGULAR ROUTINE on Wednesday, attending all his classes, but he was no more a part of the life and activity that surrounded him than is the diver in his diving bell a part of the alien world in which he is submerged. All of his energies were turned inward, focused on the problem of beguiling Dorothy into writing a suicide note or, if that could not be contrived, finding some other way to make her death seem self-induced. While in this state of labored concentration he unconsciously dropped the pretense of being undecided as to whether or not he would actually go through with his plans; he was going to kill her; he had the poison and he already knew how he was going to administer it; there was only this one problem left, and he was determined to solve it. At times during the day, when a loud voice or the chalk's screech made him momentarily aware of his surroundings, he looked at his classmates with mild surprise. Seeing their brows contracted over a stanza in Browning or a sentence in Kant, he felt as though he had suddenly come upon a group of adults playing hopscotch.

A Spanish class was his last of the day, and the latter half of it was devoted to a short unannounced examination. Because it was his poorest subject, he forced himself to lower the focus of his concentration to the translating of a page of the florid Spanish novel which the class was studying.

Whether the stimulus was the actual work he was doing or the comparative relaxation which the work offered after a day of more rigorous thinking, he could not say. But in the midst of his writing the idea came to him. It rose up fully formed, a perfect plan, unlikely to fail and unlikely to arouse Dorothy's suspicion. The contemplation of it so occupied his mind that when the period ended he had completed only half the assigned page. The inevitable failing mark in the quiz troubled him very

28

little. By ten o'clock the following morning Dorothy would have written her suicide note.

That evening, his landlady having gone to an Eastern Star meeting, he brought Dorothy back to his room. During the two hours they spent there, he was as warm and tender as she had ever wished him to be. In many ways he liked her a great deal, and he was conscious of the fact that this was to be her last such experience.

Dorothy, noticing his new gentleness and devotion, attributed it to the nearness of their wedding. She was not a religious girl, but she deeply believed that the state of wedlock carried with it something of holiness.

Afterwards they went to a small restaurant near the campus. It was a quiet place and not popular with the students; the elderly proprietor, despite the pains he took to decorate his windows with blue and white crepe paper and Stoddard pennants, was irascible with the noisy and somewhat destructive university crowd.

Seated in one of the blue-painted wall booths, they had cheeseburgers and chocolate malteds, while Dorothy chattered on about a new type of bookcase that opened out into a full-size dining table. He nodded unenthusiastically, waiting for a pause in the monologue.

"Oh, by the way," he said, "do you still have that picture I gave you? The one of me?"

"Of course I do."

"Well let me have it back for a couple of days. I want to have a copy made to send to my mother. It's cheaper than getting another print from the studio."

She took a green wallet from the pocket of the coat folded on the seat beside her. "Have you told your mother about us?"

"No, I haven't."

"Why not?"

He thought for a moment. "Well, as long as you can't tell your family until after, I thought I wouldn't tell my mother. Keep it our secret." He smiled. "You haven't told anyone, have you?"

"No," she said. She was holding a few snapshots she had taken from the wallet. He looked at the top one from across the table. It was of Dorothy and two other girls,—her sisters, he supposed. Seeing his glance, she passed the picture to him. "The middle one is Ellen, and Marion's on the end."

The three girls were standing in front of a car, a Cadillac, he noticed. The sun was behind them, their faces shadowed, but he could still discern a resemblance among them. All had the same wide eyes and prominent cheekbones. Ellen's hair seemed to be of a shade midway between Dorothy's light and Marion's dark. "Who's the prettiest?" he asked. "After you, I mean."

"Ellen," Dorothy said. "And before me. Marion could be very pretty too, only she wears her hair like this." She pulled her hair back severely and frowned. "She's the intellectual. Remember?"

"Oh. The Proust fiend."

She handed him the next snapshot, which was of her father. "Grrrrr," he growled, and they both laughed. Then she said, "And this is my fiancé," and passed him his own picture.

He looked at it speculatively, seeing the symmetry of the clear planes. "I don't know," he drawled, rubbing his chin. "Looks kind of dissolute to me."

"But so handsome," she said. "So very handsome." He smiled and pocketed the picture with a satisfied air. "Don't lose it," she warned seriously.

"I won't." He looked around, his eyes bright. On the wall next to them was a selector for the jukebox at the rear of the restaurant. "Music," he announced, producing a nickel and dropping it into the slot. He traced a finger up and down the twin rows of red buttons as he read the names of the songs. He paused at the button opposite *Some Enchanted Evening*, which was one of Dorothy's favorites, but then his eyes caught *On Top of Old Smoky* further down the row, and he thought a moment and chose that instead. He pushed the button. The jukebox bloomed into life, casting a pink radiance on Dorothy's face.

She looked at her wristwatch, then leaned back, eyes closed rapturously. "Oh gee, just think . . ." she murmured, smiling. "Next week no rushing back to the dorm!" Introductory guitar chords sounded from the jukebox. "Shouldn't we put in an application for one of the trailers?"

"I was down there this afternoon," he said. "It may take a couple of weeks. We can stay at my place. I'll speak to my landlady." He took a paper napkin and began tearing careful bits from its folded edges.

A girl's voice sang:

> On top of old Smoky,
> All covered with snow,
> I lost my true loved one,
> For courtin' too slow . . .

"Folk songs," Dorothy said, lighting a cigarette. The flame glinted on the copper-stamped matchbook.

"The trouble with you," he said, "is you're a victim of your aristocratic upbringing."

> Now courtin's a pleasure,
> But partin's a grief,
> And a false-hearted lover
> Is worse than a thief . . .

"Did you take the blood test?"

"Yes. I did that this afternoon too."

"Don't I have to take one?"

"No."

"I looked in the Almanac. It said 'blood test required' for Iowa. Wouldn't that mean for both?"

"I asked. You don't have to." His fingers picked precisely at the napkin.

> A thief he will rob you,
> And take what you have,
> But a false-hearted lover
> Will lead you to the grave . . .

"It's getting late . . ."

"Just let's stay to the end of the record, okay? I like it." He opened the napkin; the torn places multiplied symmetrically and the paper became a web of intricate lace. He spread his handiwork on the table admiringly.

> The grave will decay you,
> And turn you to dust.
> Not one man in a hundred
> A poor girl can trust . . .

"See what we women have to put up with?"

"A pity. A real pity. My heart bleeds."

Back in his room, he held the photograph over an ashtray and touched a lighted match to its lowest corner. It was a print of the yearbook photo and a good picture of him; he hated to burn it, but he had written "To Dorrie, with all my love" across the bottom of it.

7

As usual she was late for the nine o'clock class. Sitting in the back of the room, he watched the rows of seats fill up with students. It was raining outside and ribbons of water sluiced down the wall of windows. The seat on his left was still empty when the lecturer mounted the platform and began talking about the City Manager form of government.

He had everything in readiness. His pen was poised over the notebook opened before him and the Spanish novel, *La Casa de las Flores Negras*, was balanced on his knee. A sudden heart-stopping thought hit him; what if she picked today to

31

cut? Tomorrow was Friday, the deadline. This was the only chance he would have to get the note, and he had to have it by tonight. What would he do if she cut?

At ten past nine, though, she appeared; out of breath, her books in one arm, her raincoat over the other, a smile for him lighting her face the moment she eased through the door. Tiptoeing across the room behind him, she draped the raincoat over the back of her chair and sat down. The smile was still there as she sorted her books, keeping a notebook and a small assignment pad before her and putting the remaining books in the aisle between their seats.

Then she saw the book that he held open on his knee, and her eyebrows lifted questioningly. He closed the book, keeping his finger between the pages, and tilted it towards her so that she could see the title. Then he opened it again and with his pen ruefully indicated the two exposed pages and his notebook, meaning that that was how much translation he had to do. Dorothy shook her head condolingly. He pointed to the lecturer and to her notebook—she should take notes and he would copy them later. She nodded.

After he had worked for a quarter of an hour, carefully following the words of the novel, slowly writing in his notebook, he glanced cautiously at Dorothy and saw that she was intent on her own work. He tore a piece of paper about two inches square from the corner of one of the notebook's pages. One side of it he covered with doodling; words written and crossed out, spirals and zigzagging lines. He turned that side downward. With a finger stabbing the print of the novel, he began shaking his head and tapping his foot in impatient perplexity.

Dorothy noticed. Inquiringly, she turned to him. He looked at her and expelled a troubled sigh. Then he lifted his finger in a gesture that asked her to wait a moment before returning her attention to the lecturer. He began to write, squeezing words onto the small piece of paper, words that he was apparently copying from the novel. When he was through, he passed the paper to her.

Traducción, por favor, he had headed it. Translation, please:

> *Querido,*
>
>   *Espero que me perdonares por la
> infelicidad que causaré. No hay
> ninguna otra cosa que puedo hacer.*

She gave him a mildly puzzled glance, because the sentences were quite simple. His face was expressionless, waiting. She picked up her pen and turned the paper over, but the back of it was covered with doodling. So she tore a page from her assignment pad and wrote on that.

32

She handed him the translation. He read it and nodded. *"Muchas gracias,"* he whispered. He hunched forward and wrote in his notebook. Dorothy crumpled the paper on which he had written the Spanish and dropped it to the floor. From the corner of his eye he saw it land. There was another bit of paper near it, and some cigarette butts. At the end of the day they would all be swept together and burned.

He looked at the paper again, at Dorothy's small slanted handwriting:

> *Darling,*
>   *I hope you will forgive me for the*
> *unhappiness that I will cause. There*
> *is nothing else that I can do.*

He tucked the paper carefully into the pocket on the inner cover of the notebook, and closed it. He closed the novel and placed it on top of the notebook. Dorothy turned, looked at the books and then at him. Her questioning glance asked if he were finished.

He nodded and smiled.

They were not to see each other that evening. Dorothy wanted to wash and set her hair and pack a small valise for their weekend honeymoon at the New Washington House. But at eight-thirty the phone on her desk rang.

"Listen, Dorrie. Something's come up. Something important."

"What do you mean?"

"I've got to see you right away."

"But I can't. I can't come out. I just washed my hair."

"Dorrie, this is important."

"Can't you tell me now?"

"No. I have to see you. Meet me at the bench in half an hour."

"It's *drizzling* out. Can't you come to the lounge downstairs?"

"No. Listen, you know that place where we had the cheeseburgers last night? Gideon's? Well, meet me there. At nine."

"I don't see why you can't come to the lounge . . ."

"Baby, please . . ."

"Is—is it anything to do with tomorrow?"

"I'll explain everything at Gideon's."

"Is it?"

"Well, yes and no. Look, everything's going to be all right. I'll explain everything. You just be there at nine."

"All right."

At ten minutes of nine he opened the bottom drawer of his

bureau and took two envelopes from under the pajamas. One envelope was stamped, sealed, and addressed:

> *Miss Ellen Kingship*
> *North Dormitory*
> *Caldwell College*
> *Caldwell, Wisconsin*

He had typed the address that afternoon in the Student Union lounge, on one of the typewriters available for general student use. In the envelope was the note that Dorothy had written in class that morning. The other envelope contained the two capsules.

He put one envelope in each of the inner pockets of his jacket, taking care to remember which envelope was on which side. Then he put on his trenchcoat, belted it securely, and with a final glance in the mirror, left the room.

When he opened the front door of the house he was careful to step out with his right foot forward, smiling indulgently at himself as he did so.

8

GIDEON'S WAS PRACTICALLY EMPTY when he arrived. Only two booths were occupied; in one, a pair of elderly men sat frozen over a chessboard; in the other, across the room, Dorothy sat with her hands clasped around a cup of coffee, gazing down at it as though it were a crystal ball. She had a white kerchief tied about her head. The hair that showed in front was a series of flattened damp-darkened rings, each transfixed by a bobby pin.

She became aware of him only when he was standing at the head of the booth taking off his coat. Then she looked up, her brown eyes worried. She had no make-up on. Her pallor and the closeness of her hair made her seem younger. He put his coat on a hook beside her raincoat and eased into the seat opposite her. "What is it?" she asked anxiously.

Gideon, a sunken cheeked old man, came to their table. "What's yours?"

"Coffee."

"Just coffee?"

"Yes."

Gideon moved away, his slippered feet dragging audibly. Dorothy leaned forward. "What is it?"

He kept his voice low, matter-of-fact. "When I got back to my place this afternoon there was a message for me. Hermy Godsen called."

Her hands squeezed tighter around the coffee cup. "Hermy Godsen . . ."

"I called him back." He paused for a moment, scratching the tabletop. "He made a mistake with those pills the other day. His uncle—" He cut off as Gideon approached with a cup of coffee rattling in his hand. They sat motionless, eyes locked, until the old man was gone. "His uncle switched things around in the drugstore or something. Those pills weren't what they were supposed to be."

"What were they?" She sounded frightened.

"Some kind of emetic. You said you threw up. Lifting his cup, he put a paper napkin in the saucer to absorb the coffee that Gideon's shaking hand had spilled. He pressed the bottom of the cup into the napkin to wipe it.

She breathed relief. "Well that's all *over* with. They didn't hurt me. The way you spoke on the phone, you got me so worried . . ."

"That's not the point, baby." He put the soggy napkin to one side. "I saw Hermy just before I called you. He gave me the right pills, the ones we should have had last time."

Her face sagged. "No . . ."

"Well there's nothing tragic. We're right where we were Monday, that's all. It's a second chance. If they work, everything's rosy. If not, we can still get married tomorrow." He stirred his coffee slowly, watching it swirl. "I've got them with me. You can take them tonight."

"But . . ."

"But what?"

"I don't *want* a second chance. I don't *want* any more pills . . ." She leaned forward, hands knotted white on the table. "All I've been thinking about is tomorrow, how wonderful, how happy . . ." She closed her eyes, the lids pressing out tears.

Her voice had risen. He glanced across the room to where the chess players sat with Gideon watching. Fishing a nickel from his pocket, he pushed it into the jukebox selector and jabbed one of the buttons. Then he clasped her clenched hands, forced them open, held them. "Baby, baby," he soothed, "do we have to go through it all again? It's you I'm thinking of. You, not me."

"No." She opened her eyes, staring at him. "If you were thinking of me you'd want what I want." Music blared up, loud brassy jazz.

"What *do* you want, baby? To starve? This is no movie; this is real."

"We *wouldn't* starve. You're making it worse than it would be. You'd get a good job even if you didn't finish school. You're smart, you're—"

"You don't know," he said flatly. "You just don't know. You're a kid who's been rich all her life."

Her hands tried to clench within his. "Why must everyone always throw that at me? Why must *you?* Why do you think that's so important?"

"It is important, Dorrie, whether you like it or not. Look at you,—a pair of shoes to match every outfit, a handbag to match every pair of shoes. You were brought up that way. You can't—"

"Do you think that matters? Do you think I care?" She paused. Her hands relaxed, and when she spoke again the anger in her voice had softened to a straining earnestness. "I know you smile at me sometimes, at the movies I like . . . at my being romantic . . . Maybe it's because you're five years older than I am, or because you were in the Army, or because you're a man,—I don't know . . . But I believe, I truly believe, that if two people really love each other . . . the way I love you . . . the way you say you love me . . . then nothing else matters very much . . . money, things like that, they just don't matter. I believe that . . . I really do . . ." Her hands pulled away from his and flew to her face.

He drew a handkerchief from his breast pocket and touched it to the back of her hand. She took it and held it against her eyes. "Baby, I believe that too. You know I do," he said gently. "Do you know what I did today?" He paused. "Two things. I bought a wedding ring for you, and I put a classified ad in the Sunday *Clarion.* An ad for a job. Night work." She patted her eyes with the handkerchief. "Maybe I did paint things too black. Sure, we'll manage to get along, and we'll be happy. But let's be just a *little* realistic, Dorrie. We'll be even happier if we can get married this summer with your father's approval. You can't deny that. And all you have to do for us to have a chance at that extra happiness is just take these pills." He reached into his inner pocket and brought out the envelope, pressing it to make sure it was the right one. "There isn't one logical reason why you should refuse."

She folded the handkerchief and turned it in her hands, looking at it. "Since Tuesday morning I've been dreaming about tomorrow. It changed everything . . . the whole world." She pushed the handkerchief over to him. "All my life I've been arranging things to suit my father."

"I know you're disappointed, Dorrie. But you've got to think of the future." He extended the envelope to her. Her hands, folded on the table, made no move to accept it. He put it on the table between them, a white rectangle slightly swollen by the capsules inside. "I'm prepared to take a night job now, to quit school at the end of this term. All I'm asking you to do is to swallow a couple of pills."

Her hands remained folded, her eyes on the sterile whiteness of the envelope.

He spoke with cool authority: "If you refuse to take them,

36

Dorothy, you're being stubborn, unrealistic, and unfair. Unfair more to yourself than to me."

The jazz record ended, the colored lights died, and there was silence.

They sat with the envelope between them.

Across the room there was the whisper of a chessman being placed and an old man's voice said "Check."

Her hands parted slightly and he saw the glisten of sweat in her palms. His own hands were sweating too, he realized. Her eyes lifted from the envelope to meet his.

"Please, baby . . ."

She looked down again, her face rigid.

She took the envelope. She pushed it into the handbag on the bench beside her and then sat gazing at her hands on the table.

He reached across the table and touched her hand, caressed the back of it, clasped it. With his other hand he pushed his untouched coffee over to her. He watched her lift the cup and drink. He found another nickel in his pocket and, still holding her hand, dropped the coin into the selector and pressed the button opposite *Some Enchanted Evening*.

They walked the wet concrete paths in silence, divorced by the privacy of their thoughts, holding hands through habit. The rain had stopped, but face-tingling moisture filled the air, defining the scope of each streetlamp in shifting gray.

Across the street from the dorm, they kissed. Her lips under his were cool and compressed. When he tried to part them she shook her head. He held her for a few minutes, whispering persuasively, and then they exchanged goodnights. He watched as she crossed the street and passed into the yellow-lighted hall of the building.

He went to a nearby bar, where he drank two glasses of beer and tore a paper napkin into a delicate filigreed square of admirable detail. When half an hour had passed, he stepped into the telephone booth and dialed the number of the dorm. He asked the girl at the switchboard for Dorothy's room.

She answered after two rings. "Hello?"

"Hello, Dorrie?" Silence at her end. "Dorrie, did you do it?"

A pause. "Yes."

"When?"

"A few minutes ago."

He drew a deep breath. "Baby, does that girl on the switchboard ever listen in?"

"No. They fired the last girl for—"

"Well listen, I didn't want to tell you before, but . . . they might hurt a little." She said nothing. He continued, "Hermy said you'll probably throw up, like before. And you might get a sort of burning sensation in your throat and some pains

37

in your stomach. Whatever happens, don't get frightened. It'll just mean that the pills are working. Don't call anyone." He paused, waiting for her to say something, but she was silent. "I'm sorry I didn't tell you before but, well, it won't hurt too much. And it'll be over before you know it." A pause. "You're not angry with me, are you, Dorrie?"

"No."

"You'll see, it'll all be for the best."

"I know. I'm sorry I was stubborn."

"That's all right, baby. Don't apologize."

"I'll see you tomorrow."

"Yes."

There was silence for a moment and then she said, "Well, good night."

"Good-by, Dorothy," he said.

9

STRIDING INTO THE CLASSROOM Friday morning he felt weightless and tall and wonderful. It was a beautiful day; sunlight poured into the room and bounced off the metal chairs to spangle the walls and ceiling. Taking his seat in the back of the room, he stretched his legs all the way out and folded his hands across his chest, watching the other students crowd in. The morning's radiance had inflamed them all, and tomorrow was the first Varsity baseball game, with the Spring Dance in the evening; there was chattering, shouting, grinning and laughter.

Three girls stood off to the side and whispered excitedly. He wondered if they were dorm girls, if they could possibly be talking about Dorothy. She couldn't have been found yet. Why would anyone enter her room? They would think she wanted to sleep late. He was counting on her not being found for several hours; he held his breath until the girls' whispering erupted into laughter.

No, it was unlikely that she would be found before one o'clock or so. "Dorothy Kingship wasn't at breakfast and she wasn't at lunch either"—then they would knock on her door and get no answer. They'd most likely have to get the house mother or someone with a key. Or it might not even happen then. Many of the dorm girls slept through breakfast, and some of them ate lunch out occasionally. Dorrie hadn't any close friends who would miss her right away. No, if his luck held, they might not find her until Ellen's phone call came.

The night before, after saying good-by to Dorothy on the telephone, he had returned to the dorm. In the mailbox on the corner he had posted the envelope addressed to Ellen Kingship, the envelope containing Dorothy's suicide note. The first mail collection of the morning was at six; Caldwell was only a hundred miles away and so the letter would be delivered this afternoon. If Dorothy were found in the morning, Ellen, notified by her father, might leave Caldwell for Blue River before the letter arrived, which would mean that an investigation of some sort would almost certainly be launched, because the suicide note would not be found until Ellen returned to Caldwell. It was the only risk, but it was a small one and unavoidable; it had been impossible for him to sneak into the Girl's Dormitory to plant the note in Dorothy's room, and impractical to secrete it in the pocket of her coat or in one of her books prior to giving her the pills, in which case there would have been the far greater risk of Dorothy finding the note and throwing it away or, still worse, putting two and two together.

He had decided upon noon as the safety mark. If Dorothy were found after twelve, Ellen would have received the note by the time the school authorities contacted Leo Kingship and Kingship in turn contacted her. If his luck *really* held, Dorothy would not be discovered until late afternoon, a frantic phone call from Ellen leading to the discovery. Then everything would be neat and in its proper order.

There would be an autopsy, of course. It would reveal the presence of a great deal of arsenic and a two-month embryo—the way and the why of her suicide. That and the note would more than satisfy the police. Oh, they would make a perfunctory check of the local drugstores, but it would net them only a fat zero. They might even consider the Pharmacy supply room. They would ask the students, "Did you see this girl in the supply room or anywhere in the Pharmacy Building?"—displaying photograph of the deceased. Which would produce another zero. It would be a mystery, but hardly an important one; even if they couldn't be sure of the source of arsenic, her death would still be an indisputable suicide.

Would they look for the man in the case, the lover? He considered that unlikely. For all they knew she was as promiscuous as a bunny. That was hardly their concern. But what about Kingship? Would outraged morality inaugurate a private inquiry? "Find the man who ruined my daughter!" Although, from the description of her father that Dorothy had painted, Kingship would be more likely to think "Aha, she was ruined all along. Like mother, like daughter." Still, there might be an inquiry . . .

He would certainly be dragged into that. They had been seen together, though not as frequently as might be expected. In the beginning, when success with Dorothy had been in question, he had not taken her to popular places; there had been that other rich girl last year, and if Dorothy didn't work out as he planned there would be others in the future; he didn't want the reputation of a money-chaser. Then, when

Dorothy did work out, they had gone to movies, to his room, and to quiet places like Gideon's. Meeting at the bench rather than in the dorm lounge had become a custom.

He would be involved in any inquiry all right, but Dorothy hadn't told anyone they were going steady, so other men would be involved too. There was the red-headed one she'd been chatting with outside the classroom the day he first saw her and noticed the copper-stamped *Kingship* on her matches, and the one she'd started knitting argyle socks for, and every man she'd dated once or twice,—they would *all* be brought into it, and then it would be anybody's guess as to who had "ruined" her because all would deny it. And as thorough as the investigation might be, Kingship could never be certain that he hadn't completely overlooked the "guilty" party. There would be suspicion directed at all the men, proof against none.

No, everything would be perfect. There would be no quitting school, no shipping clerk's job, no oppressing wife and child, no vengeful Kingship. Only one tiny shadow . . . Suppose he were pointed out around campus as one of the men who'd gone with Dorothy. Suppose that the girl who had let him into the supply room should see him again, hear who he was, learn that he wasn't a Pharmacy student at all . . . But even that was unlikely, out of twelve thousand students . . . But suppose the very worst happened. Suppose she saw him, remembered, and went to the police. Even then, it would be no evidence. So he was in the supply room. He could make up some kind of excuse and they would have to believe him, because there would still be the note, the note in Dorothy's handwriting. How could they explain . . .

The door at the side of the room opened, creating a draft that lifted the pages of his notebook. He turned to see who it was. It was Dorothy.

Shock burst over him, hot as a wave of lava. He half-rose, blood pushing to his face, his chest a block of ice. Sweat dotted his body and crawled like a million insects. He knew it was written on his face in swollen eyes and burning cheeks, written for her to see, but he couldn't stop it. She was looking at him wonderingly, the door closing behind her. Like any other day; books under her arm, green sweater, plaid skirt. Dorothy. Coming to him, made anxious by his face.

His notebook slapped to the floor. He bent down, seizing the momentary escape. He stayed with his face near the side of the seat, trying to breathe. What happened? Oh God! She didn't take the pills! She couldn't have! She lied! The bitch! The lying goddamned bitch! The note on its way to Ellen . . . Oh Jesus, Jesus!

He heard her sliding into her seat. Her frightened whisper— *"What's wrong? What's the matter?"* He picked up the notebook and sat erect, feeling the blood drain from his face, from his entire body, leaving him dead cold with sweat drops moving. *"What's wrong?"* He looked at her. Like any other day. There was a green ribbon in her hair. He tried to speak but it was as if he were empty inside with nothing to make a sound. *"What is it?"* Students were turning to look. Finally he scraped out, "Nothing . . . I'm all right . . ."

"You're sick! Your face is as gray as . . ."

"I'm all right. It's . . . it's this . . ."—touching his side where she knew he had the Army scar. "It gives me a twinge once in a while . . ."

"God, I thought you were having a heart attack or something," she whispered.

"No. I'm all right." He kept looking at her, trying for one good breath, his hands clutching his knees in rigid restraint. Oh God, what could he do? The bitch! She had planned also, planned to get married!

He saw the anxiety for him melt from her face, a flushed tension replacing it. She ripped a page from her assignment pad, scribbled on it and passed it to him:

The pills didn't work.

The liar! The goddamned liar! He crumpled the paper and squeezed it in his hand, fingernails biting into his palm. Think! Think! His danger was so enormous he couldn't grasp it all at once. Ellen would receive the note—when? Three o'clock? Four?—and call Dorothy—"What does this mean? Why did you write this?"—"Write what?"—then Ellen would read the note and Dorothy would recognize it . . . Would she come to him? What explanation could he invent? Or would she see the truth—blurt out the whole story to Ellen—call her father. If she had kept the pills—if she hadn't thrown them away, there would be proof! Attempted murder. Would she take them to a drugstore, have them analyzed? There was no figuring her now. She was an unknown quantity. He'd thought he could predict every little twitch of her goddamned brain, and now . . .

He could feel her looking at him, waiting for some kind of reaction to the words she'd written. He tore paper from his notebook and pulled open his pen. He shielded his hand so she couldn't see how it was shaking. He couldn't write. He had to print, digging the point of the pen so hard that it shredded the surface of the paper. Make it sound natural!

Okay. We tried, that's all.
Now we get married as per
schedule.

He handed it to her. She read it and turned to him, and her face was warm and radiant as the sunlight. He pressed a smile back at her, praying she wouldn't notice the stiffness of it.

It still wasn't too late. People wrote suicide notes and then stalled around before actually doing it. He looked at his watch; 9:20. The earliest Ellen could get the note would be . . . three o'clock. Five hours and forty minutes. No step by step planning now. It would have to be quick, positive. No trickery that counted on her doing a certain thing at a certain time. No poison. How else do people kill themselves? In five hours and forty minutes she must be dead.

10

AT TEN O'CLOCK THEY LEFT THE BUILDING arm in arm, going out into the crystalline air that rang with the shouts of between-class students. Three girls in cheerleaders' uniforms pushed by, one beating a tin pie pan with a wood spoon, the other two carrying a big sign advertising a baseball pep rally.

"Does your side still hurt you?" Dorothy asked, concerned for his grim expression.

"A little," he said.

"Do you get those twinges often?"

"No. Don't worry." He looked at his watch. "You're not marrying an invalid."

They stepped off the path onto the lawn. "When will we go?" She pressed his hand.

"This afternoon. Around four."

"Shouldn't we go earlier?"

"Why?"

"Well, it'll take time, and they probably close around five or so."

"It won't take long. We just fill out the application for the license and then there's someone right on the same floor who can marry us."

"I'd better bring proof that I'm over eighteen."

"Yes."

She turned to him, suddenly serious, remorse flushing her cheeks. Not even a good liar, he thought. "Are you terribly sorry the pills didn't work?" she asked anxiously.

"No, not terribly."

"You *were* exaggerating, weren't you? About how things will be?"

"Yes. We'll make out okay. I just wanted you to try the pills. For your sake."

She flushed more deeply. He turned away, embarrassed by her transparency. When he looked at her again, the joy of the moment had crowded out her compunctions and she was hugging her arms and smiling. "I *can't* go to my classes! I'm cutting."

"Good. I am too. Stay with me."

"What do you mean?"

"Until we go down to the Municipal Building. We'll spend the day together."

"I can't, darling. Not the whole day. I have to get back to the dorm, finish packing, dress . . . Don't you have to pack?"

"I left a suitcase down at the hotel when I made the reservation."

"Oh. Well you have to dress, don't you. I expect to see you in your blue suit."

He smiled. "Yes ma'am. You can give me *some* of your time, anyway. Until lunch."

"What'll we do?" They sauntered across the lawn.

"I don't know," he said. "Maybe go for a walk. Down to the river."

"In these shoes?" She lifted a foot, displaying a soft leather loafer. "I'd get fallen arches. There's no support in these things."

"Okay," he said, "no river."

"I've got an idea." She pointed to the Fine Arts Building ahead of them. "Let's go to the record room in Fine Arts and listen to some records."

"I don't know, it's such a beautiful day I'd like to stay . . ." He paused as her smile faded.

She was looking beyond the Fine Arts Building to where the needle of station KBRI's transmission tower speared the sky. "The last time I was in the Municipal Building it was to see that doctor," she said soberly.

"It'll be different this time," he said. And then he stopped walking.

"What is it?"

"Dorrie, you're right. Why should we wait until four o'clock? Let's go now!"

"Get married *now?*"

"Well, after you pack and dress and everything. Look, you go back to the dorm now and get ready. What do you say?"

"Oh, yes! Yes! Oh, I wanted to go now!"

"I'll call you up in a little while and tell you when I'll pick you up."

"Yes. Yes." She stretched up and kissed his cheek excitedly. "I love you so much," she whispered.

He grinned at her.

She hurried away, flashing a smile back over her shoulder, walking as fast as she could.

He watched her go. Then he turned and looked again at the KBRI tower, which marked the Blue River Municipal Building; the tallest building in the city; fourteen stories above the hard slabs of the sidewalk.

11

HE WENT INTO THE FINE ARTS BUILDING where a telephone booth was jammed under the slope of the main stairway. Calling Information, he obtained the number of the Marriage License Bureau.

"Marriage License Bureau."

"Hello. I'm calling to find out what hours the Bureau is open today."

"Till noon and from one to five-thirty."

"Closed between twelve and one?"

"That's right."

"Thank you." He hung up, dropped another coin into the phone and dialed the dorm. When they buzzed Dorothy's room there was no answer. He replaced the receiver, wondering what could have detained her. At the rate she had been walking she should have been in her room already.

He had no more change, so he went out and crossed the campus to a luncheonette, where he broke a dollar bill and glared at the girl who occupied the phone booth. When she finally abdicated he stepped into the perfume-smelling booth and closed the door. This time Dorothy answered.

"Hello?"

"Hi. What took you so long? I called a couple of minutes ago."

"I stopped on the way. I had to buy a pair of gloves." She sounded breathless and happy.

"Oh. Listen, it's—twenty-five after ten now. Can you be ready at twelve?"

"Well, I don't know. I want to take a shower . . ."

"Twelve-fifteen?"

"Okay."

"Listen, you're not going to sign out for the week end, are you?"

"I have to. You know the rules."

"If you sign out, you'll have to put down where you're going to be, won't you?"

"Yes."

"Well?"

"I'll put down 'New Washington House.' If the house mother asks, I'll explain to her."

"Look, you can sign out later this afternoon. We have to come back here anyway. About the trailer. We have to come back about that."

"We do?"

44

"Yes. They said I couldn't make the formal application until we were actually married."

"Oh. Well if we're coming back later, I won't take my valise now."

"No. Take it now. As soon as we're through with the ceremony we'll check in at the hotel and have lunch. It's only a block or so from the Municipal Building."

"Then I might as well sign out now too. I don't see what difference it'll make."

"Look, Dorrie, I don't think the school is exactly crazy about having out-of-town girls running off to get married. Your house mother is sure to slow us up somehow. She'll want to know if your father knows. She'll give you a lecture, try to talk you into waiting until the end of the term. That's what house mothers are there for."

"All right. I'll sign out later."

"That's the girl. I'll be waiting for you outside the dorm at a quarter after twelve. On University Avenue."

"On University?"

"Well you're going to use the side door, aren't you?—leaving with a valise and not signing out."

"That's right. I didn't think of that. Gee, we're practically eloping."

"Just like a movie."

She laughed warmly. "A quarter after twelve."

"Right. We'll be downtown by twelve-thirty."

"Good-by, groom."

"So long, bride."

He dressed meticulously in his navy blue suit, with black shoes and socks, a white-on-white shirt, and a pale blue tie of heavy Italian silk patterned with black and silver fleurs-de-lis. On surveying himself in the mirror, however, he decided that the beauty of the tie was a trifle too conspicuous, and so he changed it for a simple pearl gray knit. Viewing himself again as he refastened his jacket, he wished he could so easily exchange his face, temporarily, for one of less distinctive design. There were times, he realized, when being so handsome was a definite handicap. As a step, at least, in the direction of appearing commonplace, he reluctantly donned his one hat, a dove gray fedora, settling the unfamiliar weight cautiously, so as not to disturb his hair.

At five minutes past twelve he was on University Avenue, across the street from the side of the dorm. The sun was almost directly overhead, hot and bright. In the sultry air the occasional sounds of birds and footfalls and grinding streetcars had a rarefied quality, as though coming from behind a glass wall. He stood with his back to the dorm, staring into the window of a hardware store.

At twelve-fifteen, reflected in the window, he saw the door

45

across the street open and Dorothy's green-clad figure appear. For once in her life she was punctual. He turned. She was looking from right to left, her pivoting glance overlooking him completely. In one white-gloved hand she held a purse, in the other, a small valise covered in tan airplane cloth with wide red stripes. He lifted his arm and in a moment she noticed him. With an eager smile she stepped from the curb, waited for a break in the passing traffic, and came towards him.

She was beautiful. Her suit was dark green, with a cluster of white silk sparkling at the throat. Her shoes and purse were brown alligator, and there was a froth of dark green veil floating in her feathery golden hair. When she reached him, he grinned and took the valise from her hand. "All brides are beautiful," he said, "but you especially."

"Gracias, señor." She looked as though she wanted to kiss him.

A taxicab cruised by and slowed in passing. Dorothy looked at him inquiringly, but he shook his head. "If we're going to economize, we'd better get in practice." He peered down the avenue. In the glittering air a streetcar approached.

Dorothy drank in the world as if she had been indoors for months. The sky was a shell of perfect blue. The campus, unfolding at the front of the dorm and stretching seven blocks down University Avenue, was quiet, shaded by freshly-green trees. A few students walked the paths; others sprawled on the lawns. "Just think," she marveled, "when we come back this afternoon, we'll be married."

The streetcar clattered up and groaned to a halt. They got on.

They sat towards the back of the car, saying little, each enfolded in thoughts. The casual observer would have been uncertain as to whether or not they traveled together.

The lower eight floors of the Blue River Municipal Building were given over to the offices of the city and of Rockwell County, of which Blue River was the county seat. The remaining six floors were rented to private tenants, most of whom were lawyers, doctors and dentists. The building itself was a mixture of modern and classical architecture, a compromise between the functional trend of the thirties and resolute Iowa conservatism. Professors teaching the introductory architecture courses at Stoddard's College of Fine Arts referred to it as an architectural abortion, causing freshmen to laugh self-consciously.

Viewed from above, the building was a hollow square, an airshaft plunging down through the core of it. From the side, setbacks at the eighth and twelfth stories gave it the appearance of three blocks of decreasing size piled one atop the other. Its lines were graceless and stark, its window lintels were traced with factitious Grecian designs, and its three

46

bronze and glass revolving doors were squeezed between giant pillars whose capitals were carved into stylized ears of corn. It was a monstrosity, but on alighting from the streetcar Dorothy turned, paused, and gazed up at it as though it were the cathedral at Chartres.

It was twelve-thirty when they crossed the street, mounted the steps, and pushed through the central revolving door. The marble floored lobby was filled with people going to and from lunch, people hurrying to appointments, people standing and waiting. The sound of voices and the surf of shoes on marble hung susurrant under the vaulted ceiling.

He dropped a pace behind Dorothy, letting her lead the way to the directory board at the side of the lobby. "Would it be under R for Rockwell County or M for Marriage?" she asked, her eyes intent on the board as he came up beside her. He looked at the board as though oblivious of her presence. "There it is," she said triumphantly. "Marriage License Bureau —six-oh-four." He turned towards the elevators, which were opposite the revolving doors. Dorothy hurried along beside him. She reached for his hand but the valise was in it. He apparently did not notice her gesture, for he made no move to change hands.

One of the four elevators stood open, half filled with waiting passengers. As they approached it, he stepped back a bit, allowing Dorothy to enter first. Then an elderly woman came up and he waited until she too had gone in before entering. The woman smiled at him, pleased by his air of gallantry, doubly unexpected from a young man in a busy office building. She seemed a bit disappointed when he failed to remove his hat. Dorothy smiled at him also, over the head of the woman, who had somehow got between them. He returned the smile with an almost invisible curving of his lips.

They left the car at the sixth floor, along with two men with briefcases who turned to the right and walked briskly down the corridor. "Hey, wait for me!" Dorothy protested in an amused whisper as the elevator door clanged shut behind her. She had been the last to leave the car, and he the first. He had turned to the left and walked some fifteen feet, for all the world as though he were alone. He turned, appearing flustered, as she caught up with him and gaily took his arm. Over her head he watched the men with the briefcases reach the other end of the corridor, turn to the right and vanish down the side of the square. "Where you running?" Dorothy teased.

"Sorry," he smiled. "Nervous bridegroom." They walked along arm in arm, following the left turn the corridor made. Dorothy recited the numbers painted on the doors as they passed them. "Six-twenty, six-eighteen, six-sixteen . . ." They had to take another left turn before they reachd 604, which was at the back of the square, across from the elevators. He tried the door. It was locked. They read the hours listed on the frosted glass panel and Dorothy moaned dejectedly.

"Damn," he said. "I should have called to make sure." He put down the valise and looked at his watch. "Twenty-five to one."

"Twenty-five minutes," Dorothy said. "I guess we might as well go downstairs."

"Those crowds . . ." he muttered, then paused. "Hey, I've got an idea."

"What?"

"The roof. Let's go up on the roof. It's such a beautiful day, I bet we'll be able to see for miles!"

"Are we allowed?"

"If nobody stops us, we're allowed." He picked up the valise. "Come on, get your last look at the world as an unmarried woman."

She smiled and they began walking, retracing their path around the square to the bank of elevators where, in a few moments, there glowed above one of the doors a white arrow pointing upwards.

When they left the car at the fourteenth floor, it happened again that they were separated by the other alighting passengers. In the corridor, they waited until these had hurried around the turns or into offices, and then Dorothy said "Let's go," in a conspiratorial whisper. She was making an adventure of it.

Again they had to make a half-circuit of the building, until, next to room 1402, they found a door marked *Stairway*. He pushed it open and they entered. The door sighed closed behind them. They were on a landing, with black metal stairs leading up and down. Dim light sifted through a dirt-fogged skylight. They walked upwards; eight steps, a turn, and eight more steps. A door confronted them, heavy reddish-brown metal. He tried the knob.

"Is it locked?"

"I don't think so."

He put his shoulder to the door and pushed.

"You're going to get your suit filthy."

The door rested on a ledge, a sort of giant threshold that raised its bottom a foot above the level of the landing. The ledge jutted out, making it difficult for him to apply his weight squarely. He put down the valise, braced his shoulder against the door and tried again.

"We can go downstairs and wait," Dorothy said. "That door probably hasn't been opened in . . ."

He clenched his teeth. With the side of his left foot jammed against the base of the ledge, he swung back and then smashed his shoulder against the door with all his strength. It gave, groaning open. The chain of a counterweight clattered. A slice of electric blue sky hit their eyes, blinding after the obscurity

48

of the stairway. There was the quick flutter of pigeons' wings.

He picked up the valise, stepped over the ledge, and put the valise down again where it would be clear of the door's swing. Pushing the door further open, he stood with his back to it. He extended one hand to Dorothy. With the other he gestured towards the expanse of roof as a head waiter gestures towards his finest table. He gave her a mock bow and his best smile. "Enter, mam'selle," he said.

Taking his hand, she stepped gracefully over the ledge and onto the black tar of the roof.

12

HE WASN'T NERVOUS AT ALL. There had been a moment of near-panic when he couldn't get the door open, but it had dissolved the instant the door had yielded to the force of his shoulder, and now he was calm and secure. Everything was going to be perfect. No mistakes, no intruders. He just *knew* it. He hadn't felt so good since—Jesus, since high school!

He swung the door partly closed, leaving a half inch between it and the jamb, so that it wouldn't give him any trouble when he left. He would be in a hurry then. Bending over, he moved the valise so that he would be able to pick it up with one hand while opening the door with the other. As he straightened up he felt his hat shift slightly with the motion. He took it off, looked at it, and placed it on the valise. Christ, he was thinking of everything! A little thing like the hat would probably louse up somebody else. They would push her over and then a breeze or the force of the movement might send their hat sailing down to land beside her body. Bam! They might as well throw themselves over after it. Not he, though; he had anticipated, prepared. An act of God, the crazy kind of little thing that was always screwing up perfect plans,—and he had anticipated it. Jesus! He ran a hand over his hair, wishing there were a mirror.

"Come look at this."

He turned. Dorothy was standing a few feet away, her back towards him, the alligator purse tucked under one arm. Her hands rested on the waist-high parapet that edged the roof. He came up behind her. "Isn't it something?" she said. They were at the back of the building, facing south. The city sprawled before them, clear and sharp in the brilliant sunlight. "Look"—Dorothy pointed to a green spot far away—"I think that's the campus." He put his hands on her shoulders. A white-gloved hand reached up to touch his.

He had planned to do it quickly, as soon as he got her up

49

there, but now he was going to take it slow and easy, drawing it out as long as he safely could. He was entitled to that, after a week of nerve-twisting tension. Not just a week,—years. Ever since high school it had been nothing but strain and worry and self-doubt. There was no need to rush this. He looked down at the top of her head against his chest, the dark green veiling buoyant in the yellow hair. He blew, making the fine net tremble. She tilted her head back and smiled up at him.

When her eyes returned to the panorama, he moved to her side, keeping one arm about her shoulders. He leaned over the parapet. Two stories below, the red tiled floor of a wide balcony extended like a shelf across the width of the building. The top of the twelfth story setback. It would be on all four sides. That was bad; a two story drop wasn't what he wanted. He turned and surveyed the roof.

It was perhaps a hundred and fifty feet square, edged by the brick parapet whose coping was flat white stone, a foot wide. An identical wall rimmed the airshaft, a square hole some thirty feet across, in the center of the roof. On the left side of the roof was a vast stilt-supported water storage tank. On the right, the KBRI tower reared up like a smaller Eiffel, its girdered pattern black against the sky. The staircase entrance, a slant roofed shed, was in front of him and a bit to his left. Beyond the airshaft, at the north side of the building, was a large rectangular structure, the housing of the elevator machinery. The entire roof was dotted with chimneys and ventilator pipes that stuck up like piers from a tarry sea.

Leaving Dorothy, he walked across to the parapet of the airshaft. He leaned over. The four walls funneled down to a tiny areaway fourteen stories below, its corners banked with trash cans and wooden crates. He looked for a moment, then stooped and pried a rain-faded matchbook from the gummy surface of the roof. He held the folder out beyond the parapet —and dropped it, watching as it drifted down, down, down, and finally became invisible. He glanced at the walls of the shaft. Three were striped with windows. The fourth, which faced him and evidently backed on the elevator shafts, was blank, windowless. This was the spot. The south side of the airshaft. Right near the stairway, too. He slapped the top of the parapet, his lips pursed thoughtfully. Its height was greater than he had anticipated.

Dorothy came up behind him and took his arm. "It's so quiet," she said. He listened. At first there seemed to be absolute silence, but then the sounds of the roof asserted themselves: the throbbing of the elevator motors, a gentle wind strumming the cables that guyed the radio tower, the squeak of a slow-turning ventilator cap . . .

They began walking slowly. He led her around the airshaft and past the elevator housing. As they strolled she brushed

50

his shoulder clean of the dust from the door. When they reached the northern rim of the roof they were able to see the river, and with the sky reflected in it, it was really blue, as blue as the rivers painted on maps. "Do you have a cigarette?" she asked.

He reached into his pocket and touched a pack of Chesterfields. Then his hand came out empty. "No, I don't. Do you have any?"

"They're buried in here someplace." She dug into her purse, pushing aside a gold compact and a turquoise handkerchief, and finally produced a crushed pack of Herbert Tareytons. They each took one. He lit them and she returned the pack to her purse.

"Dorrie, there's something I want to tell you . . ."—she was blowing a stream of smoke against the sky, hardly listening—". . . about the pills."

Her face jerked around, going white. She swallowed. "What?"

"I'm glad they didn't work," he said, smiling. "I really am."

She looked at him uncomprehendingly. "You're glad?"

"Yes. When I called you last night, I was going to tell you not to take them, but you already had." Come on, he thought, confess. Get it off your chest. It must be killing you.

Her voice was shaky. "Why? You were so . . . what made you change your mind?"

"I don't know. I thought it over. I suppose I'm as anxious to get married as you are." He examined his cigarette. "Besides, I guess it's really a sin to do something like that." When he looked up again her cheeks were flushed and her eyes glistened.

"Do you mean that?" she asked breathlessly. "Are you really glad?"

"Of course I am. I wouldn't say it if I weren't."

"Oh, thank God!"

"What's the matter, Dorrie?"

"Please . . . don't be angry. I—I didn't take them." He tried to look surprised. The words poured from her lips: "You said you were going to get a night job and I knew we could manage, everything would work out, and I was counting on it so much, *so* much. I knew I was right." She paused. "You aren't angry, are you?" she beseeched. "You understand?"

"Sure, baby. I'm not angry. I told you I was glad they didn't work."

Her lips made a quivering smile of relief. "I felt like a criminal, lying to you. I thought I would never be able to tell you. I . . . I can't believe it!"

He took the neatly folded handkerchief from his breast pocket and touched it to her eyes. "Dorrie, what did you do with the pills?"

"Threw them away." She smiled shamefacedly.

51

"Where?" he asked casually, replacing the handkerchief.

"The john."

That was what he wanted to hear. There would be no questions about why she had taken such a messy way out when she had already gone to the trouble of obtaining poison. He dropped his cigarette and stepped on it.

Dorothy, taking a final puff, did the same with hers. "Oh gee," she marveled, "everything's perfect now. Perfect."

He put his hands on her shoulders and kissed her gently on the lips. "Perfect," he said.

He looked down at the two stubs, hers edged with lipstick, his clean. He picked his up. Splitting it down the middle with his thumbnail, he let the tobacco blow away and rolled the paper into a tiny ball. He flicked it out over the parapet. "That's the way we used to do it in the Army," he said.

She consulted her watch. "It's ten to one."

"You're fast," he said, glancing at his. "We've got fifteen minutes yet." He took her arm. They turned and walked leisurely away from the edge of the roof.

"Did you speak to your landlady?"

"Wha—? Oh, yes. It's all set." They passed the elevator housing. "Monday we'll move your stuff from the dorm."

Dorothy grinned. "Will they be surprised, the girls in the dorm." They strolled around the parapet of the airshaft. "Do you think your landlady'll be able to give us some more closet space?"

"I think so."

"I can leave some of my stuff, the winter things, in the attic at the dorm. There won't be too much."

They reached the south side of the airshaft. He stood with his back against the parapet, braced his hands on the top of it, and hitched himself up. He sat with his heels kicking against the side of the wall.

"Don't sit there," Dorothy said apprehensively.

"Why not?" he asked, glancing at the white stone coping. "It's a foot wide. You sit on a bench a foot wide and you don't fall off." He patted the stone on his left. "Come on."

"No," she said.

"Chicken."

She touched her rear. "My suit . . ."

He took out his handkerchief, whipped it open and spread it on the stone beside him. "Sir Walter Raleigh," he said.

She hesitated a moment, then gave him her purse. Turning her back to the parapet, she gripped the top on either side of the handkerchief and lifted herself up. He helped her. "There," he said, putting his arm around her waist. She turned her head slowly, peeking over her shoulder. "Don't look down," he warned. "You'll get dizzy."

He put the purse on the stone to his right and they sat in silence for a moment, her hands still fastened upon the front of the coping. Two pigeons came out from behind the stair-case shed and walked around, watching them cautiously, their claws ticking against the tar.

"Are you going to call or write when you tell your mother?" Dorothy asked.

"I don't know."

"I think I'll write Ellen and Father. It's an awfully hard thing to just say over the phone."

A ventilator cap creaked. After a minute, he took his arm from her waist and put his hand over hers, which gripped the stone between them. He braced his other hand on the coping and eased himself down from the parapet. Before she could do likewise he swung around and was facing her, his waist against her knees, his hands covering both of hers. He smiled at her and she smiled back. His gaze dropped to her stomach. "Little mother," he said. She chuckled.

His hands moved to her knees, cupped them, his fingertips caressing under the hem of her skirt.

"We'd better be going, hadn't we, darling?"

"In a minute, baby. We still have time."

His eyes caught hers, held them, as his hands descended and moved behind to rest curving on the slope of her calves. At the periphery of his field of vision he could make out her white-gloved hands; they still clasped the front of the coping firmly.

"That's a beautiful blouse," he said, looking at the fluffy silk bow at her throat. "Is it new?"

"New? It's as old as the hills."

His gaze became critical. "The bow is a little off center."

One hand left the stone and rose to finger the bow. "No," he said, "now you've got it worse." Her other hand detached itself from the top of the parapet.

His hands moved down over the silken swell of her calves, as low as he could reach without bending. His right foot dropped back, poised on the toe in readiness. He held his breath.

She adjusted the bow with both hands. "Is that any bett—"

With cobra speed he ducked—hands streaking down to catch her heels—stepped back and straightened up, lifting her legs high. For one frozen instant, as his hands shifted from cupping her heels to a flat grip against the soles of her shoes, their eyes met, stupefied terror bursting in hers, a cry rising in her throat. Then, with all his strength, he pushed against her fear-rigid legs.

Her shriek of petrified anguish trailed down into the shaft like a burning wire. He closed his eyes. The scream died. Silence, then a godawful deafening crash. Wincing, he remembered the cans and crates piled far below.

He opened his eyes to see his handkerchief billowing as the breeze pulled it free of the stone's rough surface. He snatched it up. Wheeling, he raced to the stairway door, grabbed hat and valise with one hand and pulled the door open, wiping the knob with the handkerchief as he did so. He stepped quickly over the threshold ledge, pulled the door closed and wiped its inner knob. He turned and ran.

He clattered down flight after flight of black metal steps, the valise banging against his legs, his right hand burning over the banisters. His heart galloped and the image of whirling walls dizzied him. When he finally stopped he was on the seventh floor landing.

He clung to the newel post, gasping. The phrase "physical release of tension" danced in his mind. That was why he had run that way—physical release of tension—not panic, not panic. He caught his breath. Putting down the valise, he re-shaped his hat, which had been crushed in his grasp. He put it on, his hands trembling slightly. He looked at them. The palms were dirty gray from the soles of . . . he wiped them clean and jammed the handkerchief into his pocket. After a few straightening tugs at his jacket, he picked up the valise, opened the door, and stepped out into the corridor.

Every door was open. People rushed across the corridor from offices on the outer circumference to those on the inner, where windows faced the airshaft. Men in business suits, stenographers with paper cuffs clipped to their blouses, shirt-sleeved men with green eyeshades; all with jaws clenched, eyes wide, faces bloodless. He walked towards the elevators at a moderate pace, pausing when someone darted before him, then continuing on his way. Passing the doorway of each inner office, he glanced in and saw the backs of people crammed around the open windows, their voices a murmur of excite-ment and tense speculation.

Shortly after he reached the bank of elevators, a down car came. He squeezed in and faced the front of the car. Behind him the other passengers avidly exchanged fragments of infor-mation, the customary elevator coldness shattered by the violence at their backs.

The easy bustle of normality filled the lobby. Most of the people there, having just entered from outside, were unaware of any disturbance. Swinging the valise lightly, he made his way across the marbled expanse and out into the bright noisy afternoon. As he jogged down the steps that fronted the build-ing, two policemen passed him, going up. He turned and watched the blue uniforms vanish into a revolving door. At the foot of the steps he paused and examined his hands once again. They were steady as rocks. Not a tremor. He smiled. Turning, he looked at the revolving doors, wondering how dangerous it would be for him to go back, mingle with the crowd, see her . . . He decided against it.

A University streetcar rumbled past. He walked double-time to the corner, where the car was detained by a red light.

Swinging himself on, he dropped a dime in the box and walked to the rear of the car. He stood looking out the window. When the car had gone about four blocks, a white ambulance clanged by, the pitch of its bell dropping as it passed. He watched it grow smaller and smaller and finally cut through traffic to pull up in front of the Municipal Building. Then the streetcar turned onto University Avenue, and he could see no more.

13

THE BASEBALL PEP RALLY began at nine that night, taking place on an empty lot next to the stadium, but the news of a student's suicide (for how could she have fallen when the *Clarion* clearly stated there was a three and a half foot wall?) put a damper on the entire affair. In the orange glow of the bonfire, the students, the girls especially, spread their blankets and sat huddled in conversation. The business manager of the baseball team and the members of the cheerleading squad tried vainly to make the rally what it should be. They spurred the boys to the gathering of more and more fuel, throwing on crates and cartons until the flaming pillar was so high it threatened to topple, but it was to no avail. Cheers wavered and died before half the school's name was spelled out.

He had not attended many of the pep rallies before, but he attended this one. He walked the dark streets from his rooming house at a slow liturgic pace, bearing a carton in his arms.

In the afternoon he had emptied Dorothy's valise, hiding her clothes under the mattress of his bed. Then, although it was a warm day, he had donned his trenchcoat, and after filling its pockets with the bottles and small containers of cosmetics that had been lodged among the clothes, he left the house with the valise, from which he had stripped the tags bearing Dorothy's New York and Blue River addresses. He had gone downtown and checked the valise in a locker at the bus terminal. From there he had walked to the Morton Street Bridge, where he dropped the locker key and then the bottles, one by one, into the umber water, opening them first so that trapped air would not keep them afloat. Ghosts of pink lotion rode the water and thinned and faded. On his way home from the bridge he stopped at a grocery store, where he secured a tan corrugated carton that had once contained cans of pineapple juice.

He carried the carton to the rally and picked his way through the mass of squatting and reclining figures orange-sketched in the darkness. Stepping gingerly between blanket

55

corners and blue-jeaned legs, he advanced to the flaming center of the field.

The heat and the glare were intense in the clearing that surrounded the roaring twelve foot fire. He stood for a moment, staring at the flames. Suddenly the baseball manager and a cheerleader came dashing around from the other side of the clearing. "That's it! That's the boy!" they cried, and seized the carton from his hands.

"Hey," the manager said, hefting the box. "This isn't empty."

"Books . . . old notebooks."

"Ah! Magnifico!" The manager turned to the encircling crowd. "Attention! Attention! The burning of the books!" A few people looked up from their conversations. The manager and the cheerleader took the carton between them, swinging it back and forth towards the rippling flames. "All the way to the top!" the manager shouted.

"Hey . . ."

"Don't worry, friend. We never miss! Book-burning a specialty!" They swung the carton; one . . . two . . . *three!* It sailed up parallel to the cone shaped pyre, arced over and landed with a gush of sparks at the very top. It teetered a moment, then held. There was a spattering of applause from the onlookers. "Hey, here comes Al with a packing case!" cried the cheerleader. He dashed around to the other side of the fire, the manager running after him.

He stood watching as the carton turned black, sheets of flame sliding up past its sides. Suddenly the foundation of the fire shifted, pushing out showers of sparks. A flaming brand hit his foot. He jumped back. Sparks glowed all over the front of his trousers. Nervously he slapped them out, his hands coppery in the fire's glare.

When the last sparks were extinguished, he looked up to make certain that the carton was still secure. It was. Flames ripped up through its top. Its contents, he thought, were probably completely burned by now.

These had included the Pharmacy lab manual, the Kingship Copper pamphlets, the tags from the valise, and the few articles of clothing that Dorothy had prepared for their brief honeymoon; a cocktail dress of gray taffeta, a pair of black suede pumps, stockings, a half slip, bra and panties, two handkerchiefs, a pair of pink satin mules, a pink negligee, and a nightgown; silk and lace, delicate, scented, white . . .

14

From the Blue River Clarion-Ledger; *Friday, April 28, 1950:*

STODDARD COED DIES IN PLUNGE

MUNICIPAL BUILDING TRAGEDY FATAL TO DAUGHTER OF COPPER MAGNATE

Dorothy Kingship, 19-year-old Stoddard University sophomore, was killed today when she fell or jumped from the roof of the 14 story Blue River Municipal Building. The attractive blonde girl, whose home was in New York City, was a daughter of Leo Kingship, president of Kingship Copper Inc.

At 12:58 PM, workers in the building were startled by a loud scream and a crashing sound from the wide airshaft which runs through the structure. Rushing to their windows, they saw the contorted figure of a young woman. Dr. Harvey C. Hess, of 57 Woodbridge Circle, who was in the lobby at the time, reached the scene seconds later to pronounce the girl dead.

The police, arriving shortly thereafter, found a purse resting on the 3½ foot wall that encircles the airshaft. In the purse were a birth certificate and a Stoddard University registration card which served to identify the girl. Police also found a fresh cigarette stub on the roof, stained with lipstick of the shade Miss Kingship wore, leading them to conclude that she had been on the roof for several minutes prior to the plunge which ended her life...

Rex Cargill, an elevator operator, told police that he took Miss Kingship to the 6th or 7th floor half an hour before the tragedy. Another operator, Andrew Vecci, believes he took a woman dressed similarly to Miss Kingship to the 14th floor shortly after 12:30, but is uncertain of the floor at which she entered his car.

According to Stoddard's Dean of Students, Clark D. Welch, Miss Kingship was doing satisfactory work in all her studies. Shocked residents of the dormitory where she lived could offer no reason why she might have taken her own life. They described her as quiet and withdrawn. "Nobody knew her too well," said one girl.

From the Blue River Clarion-Ledger; *Saturday, April 29, 1950:*

COED'S DEATH WAS SUICIDE

SISTER RECEIVES NOTE IN MAIL

The death of Dorothy Kingship, Stoddard coed who plunged from the roof of the Municipal Building yesterday afternoon, was a suicide, Chief of Police Eldon Chesser told reporters last night. An unsigned note in a handwriting definitely established to be that of the dead girl was received through the mail late yesterday afternoon by her sister, Ellen Kingship, a student in Caldwell, Wisconsin. Although the exact wording of the note has not been made public, Chief Chesser characterized it as "a clear expression of suicidal intent." The note was mailed from

Koch. "I was in bed. She came in and I was a little surprised, because we hardly knew each other. As I said, she was smiling and moving around a great deal. She was wearing a bathrobe. She asked if I would loan her the belt to my green suit. I should mention that we both have the same green suit. I got mine in Boston and she got hers in New York, but they're exactly the same. We both wore them to dinner last Saturday night, and it was really embarrassing. Anyway, she asked if I would loan her my belt because the buckle of hers was broken. I hesitated at first, because it's my new spring suit, but she seemed to want it so badly that I finally told her which drawer it was in and she got it. She thanked me very much and left."

Here Miss Koch paused and removed her eyeglasses. "Now here's the strange part. Later, when the police came and searched her room for a note, *they found my belt on her desk!* I recognized it by the way the gold finish was rubbed off the tooth of the buckle. I had been very disappointed about that, because it was an expensive suit. The police kept the belt.

"I was very puzzled by Dorothy's actions. She had pretended to want my belt, but she hadn't used it at all. She was wearing her green suit when...when it happened. The police checked and her belt buckle wasn't the least bit broken. It all seemed very mysterious.

"Then I realized that the belt must have been just a pretext to talk to me. Laying out the suit probably reminded her of me, and everyone knew I was inca-

pacitated with a cold, so she came
in and pretended she needed the
belt. She must have been desperate for someone to talk with. If
only I'd recognized the signs at
the time. I can't help feeling that
if I had gotten her to talk out
her troubles, whatever they
might have been, maybe all this
wouldn't have happened."

...As we left Annabelle Koch's
room, she added a final word.
"Even when the police return
the belt to me," she said, "I know
I won't be able to wear my green
suit again."

15

HE FOUND THE LAST SIX WEEKS OF THE SCHOOL YEAR disap-
pointingly flat. He had expected the excitement created by
Dorothy's death to linger in the air like the glow of a rocket;
instead it had faded almost immediately. He had anticipated
more campus conversations and newspaper articles, allowing
him the luxuriant superiority of the omniscient; instead—
nothing. Three days after Dorothy died campus gossip veered
away to pounce on a dozen marijuana cigarettes that had been
discovered in one of the smaller dormitories. As for the newspapers, a short paragraph announcing Leo Kingship's arrival in Blue River marked the last time the Kingship name
appeared in the *Clarion-Ledger*. No word of an autopsy nor
of her pregnancy, although surely when an unmarried girl
committed suicide without stating a reason, that must be the
first thing they looked for. Keeping it out of the papers must
have cost Kingship plenty.

He told himself he should be rejoicing. If there had been
any kind of inquiry he certainly would have been sought for
questioning. But there had been no questions, no suspicion,—
hence no investigation. Everything had fallen into place perfectly. Except that business of the belt. That puzzled him. Why
on earth had Dorothy taken that Koch girl's belt when she
hadn't wanted to wear it? Maybe she really did want to talk
to someone—about the wedding—and then had thought better
of it. Thank God for that. Or maybe the buckle of her belt
had really been broken, but she had managed to fix it after

61

she had already taken Koch's. Either way, though, it was an unimportant incident. Koch's interpretation of it only strengthened the picture of a suicide, added to the flawless success of his plans. He should be walking on air, smiling at strangers, toasting himself with secret champagne. Instead there was this dull, leaden, let-down feeling. He couldn't understand it.

His depression became worse when he returned to Menasset early in June. Here he was, right where he'd been last summer after the daughter of the farm equipment concern had told him about the boy back home, and the summer before, after he had left the widow. Dorothy's death had been a defensive measure; all his planning hadn't advanced him in the slightest.

He became impatient with his mother. His correspondence from school had been limited to a weekly postcard, and now she badgered him for details; did he have pictures of the girls he'd gone out with?—expecting them to be the most beautiful, the most sought after—Did he belong to this club, to that club?—expecting him to be the president of each—What was his standing in philosophy, in English, in Spanish?—expecting him to be the leader in all. One day he lost his temper. "It's about time you realized I'm not the king of the world!" he shouted, storming from the room.

He took a job for the summer; partly because he needed money, partly because being in the house with his mother all day made him uneasy. The job didn't do any good towards taking his mind off things though; it was in a haberdashery shop whose fixtures were of angular modern design; the glass display counters were bound with inch wide strips of burnished copper.

Towards the middle of July, however, he began to slough off his dejection. He still had the newspaper clippings about Dorothy's death, locked in a small gray strongbox he kept in his bedroom closet. He began taking them out once in a while, skimming through them, smiling at the officious certainty of Chief of Police Eldon Chesser and the half-baked theorizing of Annabelle Koch.

He dug up his old library card, had it renewed, and began withdrawing books regularly; Pearson's *Studies in Murder*, Bolitho's *Murder for Profit*, volumes in the *Regional Murder Series*. He read about Landru, Smith, Pritchard, Crippen; men who had failed where he had succeeded. Of course it was only the failures whose stories got written,—God knows how many successful ones there were. Still, it was flattering to consider how many had failed.

Until now he had always thought of what happened at the Municipal Building as "Dorrie's death." Now he began to think of it as "Dorrie's murder."

Sometimes, when he had lain in bed and read several accounts in one of the books, the enormous daring of what he had done would overwhelm him. He would get up and look at himself in the mirror over the dresser. I got away with murder, he would think. Once he whispered it aloud: "I got away with murder!"

So what if he wasn't rich yet! Hell, he was only twenty-four.

part two:

ELLEN

1

Letter from Annebelle Koch to Leo Kingship:

GIRLS' DORMITORY
STODDARD UNIVERSITY
BLUE RIVER, IOWA
March 5, 1951

DEAR MR. KINGSHIP,

I suppose you are wondering who I am, unless you remember my name from the newspapers. I am the young woman who loaned a belt to your daughter Dorothy last April. I was the last person to speak to her. I would not bring up this subject as I am sure it must be a very painful subject to you, except that I have a good reason.

As you may recall Dorothy and I had the same green suit. She came to my room and asked to borrow my belt. I loaned it to her and later the police found it (or what I thought was it) in her room. They kept it for over a month until they got around to returning it to me and by that time it was quite late in the season so I did not wear the green suit again last year.

Now spring is approaching again and last night I tried on my spring clothes. I tried on my green suit and it fitted perfectly. But when I put on the belt I found to my surprise that it was Dorothy's belt all along. You see, the notch that is marked from the buckle is two notches too big for my waist. Dorothy was quite slender but I am even more so. In fact to be frank I am quite thin. I know that I certainly did not lose any weight because the suit still fits me perfectly, as I said above, so the belt must be Dorothy's. When the police first showed it to me I thought it was mine because the gold finish on the tooth of the buckle was rubbed off. I should have realized that since both suits were made by the same manufacturer the finish would have come off of both buckles.

So now it seems that Dorothy could not wear her own belt for some reason, even though it was not broken at all, and took mine instead. I cannot understand it. At the time I thought she only pretended to need my belt because she wanted to speak to me.

Now that I know the belt is Dorothy's I would feel funny wearing it. I am not superstitious, but after all it does not belong to me and it did belong to poor Dorothy. I thought of throwing it away but I would feel funny doing that also, so I am sending it to you in a separate package and you can keep it or dispose of it as you see fit.

I can still wear the suit because all the girls here are wearing wide leather belts this year anyway.

Yours truly,
ANNABELLE KOCH

Letter from Leo Kingship to Ellen Kingship:

March 8, 1951

MY DEAR ELLEN,

I received your last letter and am sorry not to have replied sooner, but the demands of business have been expecially pressing of late.

Yesterday being Wednesday, Marion came here to dinner. She is not looking too well. I showed her a letter which I received yesterday and she suggested that I send it on to you. You will find it enclosed. Read it now, and then continue with my letter.

Now that you have read Miss Koch's letter, I will explain why I forwarded it.

Marion tells me that ever since Dorothy's death you have been rebuking yourself for your imagined callousness to her. Miss Koch's unfortunate story of Dorothy's "desperate need of someone to talk with" made you feel, according to Marion, that that someone should have been you and would have been you, had you not pushed Dorothy out on her own too soon. You believe, although this is something which Marion has only deduced from your letters, that had there been a difference in your attitude towards Dorothy, she might not have chosen the path she did.

I credit what Marion says since it explains your wishful thinking, for I can only call it that, of last April, when you stubbornly refused to believe that Dorothy's death had been a suicide, despite the incontestable evidence of the note which you yourself received. You felt that if Dorothy had committed suicide you were in some way responsible, and so it was several weeks before you were able to accept her death for what it was, and accept also the burden of an imagined responsibility.

This letter from Miss Koch makes it clear that Dorothy went to the girl because, for some peculiar reason of her own, she did want her belt; she was not in desperate need of someone to whom she could talk. She had made up her mind to do what she was going to do, and there is absolutely no reason for you to believe that she would have come to you first if you two had not had that argument the previous Christmas. (And don't forget it was she who was in a sullen mood and started the argument.) As for the initial coldness on Dorothy's part, remember that I agreed with you that she should go to Stoddard rather than Caldwell, where she would only have become more dependent on you. True, if she had followed you to Caldwell the tragedy would not have happened, but "if" is the biggest

word in the world. Dorothy's punishment may have been ex-
cessively severe, but she was the one who chose it. I am not
responsible, you are not responsible; no one is but Dorothy
herself.

The knowledge that Miss Koch's original interpretation of
Dorothy's behavior was erroneous will, I hope, rid you of any
feelings of self-recrimination that may remain.

Your loving,
FATHER

P.S. Please excuse my indecipherable handwriting. I thought
this letter too personal to dictate to Miss Richardson.

Letter from Ellen Kingship to Bud Corliss:

March 12, 1951
8:35 AM

DEAR BUD,

Here I sit in the club car with a Coke (at this hour—ugh!)
and a pen and paper, trying to keep my writing hand steady
against the motion of the train and trying to give a "lucid if not
brilliant" explanation—as Prof. Mulholland would say—of
why I am making this trip to Blue River.

I'm sorry about tonight's basketball game, but I'm sure Con-
nie or Jane will be glad to go in my place, and you can think
of me between the halves.

Now first of all, this trip is not *impulsive*; I thought about it
all last night. You'd think I was running off to Cairo, Egypt!
Second of all, I will not be missing work, because you are going to take complete notes in each class, and anyway I doubt
if I'll be gone more than a week. And besides, since when do
they flunk seniors for overcuts? Third of all, I won't be wasting
my time, because I'll never know until I've tried, and until I
try I'll never have a moment's peace.

Now that the objections are out of the way, let me explain
why I am going. I'll fill in a little background first.

From the letter I received from my father Saturday morning, you know that Dorothy originally wanted to come to Caldwell and I opposed her for her own good, or so I convinced
myself at the time. Since her death I've wondered whether it
wasn't pure selfishness on my part. My life at home had been
restrained both by my father's strictness and Dorothy's de-
pendence on me, although I didn't realize it at the time. So
when I got to Caldwell I really let go. During my first three
years I was the rah-rah girl; beer parties, hanging around with
the Big Wheels, etc. You wouldn't recognize me. So as I
say, I'm not sure whether I prevented Dorothy from coming
in order to encourage her independence or to avoid losing
mine, Caldwell being the everybody-knows-what-everybody-
else-is-doing-type place that it is.

My father's analysis (probably second-hand via Marion) of

my reaction to Dorothy's death is absolutely right. I didn't want to admit it was suicide because that meant that I was partly responsible. I thought I had other reasons for doubt besides emotional ones however. The note she sent me, for instance. It was her handwriting—I can't deny that—but it didn't sound like her. It sounded kind of stilted, and she addressed me as "Darling," when before it had always been "Dear Ellen" or "Dearest Ellen." I mentioned that to the police, but they said that naturally she was under a strain when she wrote the note and couldn't be expected to sound her usual self, which I had to admit seemed logical. The fact that she carried her birth certificate with her also bothered me, but they explained that away too. A suicide will often take pains to make sure he is immediately identified, they said. The fact that other things which she always carried in her wallet (Stoddard registration card, etc.) would have been sufficient identification didn't seem to make any impression on them. And when I told them that she just wasn't the suicidal type, they didn't even bother to answer me. They swept away every point I raised.

So there I was. Of course I finally had to accept the fact that Dorothy committed suicide—and that I was partly to blame. Annabelle Koch's story was only the clincher. The motive for Dorothy's suicide made me even more responsible, for rational girls today do not kill themselves if they become pregnant—not, I thought, unless they have been brought up to depend on someone else and then that someone else suddenly isn't there.

But Dorothy's pregnancy meant that another person had deserted her too,—the man. If I knew anything about Dorothy it was that she did not treat sex lightly. She wasn't the kind for quick flings. The fact that she was pregnant meant that there was one man whom she had loved and had intended to marry some day.

Now early in the December before her death, Dorothy had written me about a man she had met in her English class. She had been going out with him for quite some time, and this was the Real Thing. She said she would give me all the details over Christmas vacation. But we had an argument during Christmas, and after that she wouldn't even give me the right time. And when we returned to school our letters were almost like business letters. So I never even learned his name. All I knew about him was what she had mentioned in that letter; that he had been in her English class in the fall, and that he was handsome and somewhat like Len Vernon—he is the husband of a cousin of ours—which meant that Dorothy's man was tall, blond, and blue-eyed.

I told my father about this man, urging him to find out who he was and punish him somehow. He refused, saying that it would be impossible to prove he was the one who had gotten Dorothy into trouble, and futile even if we could prove it. She had punished herself for her sins; it was a closed case as far as he was concerned.

That's how things stood until Saturday, when I received my father's letter with the one from Annabelle Koch enclosed. Which brings us to my big scene.

The letters did not have the effect my father had hoped for —not at first—because as I said, Annabelle Koch's story was far from the sole cause of my melancholy. But then I began to wonder; if Dorothy's belt was in perfect condition, why had she lied about it and taken Annabelle's instead? Why couldn't Dorothy wear her own belt? My father was content to let it pass, saying she had "some peculiar reason of her own," but I wanted to know what that reason was, because there were three other seemingly inconsequential things which Dorothy did on the day of her death that puzzled me then and that still puzzled me. Here they are:

1. At 10:15 that morning she bought an inexpensive pair of white cloth gloves in a shop across the street from her dormitory. (The owner reported it to the police after seeing her picture in the papers.) First she asked for a pair of stockings, but because of a rush of business for the Spring Dance scheduled for the following night, they were out of her size. She then asked for gloves, and bought a pair for $1.50. She was wearing them when she died, yet in the bureau in her room was a beautiful pair of hand-made white cloth gloves, perfectly spotless, that Marion had given her the previous Christmas. Why didn't she wear those?

2. Dorothy was a careful dresser. She was wearing her green suit when she died. With it she wore an inexpensive white silk blouse whose floppy out-of-style bow was all wrong for the lines of the suit. Yet in her closet was a white silk blouse, also perfectly spotless, which had been specially made to go with the suit. Why didn't she wear that blouse?

3. Dorothy was wearing dark green, with brown and white accessories. Yet the handkerchief in her purse was bright turquoise, as wrong as could be for the outfit she wore. In her room were at least a dozen handkerchiefs that would have matched her outfit perfectly. Why didn't she take one of those?

At the time of her death I mentioned these points to the police. They dismissed them as quickly as they had dismissed the others I brought up. She was distracted. It was ridiculous to expect her to dress with her ordinary care. I pointed out that the glove incident was the reverse of carelessness; she had gone out of her way to get them. If there was conscious preparation behind one incident, it wasn't unreasonable to assume that all three had some kind of purpose. Their comeback was, "You can't figure a suicide."

Annabelle Koch's letter added a fourth incident which followed the pattern of the other three. Her own belt was perfectly all right, but Dorothy wore Annabelle's instead. In each

*case she rejected an appropriate item for one that was less ap-
propriate, Why?*

I batted that problem around in my head all day Saturday,
and Saturday night too. Don't ask me what I expected to prove.
I felt that there had to be some kind of meaning to it all, and
I wanted to find out as much as I could about Dorothy's state
of mind at the time. Like poking a bad tooth with your tongue,
I guess.

I'd have to write reams to tell you all the mental steps I
went through, searching for some relationship among the four
rejected items. Price, where they came from, and a thousand
other thoughts, but nothing made sense. The same thing happened when I tried to get common characteristics in the wrong
things she had actually worn. I even took sheets of paper and
headed them Gloves, Handkerchief, Blouse, and Belt, and put
down everything I knew about each, looking for a meaning.
Apparently, there just wasn't a meaning. Size, age, ownership,
cost, color, quality, place of purchase—none of the significant
characteristics appeared on all four lists. I tore up the papers
and went to bed. You can't figure a suicide.

It came to me about an hour later, so startlingly that I shot
up straight in bed, suddenly cold. The out-of-style blouse, the
gloves she'd bought that morning. Annabelle Koch's belt, the
turquoise handkerchief . . . Something old, something new,
something borrowed, and something blue.

It might—I keep telling myself—be a coincidence. But in
my heart I don't believe that.

Dorothy went to the Municipal Building, not because it is
the tallest building in Blue River, but because a Municipal
Building is where you go when you want to get married. She
wore something old, something new, something borrowed and
something blue—poor romantic Dorothy—and she carried her
birth certificate with her to prove she was over eighteen. And
you don't make a trip like that alone. Dorothy can only have
gone with one person—the man who made her pregnant, the
man she'd been going with for a long time, the man she loved
—the handsome blue-eyed blond of her fall English class. He
got her up to the roof somehow. I'm almost certain that's the
way it was.

The note? All it said was "I hope you will forgive me for the
unhappiness I will cause. There is nothing else that I can do."
Where is there mention of suicide? She was referring to the
marriage! She knew Father would disapprove of a hasty step
like that, but there was nothing else she could do because she
was pregnant. The police were right when they said the stilted
tone was the result of strain, only it was the strain of an eloping
bride, not of a person contemplating suicide.

"Something old, something new" was enough to set me
going, but it would never be enough to make the police re-
classify a suicide with note as an unsolved murder, especially

70

*when they would be prejudiced against me—the crank who
pestered them last year. You know that's true. So I'm going
to find this man and do some very cautious Sherlocking. As
soon as I turn up anything that supports my suspicions, anything strong enough to interest the police, I promise to go
straight to them. I've seen too many movies where the heroine
accuses the murderer in his soundproof penthouse and he says
"Yes, I did it, but you'll never live to tell the tale." So don't
worry about me, and don't get impatient, and don't write my
father as he would probably explode. Maybe it is "crazy and
impulsive" to rush into it this way, but how can I sit and wait
when I know what has to be done and there is no one else to
do it?*

*Perfect timing. We're just entering Blue River now. I can
see the Municipal Building from the window.*

*I'll wind this letter up later in the day, when I'll be able to
tell you where I'm staying and what progress, if any, I've made.
Even though Stoddard is ten times as big as Caldwell, I have
a pretty good idea of how to begin. Wish me luck . . .*

2

DEAN WELCH WAS PLUMP, with round gray eyes like buttons
pressed into the shiny pink clay of his face. He favored suits of
clergy-black flannel, single breasted so as to expose his Phi
Beta Kappa key. His office was dim and chapel-like, with dark
wood and draperies and, in its center, a broad field of meticulously accoutred desktop.

After releasing the button on the inter-office speaker, the
Dean rose and faced the door, his customary moist-lipped
smile replaced by an expression of solemnity suitable for
greeting a girl whose sister had taken her own life while
nominally under his care. The ponderous notes of the noonday
carillon floated into the chamber, muffled by distance and
draperies. The door opened and Ellen Kingship entered.

By the time she had closed the door and approached his
desk, the Dean of Students had measured and evaluated her
with the complacent certainty of one who has dealt with
younger people for many years. She was neat; he liked that.
And quite pretty. Red-brown hair in thick bangs, brown eyes,
a smile whose restraint acknowledged the unfortunate past . . .
Determined looking. Probably not brilliant, but a plodder . . .
second quarter of her class. Her coat and dress were shades of
dark blue, a pleasant contrast to the usual student polychrome.
She seemed a bit nervous, but then, weren't they all?

"Miss Kingship . . ." he murmured with a nod, indicating

71

the visitor's chair. They sat. The Dean folded his pink hands. "Your father is well, I hope."

"Very well, thank you." Her voice was low-pitched and breathy.

The Dean said, "I had the pleasure of meeting him . . . last year." There was a moment of silence. "If there's anything I can do for you . . ."

She shifted in the stiff-backed chair. "We—my father and I—are trying to locate a certain man, a student here." The Dean's eyebrows lifted in polite curiosity. "He lent my sister a fairly large sum of money a few weeks before her death. She wrote me about it. I happened to come across her checkbook last week and it reminded me of the incident. There's nothing in the checkbook to indicate that she ever repaid the debt, and we thought he might have felt awkward about claiming it."

The Dean nodded.

"The only trouble," Ellen said, "is that I don't recall his name. But I do remember Dorothy mentioning that he was in her English class during the fall semester, and that he was blond. We thought perhaps you could help us locate him. It was a fairly large sum of money . . ." She took a deep breath.

"I see," said the Dean. He pressed his hands together as though comparing their size. His lips smiled at Ellen. "Can do," he snapped with military briskness. He held the pose for an instant, then jabbed one of the buttons on the inter-office speaker. "Miss Platt," he snapped, and released the button.

He brought his chair into more perfect alignment with the desk, as if he were preparing for a long campaign.

The door opened and a pale efficient-looking woman stepped into the room. The Dean nodded at her and then leaned back in his chair and stared at the wall beyond Ellen's head, mapping his strategy. Several moments passed before he spoke. "Get the program card of Kingship, Dorothy, fall semester, nineteen forty-nine. See which English section she was in and get the enrollment list for that section. Bring me the folders of all the male students whose names appear on the list." He looked at the secretary. "Got that?"

"Yes, sir."

He made her repeat the instructions.

"Fine," he said. She went out. "On the double," he said to the closed door. He turned back to Ellen and smiled complacently. She returned the smile.

By degrees the air of military efficiency faded, giving way to one of avuncular solicitude. The Dean leaned forward, his fingers softly clustered on the desk. "Surely you haven't come to Blue River solely for this purpose," he said.

"I'm visiting friends."

"Ahh."

Ellen opened her handbag. "May I smoke?"

"By all means." He pushed a crystal ashtray to her side of

72

the desk. "I smoke myself," he admitted graciously. Ellen offered him a cigarette, but he demurred. She lit hers with a match drawn from a white folder on which *Ellen Kingship* was printed in copper letters.

The Dean regarded the matchbook thoughtfully. "Your conscientiousness in financial matters is admirable," he said, smiling. "If only everyone we dealt with were similarly conscientious." He examined a bronze letter opener. "We are at present beginning the construction of a new gymnasium and fieldhouse. Several people who pledged contributions have failed to live up to their words."

Ellen shook her head sympathetically.

"Perhaps your father would be interested in making a contribution," the Dean speculated. "A memorial to your sister . . ."

"I'll be glad to mention it to him."

"Would you? I would certainly appreciate that." He replaced the letter opener. "Such contributions are tax-deductible," he added.

A few minutes later the secretary entered with a stack of Manila folders in her arm. She set them before the Dean. "English fifty-one," she said, "section six. Seventeen male students."

"Fine," said the Dean. As the secretary left he straightened his chair and rubbed his hands, the military man once more. He opened the top folder and leafed through its contents until he came to an application form. There was a photograph pasted in the corner of it. "Dark hair," he said, and put the folder on his left.

When he had gone through all of them, there were two uneven piles. "Twelve with dark hair and five with light," the Dean said.

Ellen leaned forward. "Dorothy once told me he was handsome . . ."

The Dean drew the pile of five folders to the center of his desk blotter and opened the first one. "George Speiser," he said thoughtfully. "I doubt if you'd call Mr. Speiser handsome." He lifted out the application form and turned it towards Ellen. The face in the photograph was a chinless, gimlet-eyed teen-ager. She shook her head.

The second was an emaciated young man with thick eyeglasses.

The third was fifty-three years old and his hair was white, not blond.

Ellen's hands were damp on her purse.

The Dean opened the fourth folder. "Gordon Gant," he said. "Does that sound like the name?" He turned the application form towards her.

He was blond and unarguably handsome; light eyes under

73

full brows, a long firm jaw and a cavalier grin. "I think so . . ." she said. "Yes, I think he . . ."

"Or could it be Dwight Powell?" the Dean asked, displaying the fifth application form in his other hand.

The fifth photograph showed a square-jawed, serious-looking young man, with a cleft chin and pale-toned eyes.

"Which name sounds familiar?" the Dean asked.

Ellen looked impotently from one picture to the other.

They were both blond; they were both blue-eyed; they were both handsome.

She came out of the Administration Building and stood at the head of the stone steps surveying the campus, dull gray under a clouded sky. Her purse was in one hand, a slip of paper from the Dean's memo pad in the other.

Two . . . It would slow her up a little, that's all. It should be simple to find out which was the one . . . and then she would watch him, even meet him perhaps—through not as Ellen Kingship. Watch for the darting eye, the guarded answer. Murder must leave marks. (It *was* murder. It *must* have been murder.)

She was getting ahead of herself. She looked at the paper in her hand:

> *Gordon C. Gant*
> *1312 West 26th Street*
>
> *Dwight Powell*
> *1520 West 35th Street*

3

HER LUNCH, EATEN IN A SMALL RESTAURANT across the street from the campus, was a hasty mechanical affair, her mind racing with swift thoughts. How to begin? Ask a few discreet questions of their friends? But where do you start? Follow each man, learn the identity of his friends, meet them, find the ones who had known him last year? Time, time, time . . . If she remained in Blue River too long, Bud might call her father. Her fingers tapped impatiently. Who would be *sure* to know about Gordon Gant and Dwight Powell? Their families. Or if they were from out of town, a landlady or a roommate. It would be impetuous to go straight to the center of things, to the people nearest them, but still, no time would be wasted . . . She bit her lower lip, her fingers still tapping.

After a minute she put down her half finished cup of coffee, rose from the table and threaded her way to the phone booth.

Hesitantly she ruffled the pages of the thin Blue River book. There was no Gant at all, no Powell on 35th Street. That meant they either had no phones, which seemed unlikely, or they were living with families other than their own.

She called Information and obtained the number of the telephone at 1312 West 26th Street; 2-2014:

"Hello?" The voice was a woman's; dry, middle-aged.

"Hello." Ellen swallowed. "Is Gordon Gant there?"

A pause. "Who's calling?"

"A friend of his. Is he there?"

"No." Snapped out sharply.

"Who is this?"

"His landlady."

"When do you expect him back?"

"Won't be back till late tonight." The woman's voice was quick with annoyance. There was a click as she hung up.

Ellen looked at the dead receiver and placed it on the hook. When she got back to her table the coffee was cold.

He would be gone all day. Go there? . . . A single conversation with the landlady might establish that Gant was the one who had gone with Dorothy. Or, by elimination, it might prove that Powell was the one. Speak to the landlady . . . but under what pretext?

Why, any pretext! Provided the woman believed it, what harm could the wildest story do?—even if its falseness were completely obvious to Gant when the landlady reported it. Either he wasn't the man, in which case let him puzzle over a mysterious questioner pretending to be a friend or a relative, or he *was* the man, in which case: A) He had not killed Dorothy—again let him puzzle over a mysterious questioner, or: B) He *had* killed Dorothy—and the story of a girl seeking information about him would make him uneasy. Yet his uneasiness would not interfere with her plans, for should she later make his acquaintance, he would have no reason to associate her with the girl who had questioned his landlady. Uneasiness on his part might even be a help to her, making him tense, more likely to betray himself. Why, he might even decide to take no chances and leave town—and that would be all she'd need to convince the police that there was a sound basis to her suspicions. They would investigate, find the proof . . .

Go straight to the center of things. Impetuous? When you thought about it, it was really the most logical thing to do.

She looked at her watch. Five past one. Her visit shouldn't be made too soon after the telephone call or the landlady might connect the two and become suspicious. Forcing herself to sit back in the chair, Ellen caught the waitress' eye and ordered another cup of coffee.

At a quarter of two she entered the 1300 block of West 26th

Street. It was a quiet, tired-looking street, with pallid two
story frame houses sitting behind pocked brown lawns still
hard from winter. A few old Fords and Chevvies stood immobile along the curb, some aging naturally, some trying to stay
young with unprofessional paint jobs, bright colored but luster-
less. Ellen walked with the enforced slowness of attempted
nonchalance, the sound of her heels the only sound in the
still air.

The house where Gordon Gant lived, 1312, was the third
one in from the corner; mustard colored, its brown trim the
shade of stale chocolate. After looking at it for a moment,
Ellen walked up the cracked concrete path that bisected the
dead lawn and led to the porch. There she read the nameplate
on the mailbox affixed to one of the posts: *Mrs. Minna Arquette*. She stepped to the door. Its bell was of the old-fashioned kind; a fan-shaped metal tab protruded from the center
of the door. Drawing a deep initiatory breath, she gave the
tab a quick twist. The bell within rang gratingly. Ellen waited.

Presently footsteps sounded inside, and then the door
opened. The woman who stood in the doorway was tall and
lank, with frizzy gray hair clustered above a long equine face.
Her eyes were pink and rheumy. A busily printed housedress
hung from her sharp shoulders. She looked Ellen up and down.
"Yes?"—the dry Midwestern voice of the telephone.

"You must be Mrs. Arquette," Ellen declared.

"That's right." The woman twitched a sudden smile, displaying teeth of an unnatural perfection.

Ellen smiled back at her. "I'm Gordon's cousin."

Mrs. Arquette arched thin eyebrows. "His cousin?"

"Didn't he mention that I'd be here today?"

"Why, no. He didn't say anything about a cousin. Not a
word."

"That's funny. I wrote him I'd be passing through. I'm on
my way to Chicago and I purposely came this way so I could
stop off and see him. He must have forgotten to—"

"When did you write him?"

Ellen hesitated. "The day before yesterday. Saturday."

"Oh." The smile flashed again. "Gordon leaves the house
early in the morning and the first mail don't come till ten.
Your letter is probably sitting in his room this minute."

"Ohh . . ."

"He isn't here right—"

"Couldn't I come in for a few minutes?" Ellen cut in quickly.
"I took the wrong streetcar from the station and I had to walk
about ten blocks."

Mrs. Arquette took a step back into the house. "Of course.
Come on in."

"Thank you very much." Ellen crossed the threshold, entering a hallway that was stale-smelling and—once the front door
was closed—dimly lighted. A flight of stairs rose along the

76

right wall. On the left an archway opened onto a parlor which had the stiff look of seldom used rooms.

"Miz Arquette?" a voice called from the back of the house.

"Coming!" she answered. She turned to Ellen. "You mind sitting in the kitchen?"

"Not at all," Ellen said. The Arquette teeth shone again, and then Ellen was following the tall figure down the hallway, wondering why the woman, so pleasant now, had been so irritable over the telephone.

The kitchen was painted the same mustard color as the exterior of the house. There was a white porcelain-topped table in the middle of the room, with a set of anagrams laid out on it. An elderly bald-headed man with thick eyeglasses sat at the table, pouring the last of a bottle of Dr. Pepper into a flowered jar that had once held cheese. "This is Mr. Fishback from next door," said Mrs. Arquette. "We play anagrams."

"Nickel a word," added the old man, raising his eyeglasses to look at Ellen.

"This is Miss. . ." Mrs. Arquette waited.

"Gant," said Ellen.

"Miss Gant, Gordon's cousin."

"How do you do," said Mr. Fishback. "Gordon's a nice boy." He dropped his glasses back into place, his eyes swelling up behind them. "It's your go," he said to Mrs. Arquette.

She took the seat opposite Mr. Fishback. "Sit down," she said to Ellen, indicating one of the empty chairs. "You want some pop?"

"No, thank you," Ellen said, sitting. She slipped her arms from the sleeves of her coat and dropped it back over the chair.

Mrs. Arquette stared at the dozen turned up letters in the ring of blank-backed wooden squares. "Where you on your way from?" she inquired.

"California."

"I didn't know Gordon had family in the West."

"No, I was just visiting there. I'm from the East."

"Oh." Mrs. Arquette looked at Mr. Fishback. "Go ahead, I give up. Can't do anything with no vowels."

"It's my turn?" he asked. She nodded. With a grin Mr. Fishback snatched at the turned up letters. "You missed it, you missed it!" he crowed. "C-R-Y-P-T. Crypt. What they bury folks in." He pushed the letters together and added the word to the others ranged before him.

"That's not fair," Mrs. Arquette protested. "You had all that time to think while I was at the door."

"Fair is fair," Mr. Fishback declared. He turned up two more letters and placed them in the center of the ring.

"Oh, shoot," Mrs. Arquette muttered, sitting back in her chair.

"How is Gordon these days?" Ellen asked.

"Oh, fine," said Mrs. Arquette. "Busy as a bee, what with school and the program."

"The program?"

"You mean you don't know about Gordon's program?"

"Well, I haven't heard from him in quite a while . . ."

"Why, he's had it for almost three months now!" Mrs. Arquette drew herself up grandly. "He plays records and talks. A disc jockey. 'The Discus Thrower' he's called. Every night except Sunday, from eight to ten over KBRI."

"That's wonderful!" Ellen exclaimed.

"Why, he's a real celebrity," the landlady continued, turning up a letter as Mr. Fishback nodded to her. "They had an interview on him in the paper a couple of Sundays back. Reporter come here and everything. And girls he don't even know calling him up at all hours. Stoddard girls. They get his number out of the Student Directory and call up just to hear his voice over the telephone. He don't want anything to do with them, so I'm the one's got to answer. It's enough to drive a person crazy." Mrs. Arquette frowned at the anagrams. "Go ahead, Mr. Fishback," she said.

Ellen fingered the edge of the table. "Is Gordon still going out with that girl he wrote me about last year?" she asked.

"Which one's that?"

"A blonde girl, short, pretty. Gordon mentioned her in a few of his letters last year,—October, November, all the way up through April. I thought he was really interested in her. But he stopped writing about her in April."

"Well I'll tell you," Mrs. Arquette said, "I don't ever get to see the girls Gordon goes out with. Before he got the program he used to go out three-four times a week, but he never brought any of the girls here. Not that I'd expect him to. I'm only his landlady. He never talks about them neither. Other boys I had here before him used to tell me all about their girls, but college boys were younger then. Nowadays they're mostly veterans and I guess they get a little older, they don't chatter so much. Least Gordon don't. Not that I'd want to pry, but I'm interested in people." She turned over a letter. "What was that girl's name? You tell me her name I can probably tell you if he's still going out with her, because sometimes when he's using the phone over by the stairs there, I'm in the parlor and can't help hearing part of the conversation."

"I don't remember her name," Ellen said, "but he was going with her last year, so maybe if *you* remember the names of some of the girls he spoke to then, I'll be able to recognize it."

"Let's see," Mrs. Arquette pondered, mechanically arranging anagrams in search of a word. "There was a Louella. I remember that one because I had a sister-in-law by that name. And then there was a . . ."—her watery eyes closed in concentration—". . . a Barbara. No, that was the year before, his first

78

year. Let's see, Louella . . ." She shook her head. "There was others, but I'm hanged if I can remember them."

The game of anagrams went on in silence for a minute. Finally Ellen said, "I think this girl's name was Dorothy."

Mrs. Arquette waved a go-ahead at Mr. Fishback. "Dorothy . . ." Her eyes narrowed. "No . . . if the name's Dorothy, I don't think he's still going out with her. I haven't heard him talking to any Dorothy lately, I'm sure of that. Of course he goes down to the corner sometimes to make a real personal call or a Long Distance."

"But he *was* going with a Dorothy last year?"

Mrs. Arquette looked up at the ceiling. "I don't know . . . I don't *remember* a Dorothy, but I don't *not remember* one either, if you know what I mean."

"Dottie?" Ellen tried.

Mrs. Arquette considered for a moment and then gave a noncommittal shrug.

"Your go," Mr. Fishback said petulantly.

The wooden squares clicked softly as Mrs. Arquette maneuvered them about. "I think," said Ellen, "that he must have broken up with this Dorothy in April when he stopped writing about her. He must have been in a bad mood around the end of April. Worried, nervous . . ." She looked at Mrs. Arquette questioningly.

"Not Gordon," she said. "He had real spring fever last year. Going around humming. I joshed him about it." Mr. Fishback fidgeted impatiently. "Oh, go ahead," Mrs. Arquette said.

Choking over his Dr. Pepper, Mr. Fishback pounced on the anagrams. "You missed one again!" he cried, clawing up letters. "F-A-N-E. Fane!"

"What're you talking about, fane? No such word!" Mrs. Arquette turned to Ellen. "You ever hear of a word 'fane'?"

"You should know better'n to argue with me!" Mr. Fishback shrilled. "I don't know what it means, but I know it's a word. I seen it!" He turned to Ellen. "I read three books a week, regular as clockwork."

"Fane," snorted Mrs. Arquette.

"Well look it up in the dictionary!"

"That little pocket one with nothing in it? Every time I look up one of your words and it ain't there you blame it on the dictionary!"

Ellen looked at the two glaring figures. "Gordon must have a dictionary," she said. She stood up. "I'll be glad to get it if you'll tell me which room is his."

"That's right," Mrs. Arquette said decisively. "He *does* have one." She rose. "You sit down, dear. I know just where it is."

"May I come along then? I'd like to see Gordon's room. He's told me what a nice place . . ."

"Come on," said Mrs. Arquette, stalking out of the kitchen. Ellen hurried after her.

"You'll see," Mr. Fishback's voice chased them, "I know more words than you'll *ever* know, even if you live to be a hundred!"

They sped up the darkwood stairs, Mrs. Arquette in the fore muttering indignantly. Ellen followed her through a door adjacent to the head of the stairway.

The room was bright with flowered wallpaper. There was a green-covered bed, a dresser, easy chair, table . . . Mrs. Arquette, having snatched a book from the top of the dresser, stood by the window ruffling the pages. Ellen moved to the dresser and scanned the titles of the books ranked across its top. A diary maybe. Any kind of notebook. *Prize Stories of 1950. An Outline of History, Radio Announcer's Handbook of Pronunciation, The Brave Bulls, A History of American Jazz, Swann's Way, Elements of Psychology, Three Famous Murder Novels* and *A Sub-Treasury of American Humor.*

"Oh, shoot," said Mrs. Arquette. She stood with her forefinger pressed to the open dictionary. "Fane," she read, "a temple; hence a church." She slammed the book shut. "Where does he get words like that?"

Ellen eased over to the table, where three envelopes were fanned out. Mrs. Arquette, putting the dictionary on the dresser, glanced at her. "The one without a return address is yours, I guess."

"Yes, it is," Ellen said. The two letters with return addresses were from *Newsweek* and the National Broadcasting Company.

Mrs. Arquette was at the door. "Coming?"

"Yes," Ellen said.

They trudged down the stairs and walked slowly into the kitchen, where Mr. Fishback was waiting. As soon as he observed Mrs. Arquette's dejection he burst into gleeful cackling. She gave him a dirty look. "It means a church," she said, slumping into her chair. He laughed some more. "Oh, shut up and get on with the game," Mrs. Arquette grumbled. Mr. Fishback turned over two letters.

Ellen took her purse from the coat-draped chair in which she had sat. "I guess I'll be going now," she said dispiritedly.

"Going?" Mrs. Arquette looked up, the thin eyebrows arching.

Ellen nodded.

"Well for goodness' sake, aren't you going to wait for Gordon?" Ellen went cold. Mrs. Arquette looked at the clock on the refrigerator next to the door. "It's ten after two," she said. "His last class ended at two o'clock. He should be here any minute."

She couldn't speak. The image of Mrs. Arquette's upturned face swayed sickeningly. "You . . . you told me he would be gone all day . . ." she strained out finally.

Mrs. Arquette looked injured. "Why, I never told you no uch thing! Why on earth you been sitting here if not waiting or him?"

"The telephone . . ."

The landlady's jaw dropped. "Was that you? Around one 'clock?"

Ellen nodded helplessly.

"Well why didn't you tell me it was you? I thought it was ne of those fool girls. Whenever someone calls and won't give a name I tell them he's gone for the day. Even if he's here. He old me to. He . . ." The expression of earnestness drained from Mrs. Arquette's face. The dull eyes, the thin-lipped mouth became grim, suspicious. "If you thought he was out for he day," she demanded slowly, "then why did you come here at all?"

"I . . . I wanted to meet you. Gordon wrote so much . . ."

"Why were you asking all those questions?" Mrs. Arquette stood up.

Ellen reached for her coat. Suddenly Mrs. Arquette was holding Ellen's arms, the long bony fingers clutching painfully. "Let go of me . . . Please . . ."

"Why were you snooping in his room?" The horselike face pressed close to Ellen's, the eyes swelling with anger, the rough skin red. "What did you want in there? You take something while my back was turned?"

Behind Ellen, Mr. Fishback's chair scraped and his voice piped frightenedly "Why'd she want to steal anything from her own cousin?"

"Who says she's his cousin?" Mrs. Arquette snapped.

Ellen worked futilely in her grasp. "Please, you're hurting me . . ."

The pale eyes narrowed. "And I don't think she's one of those damn girls looking for a souvenir or something either. Why was she asking all those questions?"

"I'm his cousin! I am!" Ellen tried to steady her voice. "I want to go now. You can't keep me here. I'll see him later."

"You'll see him now," Mrs. Arquette said. "You're staying here until Gordon comes." She glanced over Ellen's shoulder. "Mr. Fishback, get over by the back door." She waited, her eyes following Mr. Fishback's slow passage, and then she released Ellen. Moving quickly to the front doorway, she blocked it, her arms folded across her chest. "We'll find out what this is all about," she said.

Ellen rubbed her arms where Mrs. Arquette's fingers had clamped them. She looked at the man and woman blocking the doors at either end of the kitchen; Mr. Fishback with his glass-magnified eyes blinking nervously; Mrs. Arquette standing grim, monolithic. "You can't do this." She retrieved her purse from the floor. She took her coat from the chair and put it over her arm. "Let me out of here," she said firmly.

Neither of them moved.

They heard the front door slam and footsteps on the stairs. "Gordon!" Mrs. Arquette shouted, "Gordon!" The footsteps stopped. "What is it, Mrs. Arquette?" The landlady turned and ran down the hallway.

Ellen faced Mr. Fishback. "Please," she implored, "let me out of here. I didn't mean any harm."

He shook his head slowly.

She stood motionless, hearing the excited rasping of Mrs. Arquette's voice far behind her. Footsteps approached and the voice grew louder. "She kept asking all kinds of questions about what girls you were going out with last year, and she even tricked me into taking her to your room. She was looking at your books and the letters on your table . . ." Mrs. Arquette's voice suddenly flooded the kitchen. "There she is!"

Ellen turned. Mrs. Arquette stood to the left of the table, one arm lifted, pointing accusation. Gant was in the doorway leaning against the jamb, tall and spare in a pale-blue topcoat, books in one hand. He looked at her for a moment, then his lips curved a smile over his long jaw and one eyebrow lifted slightly.

He detached himself from the jamb and stepped into the room, putting his books on the refrigerator without taking his eyes from her. "Why, Cousin Hester . . ." he marveled softly, his eyes flicking down then up again in considered appraisal. "You've passed through adolescence magnificently . . ." He ambled around the table, placed his hands on Ellen's shoulders, and kissed her fondly on the cheek.

4

"YOU . . . YOU MEAN she really *is* your cousin?" Mrs. Arquette gasped.

"Arquette, my love," said Gant, moving to Ellen's left, "ours was a communal teething ring." He patted Ellen's shoulder. "Wasn't it, Hester?"

She eyed him crazily, her face flushed, her mouth slack. Her gaze moved to Mrs. Arquette at the left of the table, to the hallway beyond it, to the coat and purse in her hands . . . She darted to the right, sped around the table and through the door and down the hallway hearing Arquette's "Running away!" and Gant's pursuing shout: "She's from the psychotic side of the family!" Wrenching open the heavy front door, she fled from the house, her toes biting the concrete path. At the sidewalk she turned to the right and reined to swift bitter trides, wrestling into her tangled coat. Oh God, everything messed up! She clenched her teeth, feeling the hot pressure of tears behind her eyes. Gant caught up with her and matched her strides with long easy legs. She flung a fiery glance at the grinning face and then glared straight ahead, her whole being compressed with unreasoned fury at herself and him.

"Isn't there a secret word?" he asked. "Aren't you supposed to press a message into my hand and whisper 'Southern Comfort' or something? Or is this the one where the heavy in the dark suit has been following you all day and you sought refuge in the nearest doorway? I like them equally well, so whichever it is . . ." She strode along in acid silence. "You ever read the Saint stories? I used to. Old Simon Templar was *always* running into beautiful women with strange behavior patterns. Once one of them swam onto his yacht in the middle of the night. Said she was a channel swimmer gone astray, I believe. Turned out to be an insurance investigator." He caught her arm. "Cousin Hester, I have the most insatiable curiosity . . ."

She pulled her arm free. They had reached an interesecting avenue along the other side of which a taxi cruised. She waved and the cab began a U turn. "It was a joke," she said tightly. "I'm sorry. I did it on a bet."

"That's what the girl on the yacht told the Saint." His face went serious. "Fun is fun, but why all the questions about my sordid past?"

The cab pulled up. She tried to open the door but he braced his hand against it. "Look here, cousin, don't be fooled by my disc jockey dialogue. I'm not kidding . . ."

"Please," she moaned exhaustedly, tugging at the door handle. The cabbie appeared at the front window, looking up at them and appraising the situation. "Hey mister . . ." he said. His voice was a menacing rumble.

With a sigh, Gant released the door. Ellen opened it, ducked in and slammed it closed. She sank into soft worn leather. Outside Gant was leaning over, his hands on the door, staring in at her through the glass as though trying to memorize the details of her face. She looked away.

She waited until the cab had left the curb before telling the driver her destination.

It took ten minutes to reach the New Washington House, where Ellen had registered before calling on the Dean,—ten minutes of lip-biting and quick-handed smoking and bitter self-denunciation, the release of the tension which had been built up before Gant's arrival and which had been left hanging, unspent, by his anticlimactic assinine banter. Cousin Hester! Oh, she had really messed things up! She had bet half her chips and got nothing in return. Still in the dark as to whether or not he was *the* man, she had made further questioning of him or his landlady completely impossible. If investigation of

Powell should show he wasn't the man, proving that Gant was
she might as well give up and go back to Caldwell, because if—
always the second, the big "if"—if Gant had killed Dorothy
he would be on guard, knowing Ellen's face and knowing
what she was after by the questions she had asked Mrs. Ar
quette. A killer on guard, ready perhaps to kill again. She
wouldn't risk tangling with that—not when he had seen her
face. Better to live in doubt than to die in certainty. Her only
other course would be to go to the police, and she would still
have nothing more to offer them than something old, some
thing new," so they would nod solemnly and usher her politely
from the station.

Oh, she had made a fine start!

The hotel room had beige walls and clumsy brown furniture
and the same clean, impersonal, transient air as the miniature
paper-wrapped cake of soap in the adjoining bathroom. The
only mark of its occupancy was the suitcase with the Caldwell
stickers on the rack at the foot of the double bed.

After hanging her coat in the closet, Ellen seated herself at
the writing table by the window. She took her fountain pen and
the letter to Bud from her purse. Staring down at the addressed
but still unsealed envelope, she debated whether or not to mention, in addition to an outline of the interview with Dear
Welch, the story of the Gant fiasco. No . . . if Dwight Powell
turned out to be the one, then the Gant business meant nothing. It *must* be Powell. Not Gant, she told herself,—not with
that lighthearted chatter. But what had he said?—Don't be
fooled by my disc jockey dialogue. I'm not kidding . . .

There was a knock at the door. She jumped to her feet.
"Who is it?"

"Towels," a high feminine voice answered.

Ellen crossed the room and grasped the doorknob. "I . . .
I'm not dressed. Could you leave them outside please?"

"All right," the voice said.

She stood there for two minutes, hearing occasional passing
footsteps and the muffled sound of the elevator down the hall,
while the knob grew damp in her hand. Finally she smiled at
her nervousness, visualizing herself peering under the bed old-
maid fashion before going to sleep. She opened the door.

Gant lounged with one elbow against the jamb, the hand
propping up his blond head. "Hi, Cousin Hester," he said.
"I believe I mentioned my insatiable curiosity." She tried to
close the door, but his foot was in the way, immovable. He
smiled. "Much fun. Follow that cab!" His right hand described
a zigzag course. "Shades of the Warner Brothers. The driver
got such a kick out of it he almost refused the tip. I told him
you were running away from my bed and board."

"Get away!" she whispered fiercely. "I'll call the manager!"

"Look, Hester,"—the smile dropped—"I think I could have

84

you arrested for illegal entry or impersonating a cousin or something like that, so why don't you invite me in for a small confab? If you're worried about what the bellhops will think, you can leave the door open." He pushed gently on the door, forcing Ellen to retreat a step. "That's a good girl," he said as he eased through the opening. He eyed her dress with exaggerated disappointment. " 'I'm not dressed,' she says. I should have known you were a habitual liar." He strolled to the bed and sat down on the edge of it. "Well for pity's sake, coz, stop shaking! I'm not going to eat you."

"What . . . what do you want?"

"An explanation."

She swung the door all the way open and remained standing in the doorway, as though it were his room and she the visitor. "It's . . . very simple. I listen to your program all the time . . ."

He glanced at the suitcase. "In Wisconsin?"

"It's only a hundred miles away. We get KBRI. We really do."

"Go ahead."

"I listen to you all the time, and I like your program very much . . . I'm in Blue River, so I thought I'd try to meet you."

"And when you meet me you run away."

"Well what would you have done? I didn't plan it *that* way. I pretended to be your cousin because I . . . I wanted to get information about you—what kind of girls you like . . ."

Rubbing his jaw doubtfully, he stood up. "How did you get my phone number?"

"From the Student Directory."

He moved to the foot of the bed and touched the suitcase. "If you go to Caldwell, how did you get a Stoddard directory?"

"From one of the girls here."

"Who?"

"Annabelle Koch. She's a friend of mine."

"Annabelle . . ." He had recognized the name. He squinted at Ellen incredulously. "Hey, is this really on the level?"

"Yes." She looked down at her hands. "I know it was a crazy thing to do, but I like your program so much . . ." When she looked up again he was by the window.

He said, "Of all the stupid, idiotic . . ."—and suddenly he was staring at the hallway beyond her, his eyes baffled. She turned. There was nothing out of the ordinary to be seen. She looked back at Gant and he was facing the window, his back to her. "Well, Hester," he said, "that was a flattering explanation" —he turned, taking his hand from inside his jacket—"and one I shall long remember." He glanced at the partially open bathroom door. "Do you mind if I utilize your facilities?" he asked, and before she could say anything he had ducked into the bathroom and closed the door. The lock clicked.

Ellen gazed blankly at the door, wondering whether or not Gant had believed her. Her knees quivered. Drawing a deep steadying breath, she crossed the room to the writing table and took a cigarette from her purse. She broke two matches before she got it lighted, and then she stood looking out the window, nervously rolling her fountain pen back and forth over the surface of the table which was bare except for her purse. Bare . . . the letter . . . The letter to Bud! Gant had been standing near the table and he had tricked her into turning towards the hallway and then he had been facing the window and he turned, taking his hand from inside his jacket! . . .

Frantically she hammered on the bathroom door. "Give me that letter! Give it to me!"

Several seconds passed before Gant's deep-toned voice said, "My curiosity is especially insatiable when it comes to phony cousins and flimsy stories."

She stood in the doorway with one hand on the jamb and her coat in the other, looking from the still-closed bathroom door to the hallway and smiling inanely at the occasional passers-by. A bellhop asked if there were anything he could do for her. She shook her head.

Gant finally came out. He was folding the letter carefully into its envelope. He put it on the writing table. "Well," he said. He viewed her ready-to-flee figure. "Well." He smiled somewhat uncomfortably. "As my grandmother said when the man on the phone asked for Lana Turner, 'Boy, have you got the wrong number.'"

Ellen did not move.

"Look," he said. "I didn't even know her. I said hello to her once or twice. There were other blond guys in that class. I didn't even know her name until her picture was in the papers. The teacher had taken attendance by seat numbers, never called the roll. I didn't even know her name."

Ellen didn't move.

"Well for God's sake, if you want to break a speed record that coat's only going to be in the way."

She didn't move.

In two swift strides he was at the bedside table, snatching up the Gideon Bible. He raised his right hand. "I swear on this Bible that I never went out with your sister, or said more than two words to her . . . or anything . . ." He put the Bible down. "Well?"

"If Dorothy was killed," Ellen said, "the man who did it would swear on a dozen Bibles. And if she thought he loved her, then he was a good actor too."

Gant rolled his eyes heavenward and extended his wrists for the handcuffs. "All right," he said, "I'll go quietly."

"I'm glad you think this is something to joke about."

He lowered his hands. "I'm sorry," he said sincerely. "But how the hell am I supposed to convince you that—"

"You can't," Ellen said. "You might as well go."

86

"There were other blond guys in the class," he insisted. He snapped his fingers. "There was one she used to come in with all the time! Cary Grant chin, tall . . ."

"Dwight Powell?"

"That's right!" He stopped short. "Is he on your list?"

She hesitated a moment, and then nodded.

"He's the one!"

Ellen looked at him suspiciously.

He threw up his hands. "Okay. I give up. You'll see, it was Powell." He moved towards the door; Ellen backed into the hallway. "I would just like to leave, as you suggested," Gant said loftily.

He came into the hallway. "Unless you want me to go on calling you Hester, you ought to tell me what your name really is."

"Ellen."

Gant seemed reluctant to go. "What are you going to do now?"

After a moment she said, "I don't know."

"If you barge into Powell's place, don't pull a fluff like you did this afternoon. He may be no one to fool around with."

Ellen nodded.

Gant looked her up and down. "A girl on a mission," he mused. "Never thought I'd live to see the day." He started to go and then turned back. "You wouldn't be in the market for a Watson, would you?"

"No, thanks," she said in the doorway. "I'm sorry but . . ."

He shrugged and smiled. "I figured my credentials wouldn't be in order. Well, good luck . . ." He turned and walked down the hallway.

Ellen backed into her room and slowly closed the door.

. . . It's 7:30 now, Bud, and I'm comfortably settled in a very nice room at the New Washington House—just had dinner and am ready to take a bath and turn in after a full day.

I spent most of the afternoon in the waiting room of the Dean of Students. When I finally got to see him I told a fabulous story about an unpaid debt which Dorothy owed to a handsome blond in her fall English class. After much digging through records and examining a rogues gallery of application blank photos, we came up with the man—Mr. Dwight Powell of 1520 West 35th Street, on whom the hunting season opens tomorrow morning.

How's that for an efficient start? Never underestimate the power of a woman!

Love,
ELLEN

At eight o'clock she paused in her undressing and dropped a quarter into the coin-operated bedside radio. She pushed the button marked KBRI. There was a low humming and then, smooth and sonorous, Gant's voice swelled into the room. ". . . another session with The Discus Thrower, or as our engineer puts it, 'Puff and Pant with Gordon Gant,' which shows the limitations of a purely scientific education. On to the agenda. The first disc of the evening is an oldie, and it's dedicated to Miss Hester Holmes of Wisconsin . . ."

A jumpy orchestral introduction, nostalgically dated, burst from the radio and faded under the singing of a sugary, little-girl voice:

> Button up your overcoat
> When the wind is free,
> Take good care of yourself,
> You belong to me . . .

Smiling, Ellen went into the bathroom. The tiled walls rang with the sound of water pounding into the tub. She kicked off her slippers and hung her robe on a hook beside the door. She reached over and turned off the water. In the sudden silence, the wispy voice sifted in from the next room:

> Don't sit on hornets' tails, ooh-ooh,
> Or on nails, ooh-ooh,
> Or third rails, ooh-ooh . . .

5

"HELLO?" THE VOICE WAS A WOMAN'S.

"Hello," Ellen said. "Is Dwight Powell there?"

"No, he isn't."

"When do you expect him back?"

"I couldn't say for sure. I know he works over at Folger's between his classes and afterwards, but I don't know to what time he works."

"Aren't you his landlady?"

"No. I'm her daughter-in-law come over to clean. Mrs. Honig is in Iowa City with her foot. She cut it last week and it got infected. My husband had to take her to Iowa City."

"Oh, I'm sorry . . ."

"If you have a message for Dwight, I can leave him a note."

"No, thanks. I have a class with him in a couple of hours, so I'll see him then. It wasn't anything important."

"Okay. Good-by."

"Good-by."

Ellen hung up. She certainly wasn't going to wait to speak

to the landlady. She was already more or less convinced that Powell was the man who had been going with Dorothy; checking with the landlady would only have been a sort of formality; verification could be obtained just as easily from Powell's friends. Or from Powell himself . . .

She wondered what kind of place it was where he worked. Folger's. It would have to be near the campus if he went there in free hours between classes. If it were a store of some sort, where he waited on customers . . .

She picked up the telephone book, turned to the F's and skimmed through the listings.

Folger Drugs 1448 UnivAv. . . .2-3800

It was between 28th and 29th Streets across the avenue from the campus; a squat brick structure with a long green sign stretched across its brow: *Folger Drugs* and in smaller letters *Prescriptions* and in still smaller letters *Fountain Service*. Ellen paused outside the glass door and smoothed her bangs. Drawing herself up as though making an entrance onto a stage, she pushed open the door and went in.

The fountain was on the left; mirrors, chrome, gray marble; fronted by a line of round-topped red leatherette stools. It was not yet noon so only a few people were seated at the forward end.

Dwight Powell was behind the counter, wearing a snug white mess jacket and a white cap which rode the waves or his fine blond hair like an overturned ship. His square-jawed face was lean and he had a moustache; a thin carefully trimmed line of almost colorless hairs, visible only when the light gleamed on it; a feature which evidently had been added some time after the taking of the photograph which the Dean had shown. Powell was squirting whipped cream from a metal cannister onto a gummy-looking sundae. There was a sullen set to his lips that made it clear he disliked his job.

Ellen walked towards the far end of the counter. As she passed Powell, who was placing the sundae before a customer, she sensed him glance up. She went on, eyes straight ahead, to the empty section. Taking off her coat, she folded it and put it with her purse on one of the row of empty stools. She seated herself on the next stool. With her hands flat on the cold marble, she examined her reflection in the mirrored wall opposite. Her hands left the marble, dropped to the bottom of her powder blue sweater and pulled it down tight.

Powell approached along the gangway behind the counter. He put a glass of water and a paper napkin before her. His eyes were deep blue, the skin immediately below them gray-shadowed. "Yes, miss?" he said in a low-pitched voice. His eyes met hers and then strayed downwards momentarily.

She looked at the mirrored wall, at the pictures of sandwiches fixed to it. The grill was directly opposite her. "A

89

cheeseburger," she said, looking back at him. His eyes were on hers again. "And a cup of coffee."

"Cheeseburger and coffee," he said, and smiled. It was a stiff smile that vanished quickly, as though his facial muscles were unaccustomed to the exercise. He turned and opened a locker under the grill, taking out a patty of meat on a piece of waxed paper. Kicking the locker door shut, he slapped the meat onto the grill and peeled the waxed paper off its back. The meat sizzled. He took a hamburger roll from a bin next to the grill and began slicing it down the center with a long knife. She watched his face in the mirror. He glanced up and smiled again. She returned the smile faintly; I am not interested, but I am not completely *un*interested. He put the two halves of the roll face down beside the hamburger and turned to Ellen. "Coffee now or later?"

"Now, please."

He produced a tan cup and saucer and a spoon from under the counter. He arranged them before her and then moved a few paces down the gangway, to return with a glass pot of coffee. He poured the steaming liquid slowly into her cup. "You go to Stoddard?" he asked.

"No, I don't."

He rested the coffee pot on the marble and with his free hand brought a jigger of cream up from under the counter.

"You?" Ellen asked.

Down the counter a spoon chinked against glass. Powell answered the call with the sullen compression returning to his lips.

He was back a minute later, picking up a spatula and turning the hamburger. He opened the locker again and took out a slice of American cheese which he put on top of the meat. They looked at each other in the mirror as he arranged the roll and a couple of slices of pickle on a plate. "You haven't been in here before, have you?" he said.

"No. I've only been in Blue River a couple of days."

"Oh. Staying or passing through?" He spoke slowly, like a circling hunter.

"Staying. If I can find a job."

"As what?"

"A secretary."

He turned around, the spatula in one hand, the plate in the other. "That should be easy to find."

"Ha," she said.

There was a pause. "Where you from?" he asked.

"Des Moines."

"It should be easier to find a job there than it is here."

She shook her head. "All the girls looking for jobs go to Des Moines."

Turning back to the grill, he lifted the cheeseburger with the spatula and slid it onto the roll. He set the plate before

90

her and produced a bottle of ketchup from below the counter. "You have relatives here?"

She shook her head. "Don't know a soul in town. Except the woman at the employment agency."

A spoon tapped glass again down the counter. "Damn," he muttered. "Maybe you want *my* job?" He stalked away.

In a few minutes he returned. He began scraping the top of the grill with the edge of the spatula. "How's the cheeseburger?"

"Fine."

"You want something else? Some more coffee?"

"No, thanks."

The grill was perfectly clean but he continued scraping it, watching Ellen in the mirror. She dabbed at her lips with the napkin. "Check, please," she said.

He turned, taking a pencil and a green pad from a clip on his belt. "Listen," he said, not looking up from his writing, "there's a very good revival at the Paramount tonight. *Lost Horizon*. You want to see it?"

"I . . ."

"You said you didn't know anybody in town."

She seemed to debate for a moment. "All right," she said finally.

He looked up and smiled, this time effortlessly. "Swell. Where can I meet you?"

"The New Washington House. In the lobby."

"Eight o'clock okay?" He tore the check from the pad. "My name is Dwight," he said. "As in Eisenhower. Dwight Powell." He looked at her, waiting.

"Mine is Evelyn Kittredge."

"Hi," he said, smiling. She flashed a broad smile in return. Something flickered over Powell's face; surprise? . . . memory? . . .

"What's wrong?" Ellen asked. "Why do you look at me that way?"

"Your smile," he said uneasily. "Exactly like a girl I used to know . . ."

There was a pause, then Ellen said decisively, "Joan Bacon or Bascomb or something. I've been in this town only two days and two people have told me I look like this Joan—"

"No," Powell said, "this girl's name was Dorothy." He folded the check. "Lunch is on me." He waved his arm, trying to attract the attention of the cashier up front. Craning his neck, he pointed to the check, to Ellen and to himself, and then tucked the check into his pocket. "All taken care of," he said.

Ellen was standing, putting on her coat. "Eight o'clock in the New Washington lobby," Powell reiterated. "Is that where you're staying?"

"Yes." She made herself smile. She could see his mind following the path; easy pick-up, stranger in town, staying at a hotel . . . "Thanks for lunch."

"Don't mention it."

She picked up her purse.

"See you tonight, Evelyn."

"Eight o'clock," she said. She turned and walked towards the front of the store, keeping her pace slow, feeling his eyes on her back. At the door she turned. He lifted a hand and smiled. She returned the gesture.

Outside, she found that her knees were shaking.

6

ELLEN WAS IN THE LOBBY AT SEVEN-THIRTY, so that Powell would not have the occasion to ask the desk clerk to ring Miss Kittredge's room. He arrived at five of eight, the thin line of his mustache glinting over an edgy smile. (Easy pick-up . . . stranger in town . . .) He had ascertained that *Lost Horizon* went on at 8:06, so they took a cab to the theater although it was only five blocks away. Midway through the picture Powell put his arm around Ellen, resting his hand on her shoulder. She kept seeing it from the corner of her eye, the hand that had caressed Dorothy's body, had pushed powerfully . . .maybe . . .

The Municipal Building was three blocks from the theater and less than two from the New Washington House. They passed it on their way back to the hotel. A few windows were lighted in the upper floors of the looming façade across the street. "Is that the tallest building in the city?" Ellen asked, looking at Powell.

"Yes," he said. His eyes were focused some twenty feet ahead on the sidewalk.

"How high is it?"

"Fourteen stories." The direction of his gaze had not altered. Ellen thought: When you ask a person the height of something that's in his presence, he instinctively turns to look at it, even if he already knows the answer. Unless he has some reason for not wanting to look at it.

They sat in a booth in the hotel's black-walled soft-pianoed cocktail lounge and drank whiskey sours. Their conversation was intermittent, Ellen pushing it against the uphill slope of Powell's slow deliberate speech. The taut buoyancy with which he had begun the evening had faded in passing the Municipal Building, had risen again on entering the hotel, and now was waning steadily the longer they sat in the red-upholstered booth.

They spoke about jobs. Powell disliked his. He had held it for two months and planned to quit as soon as he could find something better. He was saving his money for a summer study tour of Europe.

What was he studying? His major was English. What did he plan to do with it? He wasn't sure. Advertising, maybe, or get into publishing. His plans for the future seemed sketchy.

They spoke about girls. "I'm sick of these college girls," he said. "Immature . . . they take everything too seriously." Ellen thought this was the beginning of a line, the one that leads straight to "You place too much importance on sex. As long as we like each other, what's the harm in going to bed?" It wasn't though. It seemed to be something that was troubling him. He weighed his words carefully, twisting the stem of the third cocktail glass between long restless fingers. "You get one of them on your neck," he said, the blue eyes clouded, "and you can't get her off." He watched his hand. "Not without making a mess . . ."

Ellen closed her eyes, her hands damp on the slick black tabletop.

"You can't help feeling sorry for people like that," he went on, "but you've got to think of yourself first."

"People like what?" she said, not opening her eyes.

"People who throw themselves on other people . . ." There was the loud slap of his hand hitting the tabletop. Ellen opened her eyes. He was taking cigarettes from a pack on the table, smiling. "The trouble with me is too many whiskey sours," he said. His hand, holding a match to her cigarette, was unsteady. "Let's talk about you."

She made up a story about a secretarial school in Des Moines run by an elderly Frenchman who pitched spitballs at the girls when they weren't looking. When it was finished Powell said, "Look, let's get out of here."

"You mean go to another place?" Ellen asked.

"If you want to," he said unenthusiastically.

Ellen reached for the coat beside her. "If you don't mind, I'd just as soon we didn't. I was up very early this morning."

"Okay," Powell said. "I'll escort you to your door." The edgy smile which had begun the evening made its return.

She stood with her back to the door of her room, the brass-tagged key in her hand. "Thank you very much," she said. "It really was a nice evening."

His arm with both their coats over it went around her back. His lips came towards her and she turned away, catching the kiss on her cheek. "Don't be coy," he said flatly. He caught her jaw in his hand and kissed her mouth hard.

"Let's go in . . . have a last cigarette," he said.

93

She shook her head.

"Evvie . . ." His hand was on her shoulder.

She shook her head again. "Honestly, I'm dead tired." It was a refusal, but the modest curling of her voice implied that things might be different some other night.

He kissed her a second time. She pushed his hand back up to her shoulder. "Please . . . someone might . . ." Still holding her, he drew back a bit and smiled at her. She smiled back, trying to make it the same broad smile she had given him in the drugstore.

It worked. It was like touching a charged wire to an exposed nerve. The shadow flickered across his face.

He drew her close, both arms around her, his chin over her shoulder as if to avoid seeing her smile. "Do I still remind you of that girl?" she asked. And then, "I'll bet she was another girl you went out with just once."

"No," he said, "I went out with her for a long time." He pulled back. "Who says I'm going out with you just once? You doing anything tomorrow night?"

"No."

"Same time, same place?"

"If you like."

He kissed her cheek and held her close again. "What happened?" she asked.

"What do you mean?" His words vibrated against her temple.

"That girl. Why did you stop going with her?" She tried to make it light, casual. "Maybe I can profit by her mistakes."

"Oh." There was a pause. Ellen stared at the cloth of his lapel, seeing the precise weaving of the slate blue threads. "It was like I said downstairs . . . we got too involved. Had to break it off." She heard him take a deep breath. "She was very immature," he added.

After a moment Ellen made a withdrawing movement. "I think I'd better . . ."

He kissed her again, a long one. She closed her eyes sickly.

Easing from his arms, she turned and put the key in the door without looking at him. "Tomorrow night at eight," he said. She had to turn around to take her coat, and there was no avoiding his eyes. "Good night, Evvie."

She opened the door behind her and stepped back forcing a smile to her lips. "Good night." She shut the door.

She was sitting motionlessly on the bed, the coat still in her hands, when the telephone rang five minutes later. It was Gant.

"Keeping late hours, I see."

She sighed. "Is it a relief to talk to you . . ."

"Well!" he said, stretching the word. "Well, well, *well!* I gather that my innocense has been clearly and conclusively established."

94

"Yes. Powell's the one who was going with her. And I'm right about it not being suicide. I know I am. He keeps talking about girls who throw themselves on other people and take things too seriously and get involved and things like that." The words tumbled quickly, freed of the strain of guarded conversation.

"Good Lord, your efficiency astounds me. Where did you get your information?"

"From him."

"What?"

"I picked him up in the drugstore where he works. I'm Evelyn Kittredge, unemployed secretary, of Des Moines, Iowa. I just tight-roped through the evening with him."

There was a long silence from Gant's end of the line. "Tell all," he said finally, wearily. "When do you plan to beat the written confession out of him?"

She told him of Powell's sudden dejection when passing the Municipal Building, repeating as accurately as she could the remarks he had made under the influence of the doldrums and the whiskey sours.

When Gant spoke again he was serious. "Listen, Ellen, this doesn't sound like anything to play around with."

"Why? As long as he thinks I'm Evelyn Kittredge—"

"How do you know he does? What if Dorothy showed him a picture of you?"

"She had only one, and that was a very fuzzy group snapshot with our faces in the shade. If he did see it, it was almost a year ago. He couldn't possibly recognize me. Besides, if he suspected who I am he wouldn't have said the things he did."

"No, I guess he wouldn't have," Gant admitted reluctantly. "What do you plan to do now?"

"This afternoon I went down to the library and read all the newspaper reports of Dorothy's death. There were a few details that were never mentioned, little things like the color of her hat, and the fact that she was wearing gloves. I have another date with him tomorrow night. If I can get him talking about her 'suicide' maybe he'll let drop one of those things that he couldn't know unless he was with her."

"It wouldn't be conclusive evidence," Gant said. "He could claim he was in the building at the time and he saw her after she . . ."

"I'm not *looking* for conclusive evidence. All I want is something that will prevent the police from thinking that I'm just a crank with an overactive imagination. If I can prove he was anywhere near her at the time, it should be enough to start them digging."

"Well will you please tell me how the hell you expect to get him to talk in such detail without making him suspicious? He's not an idiot, is he?"

"I have to try," she argued. "What else is there to do?"

Gant thought for a moment. "I am the owner of an old ball peen hammer," he said. "We could beat him over the head, drag him to the scene of the crime, and sweat it out of him."

"You see," Ellen said seriously, "there's no other way to . . ." Her voice faded.

"Hello?"

"I'm still here," she said.

"What happened? I thought we were cut off."

"I was just thinking."

"Oh. Look, seriously . . . be careful, will you? And if it's at all possible, call me tomorrow evening, just to let me know where you are and how things are going."

"Why?"

"Just to be on the safe side."

"He thinks I'm Evelyn Kittredge."

"Well call me anyway. It can't hurt. Besides, my hair grays easily."

"All right."

"Good night," Ellen."

"Good night, Gordon."

She replaced the receiver and remained sitting on the bed, biting her lower lip and drumming her fingers the way she always did when she was toying with an idea.

7

SNAPPING SHUT HER PURSE, Ellen looked up and smiled across the lobby at Powell's approaching figure. He was wearing a gray topcoat and a navy blue suit, and the same smile he had worn the previous evening. "Hi," he said, dropping down beside her on the leather divan. "You certainly don't keep your dates waiting."

"Some of them I do."

His smile broadened. "How's the job-hunting?"

"Pretty good," she said. "I think I've got something. With a lawyer."

"Swell. You'll be staying in Blue River then, right?"

"It looks that way."

"Swell . . ." he drew the word out caressingly. Then his eyes flicked to his wristwatch. "We'd better get on our horses. I passed the Glo-Ray Ballroom on my way over here and there was a line all the way——"

"Ohh," she lamented.

"What's the matter?"

Her face was apologetic. "I've got an errand to do first. This

96

lawyer. I have to bring him a letter . . . a reference." She tapped her purse.

"I didn't know secretaries needed references. I thought they just tested your shorthand or something."

"Yes, but I mentioned that I had this letter from my last employer and he said he'd like to see it. He's going to be at his office till eight-thirty." She sighed. "I'm awfully sorry."

"That's all right."

Ellen touched his hand. "I'd just as soon not go dancing," she confided. "We can go someplace, have a few drinks . . ."

"Okay," he said more cheerfully. They stood up. "Where is this lawyer?" Powell asked, standing behind her, helping her on with her coat.

"Not far from here," Ellen said. "The Municipal Building."

At the head of the steps that fronted the Municipal Building, Powell stopped. Ellen, in the quadrant of a revolving door, relaxed her about-to-push hand and looked at him. He was pale, but that might have been the grayish light filtering out from the lobby. "I'll wait for you down here, Evvie." His jaw was rigid, the words coming out stiffly.

"I wanted you to come up with me," she said. "I could have brought this letter over here before eight o'clock, but I thought it was kind of odd, his telling me to bring it in the evening. He's a greasy looking character." She smiled. "You're my protection."

"Oh," Powell said.

Ellen pushed around through the door, and after a moment Powell followed her. She had turned and was watching him when he came out of the door. He was breathing through partially opened lips, his face barren of expression.

The vast marbled lobby was silent and empty. Three of the four elevators were black behind latticed metal gates. The fourth was a yellow-lighted cell with wooden walls the color of honey. They walked towards it side by side, their footsteps drawing whispering echoes from the domed ceiling.

In the cell a tan-uniformed Negro operator stood reading a copy of *Look*. He tucked the magazine under his arm, toed the floor button that released the big sliding metal door, and threw the latticed gate across after it. "Floor please," he said.

"Fourteen," Ellen said.

They stood in silence, watching the steadily advancing position of the lighted numeral in the row of unlighted numerals over the door. 7 . . . 8 . . . 9 . . . Powell rubbed his mustache with the side of his forefinger.

When the light jumped from 13 to 14, the car came to a smooth automatic top-floor stop. The operator drew in the gate and pulled down on the jointed bar that opened the outer door.

Ellen stepped out into the deserted corridor, Powell following her. Behind them the door slid shut with a hollow clangor.

They heard the gate closing and then the decrescent hum of the car "It's this way," Ellen said, moving towards the right. "Room fourteen-oh-five." They walked to the bend of the corridor and made the right turn. There was light behind only two of the frosted glass door panels in the stretch of straight-lined corridor before them. There was no sound except their feet on the polished rubber tiles. Ellen groped for something to say . . . "It won't take long. I just have to give him the letter."

"Do you think you'll get the job?"

"I think so. It's a good letter."

They reached the end of the corridor and turned right again. One door was lighted, up ahead in the left wall, and Powell angled towards it. "No, that's not the one," Ellen said. She went to an unlighted door on the right. Its frosted panel was inscribed *Frederic H. Clausen, Attorney at Law*. Powell came up behind her as she futilely tried the knob and looked at her watch. "How do you like that?" she said bitterly. "Not even a quarter after and he said he'd be here till eight-thirty." (The secretary on the telephone had said "The office closes at five.")

"What now?" Powell asked.

"I guess I'll leave it under the door," she said, opening her purse. She took out a large white envelope and her fountain pen. Uncapping the pen, she held the envelope flat against the purse and began to write. "It's a shame about the dancing," she said.

"That's okay," said Powell. "I wasn't too keen on it myself." He was breathing more easily, like a novice aerialist passing the middle of the taut wire and becoming less uncertain of his footing.

"On second thought," Ellen said, glancing up at him, "If I leave the letter now I'll only have to come back for it tomorrow anyway. I might just as well bring it over in the morning." She recapped the pen and put it back in her purse. She held the envelope at an angle to the light, saw that the ink was still wet, and began to wave the envelope with quick fanlike motions. Her gaze drifted to a door across the corridor, the door marked *Stairway*. Her eyes lighted. "You know what I'd like to do?" she asked.

"What?"

". . . Before we go back and have those drinks . . ."

"What?" He smiled.

She smiled back at him, waving the envelope. "Go up to the roof."

The aerialist looked down and saw the net being drawn out from under him. "What do you want to do that for?" he asked slowly.

"Didn't you see the moon? And the stars? It's a perfect night. The view must be tremendous."

"I think we might still be able to get into the Glo-Ray," he said.

"Oh, neither of us are crazy about going." She slipped the envelope into her purse and snapped it shut. "Come on," she said gaily, turning from him and crossing the corridor. "What happened to all that romance you displayed in the hall last night?" His hand reached out for her arm and caught empty air.

She pushed the door open and looked back, waiting for him to follow.

"Evvie, I . . . Heights make me dizzy." He forced a thin smile.

"You don't have to look down," she said lightly. "You don't even have to go near the edge."

"The door's probably locked . . ."

"I don't think they can lock a door to a roof. Fire laws." She frowned in mock disgust. "Oh come on! You'd think I was asking you to go over Niagrara Falls in a barrel or something!" She backed through the doorway onto the landing, holding the door, smiling, waiting for him.

He came with a slow trancelike helplessness, as though there were part of him that perversely wanted to follow her. When he was on the landing she released the door. It swung closed with a soft pneumatic hissing, cutting off the light from the corridor and leaving a 10-watt bulb to fight a losing battle against the shadows of the stairwell.

They climbed eight steps, turned, and climbed eight more. There was a dark metal door with a warning painted on it in large white letters: *Entrance Strictly Forbidden Except in Emergency.* Powell read it aloud, stressing the words 'strictly forbidden.'

"Signs," Ellen said disdainfully. She tried the knob.

"It must be locked," Powell said.

"If it were locked they wouldn't have *that*." Ellen indicated the sign. "You try."

He took the knob, pushed. "It's stuck, then."

"Oh, come on. Give a real try."

"Okay," he said, "okay okay," with to-hell-with-it abandon. He drew back and slammed his shoulders against the door full-force. It flew open almost dragging him with it. He stumbled across the high threshold onto the tarred deck. "Okay, Evvie," he said sullenly, straightening himself, holding the door wide, "come look at your gorgeous moon."

"Sourpuss," Ellen said, the light tone of her voice stripping his bitterness of significance. She stepped over the ledge and breezed a few steps past Powell, advancing from the shadow of the staircase housing out onto the expanse of roof like a cold-legged skater pretending not to worry about thin ice. She

heard the door closing behind her, and then Powell came up
on her left.

"Sorry," he said, "it's just that I almost broke my shoulder
on the damn door, that's all." He managed a starchy smile.

They were facing the KBRI tower; skeletal, black against
the blue-black star-spattered sky; at the very top of it a slowly
flashing red light whose steady pulsing flushed the roof with
intermittent rose. Between the red throbs there was the soft
light of the quarter moon overhead.

Ellen glanced at Powell's upturned tense-jawed profile; first
dim white, then bathed with red, then white again. Beyond
him she saw the wall that rimmed the airshaft, its white stone
top distinct in the night. She remembered a diagram that had
appeared in one of the newspapers; the X at the south side of
the square—the side nearest them. Suddenly she was caught
by a crazy desire to go there, look over, see where Dorothy . . .
A sick wave swept over her. The focus of her vision realigned
on Powell's wide-edged profile and involuntarily she drew
away.

It's all right, she told herself, I'm safe—safer than pushing
conversation in some cocktail lounge. I'm all right, I'm Evelyn
Kittredge . . .

He became conscious of her gaze. "I thought you wanted to
look at the sky," he said, not lowering his own skyward face.
She looked up and the sudden lifting of her head heightened
the dizziness. The stars wheeled . . .

She broke away, went to the right, to the outer edge of the
roof. Abrading her hands against the roughness of the coping,
she gasped lungfuls of the cold night air . . . This is where
he killed her. He's bound to betray himself—enough to go to
the police. I'm safe . . . Finally her head cleared. She looked
at the panorama below, the myriad lights glittering off into
blackness. "Dwight, come look."

He turned and walked towards the parapet, but he stopped
a few feet away.

"Isn't it beautiful?" She spoke without looking back.

"Yes," he said.

He looked for a moment, while a breeze plucked softly at
the tower cables, and then he turned slowly around until he
was facing the airshaft. He stared at the parapet. Then his
right foot extended itself and his legs began to walk. They
carried him forward with silent relentless efficiency, like the
legs of a reformed alcoholic carrying him to the bar for just
one little drink. They carried him straight up to the airshaft
parapet and his hands rose and set themselves flat on the cool
stone. He leaned over and looked down.

Ellen felt his absence. She turned around and probed the
quarter-moon obscurity. Then the tower light flashed on, its
crimson glow showing him at the wall of the airshaft, and her
heart jumped chokingly. The red glow vanished, but knowing

where he was she could still distinguish him in the wan moonlight. She began moving forward, her steps noiseless on the resilient tar.

He looked down. A few yellow beams from lighted windows criss-crossed the square funnel of the shaft. One light was far below, at the very bottom, illuminating the small gray concrete square that was the focus of the converging walls.

"I thought heights made you dizzy."

He whirled.

There were sweat beads on his brow and above his moustache. A nervous smile shot to his lips. "They do," he said, "but I can't help looking. Self-torture . . ." The smile faded. "That's my specialty." He took a deep breath. "You ready to go now?" he asked.

"We just got here," Ellen protested lightly. She turned and walked towards the eastern rim of the roof, threading her way between the gaunt shapes of ventilator pipes. Powell followed reluctantly. Reaching the edge, Ellen stood with her back to the parapet and gazed up at the rearing red-limned tower beside them. "It's nice up here," she said. Powell, looking out over the city, his hands folded on the parapet, said nothing. "Have you ever been here at night?" Ellen asked.

"No," he said. "I've never been here before at all."

She turned to the parapet and leaned over, looking down at the shelf of the setback two stories below. She frowned thoughtfully. "Last year," she said slowly, "I think I read about some girl falling from here . . ."

A ventilator cap creaked. "Yes," Powell said. His voice was dry. "A suicide. She didn't fall."

"Oh." Ellen kept looking at the setback. "I don't see how she could have gotten killed," she said. "It's only two stories."

He lifted a hand, the thumb pointing back over his shoulder. "Over there . . . the shaft."

"Oh, that's right." She straightened up. "I remember now. The Des Moines newspapers gave it a very big write-up." She put her purse on the ledge and held it squarely with both hands, as though testing the rigidity of its frame. "She was a Stoddard girl, wasn't she?"

"Yes," he said. He pointed far out towards the horizon. "You see that roundish building there, with the lights on it? That's the Stoddard Observatory. Had to go out there for a Physical Science project once. They have a—"

"Did you know her?"

The red light stained his face. "Why do you ask?" he said.

"I just thought you might have known her. That's a natural thing to think, both going to Stoddard . . ."

"Yes," he said sharply, "I knew her and she was a very nice girl. Now let's talk about something else."

"The only reason the story stuck in my mind," she said, "was because of the hat."

Powell gave an exasperate sigh. Wearily he said, "What hat?"

"She was wearing a red hat with a bow on it and I had just bought a red hat with a bow on it the day that it happened."

"Who said she was wearing a red hat?" Powell asked.

"Wasn't she? The Des Moines papers said . . ." . . . Tell me they were wrong, she prayed tell me it was green . . .

There was silence for a moment. "The *Clarion* never mentioned a red hat," Powell said. "I read the articles carefully, knowing her . . ."

"Just because the Blue River paper never mentioned it doesn't mean that it wasn't so," Ellen said.

He didn't say anything. She looked and saw him squinting at his wristwatch. "Look," he said brusquely, "it's twenty-five to nine. I've had enough of this magnificent view." He turned away abruptly, heading for the staircase housing.

Ellen hurried after him. "We can't go yet," she wheedled, catching his arm just outside the slant-roofed shed.

"Why not?"

Behind a smile her mind raced. "I . . . I want a cigarette."

"Oh for . . ." His hand jerked towards a pocket, then stopped short. "I don't have any. Come on, we'll get some downstairs."

"I have some," she said quickly, flashing her purse. She backed away, the position of the airshaft behind her as clear in her mind as if she were looking at the newspaper diagram. X marks the spot. Turning slightly, she sidled back towards it, opening the purse, smiling at Powell, saying inanely "It'll be nice to smoke a cigarette up here." The parapet reared against her hip. X. She fumbled in her purse. "You want one?"

He came towards her with resignation and compressed-lip anger. She shook the crumpled pack of cigarettes until one white cylinder protruded, thinking—it has to be tonight, because he won't ask Evelyn Kittredge for another date. "Here," she offered. He snatched the cigarette grimly.

Her fingertips dug for another one, and as they did her eyes roved and apparently became aware of the airshaft for the first time. She turned towards it slightly. "Is this where . . . ?" She turned back to him.

His eyes were narrowed, his jaw tightened by the last threads of a fast-raveling patience. "Listen, Evvie," he said, "I asked you not to talk about it. Now will you just do me that one favor? Will you please?" He jabbed the cigarette between his lips.

She didn't take her eyes from his face. Drawing a cigarette from the pack, she put it calmly to her lips and dropped the pack back into her purse. "I'm sorry," she said coolly, tucking

102

the purse under her left arm. "I don't know what you're so touchy about."

"Can't you understand? I *knew* the girl."

She struck a match and held it to his cigarette, the orange glow lighting his face, showing the blue eyes simmering with about-to-break strain, the jaw muscles tight as piano wires. . . . One more jab, one more jab . . . She withdrew the match from his lighted cigarette, held it before his face. "They never did say why she did it, did they?" His eyes closed painfully. "I'll bet she was pregnant," she said.

His face flared from flame orange to raw red as the match died and the tower light flashed on. The wire-tight muscles burst and the blue eyes shot open like dams exploding. . . . Now!—Ellen thought triumphantly—Now! Let it be something good, something damning! . . .

"All right!" he blazed, "all right! You know why I won't talk about it? You know why I didn't want to come up here at all? Why I didn't even want to come into this goddamn building?" —he flung away his cigarette—"Because the girl who committed suicide here was the girl I told you about last night! The one you smile like!" His eyes dropped from her face. "The girl who I—"

The words cut off guillotine-sharp. She saw his downcast eyes dilate with shock and then the tower light faded and she could see him only as a dim form confronting her. Suddenly his hand caught her left wrist, gripping it with paralyzing pressure. A scream pushed the cigarette from her lips. He was wrenching at the fingers of her captive hand, clawing at them. The purse slid out from under her arm and thudded to her feet. Futilely her right hand flailed his head. He was thumbing the muscles of her hand, forcing the fingers open . . . Releasing her, he stepped back and became a dimly outlined form again.

"What did you do?" she cried. "What did you take?" Dazedly she stooped and retrieved her purse. She flexed her left hand, her jarred senses vainly trying to recall the imprint of the object she had been holding.

Then the red light flashed on again and she saw it resting in the palm of his hand as though he had been examining it even in the dark. The matchbook. With the coppered letters glinting sharp and clear: *Ellen Kingship*.

Coldness engulfed her. She closed her eyes sickly, nauseous fear ballooning in her stomach. She swayed; her back felt the hard edge of the airshaft parapet.

8

"HER SISTER . . ." HE FALTERED, "HER SISTER . . ."

She opened her eyes. He was staring at the matchbook with glazed incomprehension. He looked up at her. "What is this?" he asked dully. Suddenly he hurled the matchbook at her feet and his voice flared loud again, "What do you want from me?"

"Nothing, nothing," she said quickly, "nothing." Her eyes darted desperately. He was standing between her and the stairway shed. If only she could circle around him . . . She began inching to her left, her back pulling against the parapet.

He rubbed his forehead. "You . . . you pick me up . . . you ask me questions about her . . . you get me up here . . ." Now his voice was entreating: "What do you *want* from me?"

"Nothing . . nothing," warily sidestepping.

"Then why did you *do* this?" His body flexed to move forward.

"Stop!" she cried.

The ball-poised feet dropped flat, frozen.

"If anything happens to me," she said, forcing herself to speak slowly, evenly, "there's somebody else who knows all about you. He knows I'm with you tonight, and he knows all about you, so if anything happens, anything at all . . ."

"If anything . . . ?" His brow furrowed. "What are you talking about?"

"You know what I mean. If I fall . . ."

"Why should you . . . ?" He stared unbelievingly. "You think I'd . . . ?" One hand gestured limply towards the parapet. "Jesus!" he whispered. "What are you, crazy?"

She was a good fifteen feet from him. She began edging away from the parapet, cutting across to get on a straight line with the stairway door that was behind him and on his right. He pivoted slowly, following her cautious transverse path. "What's this 'knows all about me'?" he demanded. "Knows what?"

"Everything," she said. "Everything. And he's waiting downstairs. If I'm not down in five minutes he's calling the police."

He slapped his forehead exhaustedly. "I give up," he moaned. "You want to go downstairs? You want to go? Well go ahead!" He turned and backed to the airshaft parapet, to the spot where Ellen had been standing originally, leaving her a clear path to the door. He stood with his elbows resting on the stone behind him. "Go ahead! Go on!"

She moved towards the door slowly, suspiciously, knowing that he could still beat her there, cut her off. He didn't move.

"If I'm supposed to be arrested," he said, "I'd just like to know what for. Or is that too much to ask?"

She made no answer until she had the door open in her hand. Then she said, "I expected you to be a convincing actor. You had to be, to make Dorothy believe you were going to marry her."

"What?" This time his surprise seemed deeper, painful. "Now listen, I never said *anything* to make her believe I was going to marry her. That was all on *her* side, all *her* idea."

"You liar," she clenched hatefully. "You filthy liar." She ducked behind the shield of the open door and stepped over the high threshold.

"Wait!" As though sensing that any forward movement would send her running, he dropped back along the parapet and then cut out from it, following the same path Ellen had taken before. He stopped when he was opposite the doorway, some twenty feet from it. Within the shed Ellen turned to face him, one hand on the doorknob, ready to pull it closed.

"For God's sake," he said earnestly, "will you just tell me what this is all about? Please?"

"You think I'm bluffing. You think we really don't know."

"Jesus . . ." he whispered furiously.

"All right," she glared. "I'll itemize it for you. One; she was pregnant. Two; you didn't want—"

"*Pregnant?*" It hit him like a rock in the stomach. He leaned forward. "Dorothy was *pregnant*? Is *that* why she did it? Is *that* why she killed herself?"

"She didn't kill herself!" Ellen cried. "You killed her!" She pulled the door shut, turned and ran.

She ran clatteringly down the metal steps, her heels ringing, clutching at the bannister and swinging round the turn at each landing and before she had gone two and a half flights she heard him thundering down after her shouting *Evvie! Ellen! Wait!* and then it was too late to take the elevator because by the time she ran all the way around the corridor and it came and took her down he would be waiting there already so there was nothing to do but keep on running with her heart beating and legs aching down the fourteen flights from roof to lobby which were really twenty-eight half-flights spiraling down through the gloomy stairwell with twenty-seven landings to swing out arm-pullingly banging against the wall with him thundering closer behind all the way down to the main floor half-slipping with the damn heels and coming out into a marble corridor and running around clattering echoing into the slippery floored cathedral of a lobby where the startled Negro head popped out of the elevator then pushing exhaustedly out through the heavy revolving door and down more steps of treacherous marble and almost bumping into a woman on the sidewalk and running down to the left down towards Washington Avenue down the smalltown night-deserted street and finally slowing with her heart hard-pumping to snatch one backward look before rounding the corner and there he was running down the marble steps waving and shouting *Wait! Wait!* She wheeled around the corner running again ignoring the couple that turned to stare and the boys in the car shouting *Want a ride*? and seeing the hotel down the block with its glass doors glowing like an ad for hotels getting nearer—he's getting nearer too but don't look back just keep on running—until at last she reached the beautiful glass doors and a man smiling amusedly held one of them open "Thank you, thank you," and finally she was in the lobby, the lobby, the safe warm lobby, with bellhops and loungers and men behind newspapers . . . She was dying to drop into one of the chairs but she went straight to the corner phone booths because if Gant went to the police with her, Gant who was a local celebrity, then they'd be more inclined to listen to her, believe her, investigate. Panting, she seized the phone book and flipped to the K's—it was five to nine so he'd be at the studio. She slapped away pages, gaspingly catching her breath. There it was: KBRI—5-1000. She opened her purse and hunted for coins. Five-one-thousand, five-one-thousand, as she turned from the phone book rack and looked up.

Powell confronted her. He was flushed and panting, his blond hair wild. She wasn't afraid; there were bright lights and people. Hate leveled her rough breathing like a glacier: "You should have run the other way. It won't do you any good, but I would start running if I were you."

And he looked at her with a sick-dog, pleading, near-tears expression that was so pathetically sad-looking it had to be true, and he said softly, hurtfully,—"Ellen, I loved her."

"I have a phone call to make," she said, "if you'll get out of the way."

"Please, I've got to talk to you," he pleaded. "Was she? Was she really pregnant?"

"I have a phone call to make."

"Was she?" he demanded.

"You know she was!"

"The papers said nothing! Nothing . . ." Suddenly his brow furrowed and his voice dropped low, intense. "What month was she in?"

"Will you please get out of my—"

"What month was she in?" His voice was demanding again. "Oh God! The second."

He let out a tremendous weight-dropping sigh of relief.

"Now will you *please* get out of my way?"

"Not until you explain what's going on. This Evelyn Kittredge act . . ."

Her glare was acid.

He whispered confusedly, "You mean you really think I
106

killed her?" and saw no change in the narrow stabbing of her eyes. "I was in New York!" he protested. "I can prove it! I was in New York all last spring!"

It shook her, but only for a moment. Then she said, "I suppose you could figure out a way to prove you were in Cairo, Egypt, if you wanted to."

"Jesus . . ." he hissed, exasperated. "Will you just let me speak to you for five minutes? Five minutes?" He glanced around and caught a glimpse of a man's head vanishing behind a quickly lifted newspaper. "People are listening," he said. "Just come into the cocktail lounge for five minutes. What harm can it do? I couldn't 'do anything' to you there, if that's what you're worried about."

"What *good* can it do?" she argued. "If you were in New York and you didn't kill her, then why did you avoid looking at the Municipal Building when we passed it last night? And why didn't you want to go up on the roof tonight? And why did you stare down into the airshaft the way you did?"

He looked at her awkwardly, painfully. "I can explain it," he said haltingly, "only I don't know whether you'll be able to understand it. You see, I felt . . ."—he groped for a word—". . . I felt *responsible* for her suicide."

Most of the booths in the black-walled lounge were empty. Glasses clinked and the soft piano dallied with some Gershwin themes. They took the seats they had occupied the night before, Ellen sitting back stiffly against the upholstered partition as though to repudiate any suggestion of intimacy. When the waiter appeared they ordered whiskey sours, and it wasn't until the drinks were in the table between them and Powell had taken the first sip of his that, realizing Ellen's intention to maintain a noncommittal silence, he began to speak. The words came slowly at first, and with embarrassment.

"I met her a couple of weeks after classes began last year," he said. "Last school year, I mean. Late September. I'd seen her before—she was in two of my classes and she'd been in one of my classes in freshman year—but I never spoke to her until this particular day because I usually wind up with a seat in the first or second row and she always sat in the back, in the corner. Well, on the night before this day when I spoke to her, I'd been talking with some guys and one of them had said how the quiet girls were the ones who . . ." He paused, fingering his glass and looking down at it. "You're more likely to have a good time with a quiet girl. So when I saw her the next day, sitting in the back in the corner where she always sat, I remembered what this guy had said.

"I started a conversation with her, going out of the room at the end of the period. I told her I'd forgotten to take down the assignment and would she give it to me, and she did. I think she knew it was just an excuse to talk, but still she responded

107

so . . . so eagerly it surprised me. I mean, usually a pretty girl will take a thing like that lightly, give you smart answers, you know . . . But she was so . . . unsophisticated, she made me feel a little guilty.

"Well anyway, we went out that Saturday night, went to a movie and to Frank's Florentine Room, and we really had a nice time. I don't mean fooling around or anything. Just a nice time. We went out again the next Saturday night and two times the week after that, and then three times until finally, just before we broke up, we were seeing each other almost every night. Once we got to know each other, she was a lot of fun. Not at all like she'd been in class. Happy. I liked her.

"Early November it turned out that that guy was right, what he said about quiet girls. About Dorothy, anyway." He glanced up, his eyes meeting Ellen's squarely. "You know what I mean?"

"Yes," she said coolly, impassive as a judge.

"This is a hell of a thing to tell a girl's sister."

"Go on."

"She was a *nice* girl," he said, still looking at her. "It was just that she was . . . love-starved. Not sex. Love." His glance fell. "She told me about things at home, about her mother— your mother, about how she'd wanted to go to school with you . . ."

A tremor ran through her; she told herself it was only the vibration caused by someone sitting down in the booth behind her.

"Things went on that way for a while," Powell continued, talking more swiftly now, his shame melting into a confessionary satisfaction. "She was really in love, hanging onto my arm and smiling up at me all the time. I mentioned once I liked argyle socks; she knitted me three pairs of them." He scratched the tabletop carefully. "I loved her too, only it wasn't the same. It was . . . sympathy-love. I felt sorry for her. Very nice of me.

"The middle of December she started to talk about marriage. Very indirectly. It was just before Christmas vacation and I was going to stay here in Blue River. I've got no family and all I've got in Chicago are a couple of cousins and some high school and Navy friends. So she wanted me to go to New York with her. Meet the family. I told her no, but she kept bringing it up again and finally there was a showdown.

"I told her I wasn't ready to get tied down yet, and she said that plenty of men were engaged and even married by twenty-two and if it was the future I was worrying about, her father would find a place for me. I didn't want that though. I had ambitions. I'll have to tell you about my ambitions some day. I was going to revolutionize American advertising. Well anyway, she said we could both get jobs when we finished school, and I said she could never live that way having been rich all

108

ner life. She said I didn't love her as much as she loved me, and I said I guessed she was right. That was it, of course, more than any of the other reasons.

"There was a scene and it was terrible. She cried and said I'd be sorry and all the things a girl says. Then after a while she changed her tack and said she was wrong; we would wait and go on the way we had been. But I'd been feeling sort of guilty all along, so I figured that since we'd had this halfway break, we might as well make it complete, and right before a vacation was the best time to do it. I told her it was all over, and there was more crying and more 'You'll be sorry' and that's the way it ended. Couple of days later she left for New York."

Ellen said, "All during that vacation she was in such a bad mood. Sulking . . . picking arguments . . ."

Powell printed wet rings on the table with the bottom of his glass. "After vacation," he said, "it was bad. We still had those two classes together. I would sit in the front of the room not daring to look back. We kept bumping into each other all over campus. So I decided I'd had enough of Stoddard and applied for a transfer to NYU." He saw the downcast expression on Ellen's face. "What's the matter?" he said. "Don't you believe me? I can prove all this. I've got a transcript from NYU and I think I've still got a note that Dorothy sent me when she returned a bracelet I'd given her."

"No," Ellen said dully. "I believe you. That's just the trouble."

He gave her a baffled look, and then continued. "Just before I left, towards the end of January, she was starting to go with another guy. I saw—"

"Another man?" Ellen leaned forward.

"I saw them together a couple of times. It hadn't been such a big blow to her after all, I thought. I left with a nice clean conscience. Even felt a bit noble."

"Who was he?" Ellen asked.

"Who?"

"The other man."

"I don't know. A man. I think he was in one of my classes. Let me finish.

"I read about her suicide the first of May, just a paragraph in the New York papers. I raced up to Times Square and got a *Clarion-Ledge* at that Out-of-Town Newspaper stand. I bought a *Clarion* every day that week, waiting for them to say what was in the note she sent you. They never did. They never said why she did it . . .

"Can you imagine how I felt? I didn't think she had done it just on account of me, but I did think that it was sort of a . . . general despondency. Which I was a major cause of.

"My work fell off after that. I was bucking too hard. I guess I felt I had to get terrific marks to justify what I'd done to her.

109

I broke into a cold sweat before every exam, and my marks turned out pretty poor. I told myself it was because of the transfer; at NYU I had to make up a lot of required courses that weren't required at Stoddard, and I'd lost about sixteen credits besides. So I decided to come back to Stoddard in September, to get myself straightened out." He smiled wryly. "Also maybe to try to convince myself that I didn't feel guilty."

"Anyway, it was a mistake. Every time I saw one of the places we used to go to, or the Municipal Building . . ." He frowned. "I kept telling myself it was her fault, that any other girl would have been mature enough to shrug it off . . . but it didn't do much good. It got to the point where I found myself going out of my way to walk past the building, needling myself, like looking into the airshaft tonight, visualizing her . . ."

"I know," Ellen said, hurrying him, "I wanted to look too. I guess it's a natural reaction."

"No," Powell said, "you don't know what it means to feel *responsible* . . ." He paused, seeing Ellen's humorless smile. "What are you smiling at?"

"Nothing."

"Well . . . that's it. Now you tell me she did it because she was pregnant . . . two months. It's a rotten thing of course, but it makes me feel a whole lot better. I guess she still wouldn't be dead if I hadn't ditched her, but I couldn't be expected to know how things would turn out, could I? I mean, there's a limit to responsibility. If you keep going back you could blame it on anyone." He drained the rest of his drink. "I'm glad to see you've stopped running for the police," he said. "I don't know where you got the idea that I killed her."

"Someone did kill her," Ellen said. He looked at her wordlessly. The piano paused between selections, and in the sudden stillness she could hear the faint cloth rustlings of the person in the booth behind her.

Leaning forward, she began talking, telling Powell of the ambiguously worded note, of the birth certificate, of something old, something new, something borrowed and something blue.

He was silent until she had finished. Then he said, "My God . . . It *can't* be a coincidence,"—as eager as she to disprove suicide.

"This man you saw her with," Ellen said. "You're sure you don't know who he was?"

"I think he was in one of my classes that semester, but the two times I saw them together were fairly late in January, when exams had started and there were no more classes, so I couldn't make sure or find out his name. And right afterwards I left for New York."

"Haven't you seen him again?"

"I don't know," Powell said. "I'm not sure. Stoddard's a big campus."

"And you're absolutely certain you don't know his name?"

"I don't know it now," Powell said, "but I can find it out in about an hour." He smiled. "You see, I've got his address."

9

'I TOLD YOU I SAW THEM TOGETHER a couple of times," he said. "Well the second time was one afternoon in a luncheonette across from the campus. I never expected to see Dorothy there; it wasn't a very popular place. That's why I was there. I didn't notice them until I'd sat down at the counter and then I didn't want to get up and leave because she'd already seen me in the mirror. I was sitting at the end of the counter, then two girls, then Dorothy and this guy. They were drinking malteds.

"The minute she saw me she started talking to him and touching his arm a lot; you know, trying to show me she had someone new. It made me feel awful, her doing that. Embarrassed for her. Then, when they were ready to leave, she gave a nod to those two girls sitting between us, turned to him and said in a louder-than-necessary voice, 'Come on, we can drop our books at your place.' To show me how chummy they were, I figured.

"As soon as they were gone one of the girls commented to the other about how good-looking he was. The other one agreed, and then she said something like 'He was going with so-and-so last year. It looks as if he's only interested in the ones who have money.'

"Well, I figured that if Dorothy was a sitting duck because she was on the rebound from me, then I ought to make sure that she wasn't being taken in by some gold-digger. So I left the luncheonette and followed them.

"They went to a house a few blocks north of the campus. He rang the bell a couple of times and then he took some keys out of his pocket and unlocked the door and they went in. I walked by on the other side of the street and copied down the address on one of my notebooks. I thought I would call up later, when someone else was there, and find out his name. I had a vague idea about speaking to some of the girls around school about him.

"I never did it though. On the way back to the campus, the . . . presumption of the whole thing hit me. I mean, where did I come off asking questions about this guy just on the basis of some remark made by a girl who probably had a bad case of sour grapes? It was a cinch he couldn't treat Dorothy any worse than I had. And that 'on the rebound' stuff; how did I know they weren't fine for each other?"

"But you still have the address?" Ellen asked anxiously.

"I'm pretty sure I do. I've got all my old notes in a suitcase in my room. We can go over there and get it right now if you want."

"Yes," she agreed quickly. "Then all we'll have to do is call up and find out who he is."

"He isn't necessarily the right one," Powell said, taking out his wallet.

"He must be. It can't be anyone she started going with much later than that." Ellen stood up. "There's still a phone call I'd like to make before we go."

"To your assistant? The one who was waiting downstairs ready to call the police of you didn't show up in five minutes?"

"That's right," she admitted, smiling. "He wasn't waiting downstairs, but there really is someone."

She went to the back of the dimly lit room, where a telephone booth painted black to match the walls stood like an up-ended coffin. She dialed 5-1000:

"KBRI, good evening," a woman's voice chirruped.

"Good evening. May I speak to Gordon Gant please?"

"I'm sorry, but Mr. Gant's program is on the air now. If you call again at ten o'clock you might be able to catch him before he leaves the building."

"Couldn't I speak to him while a record is on?"

"I'm sorry, but no telephone calls may be directed to a studio from which a program is being broadcast."

"Well would you take a message for him?"

The woman sing-songed that she would be glad to take a message, and Ellen told her that Miss Kingship—spelled out— said that Powell—spelled out—was all right but had an idea as to who wasn't and Miss Kingship was going to Powell's home and would be there at ten o'clock, when Mr. Gant could call her.

"Any telephone numbers?"

"Darn," Ellen said, opening the purse in her lap. "I don't have the number, but the address"—managing to unfold the slip of paper without dropping the purse—"is Fifteen-Twenty West Thirty-Fifth Street."

The woman read the message back. "That's right," Ellen said. "You'll be sure he gets it?"

"Of course I will," the woman declared frostily.

"Thank you very much."

Powell was feeding coins onto a small silver tray in the hand of a rapt waiter when Ellen returned to their booth. A smile appeared momentarily on the waiter's face and he vanished, trailing a mumbled thank you. "All set," Ellen said. She reached for her coat which was folded on the banquette where she had been sitting. "By the way, what does he look like, our man? Aside from being so handsome that girls comment on it."

"Blond, tall . . ." Powell said, pocketing his wallet.

"Another blond," sighed Ellen.

"Dorothy went for us Nordic types."

Ellen smiled, pulling on her coat. "Our father is blond—or was until he lost his hair. All three of us—" Ellen's empty coat-sleeve slapped over the top of the booth partition as her hand groped for it. "Excuse me," she said, glancing back over her shoulder, and then she saw that the next booth had been vacated. There were a cocktail glass and a dollar bill on the table, and a paper napkin which had been carefully torn into a delicate lacework web.

Powell helped her with the obstinate sleeve. "Ready?" he asked, putting on his own coat.

"Ready," she said.

It was 9:50 when the cab pulled up in front of Powell's house. West 35th Street was silent, feebly lighted by street-lamps whose beams had to strain their way through meshing tree branches. Yellow windowed houses faced each other on either side, like timid armies showing flags across no-man's-land.

As the roar of the departing cab faded away, Ellen and Powell mounted the steps of a dark, creaking-floored porch. After a few unsuccessful stabs for the keyhole, Powell un-locked the door and pushed it open. He stepped aside and fol-lowed Ellen in, throwing the door closed with one hand and flicking a light switch with the other.

They were in a pleasant-looking living room full of fat chintz-and-maple furniture. "You'd better stay down here," Powell said, going towards a staircase at the left side of the room. "Everything's in a mess upstairs. My landlady is in the hospital and I wasn't expecting company." He paused on the first step. "It'll probably take me a few minutes to find that book. There's some instant coffee in the kitchen back there. You want to fix some?"

"All right," Ellen said, slipping out of her coat.

Powell jogged up the stairs and swung around the newel post. The door to his room was opposite the side of the stair-well. He went in, flipping on the light, and shucked off his coat. The unmade bed, on the right against the windows, was littered with pajamas and discarded clothes. He tossed his coat on top of the whole business and squatted down, about to pull a suitcase from under the bed; but with a sharp fingersnap he straightened up, turned, and stepped over to the bureau, which stood squeezed between a closet door and an armchair. He opened the top drawer and rummaged through papers and small boxes and scarves and broken cigarette lighters. He found the paper he wanted at the bottom of the drawer. Pulling it free with a flourish, he went into the hall and leaned over the stairwell bannister. "Ellen!" he called.

In the kitchen, Ellen adjusted the sighing gas flame under a pan of water. "Coming!" she answered. She hurried through the dining room and into the living room. "Got it already?" she asked, going to the stairs and looking up.

Powell's head and shoulders jutted into the stairwell. "Not yet," he said. "But I thought you'd like to see this." He let go of a stiff sheet of paper that came side-slipping down. "Just in case you have any lingering doubts."

It landed on the stairs before her. Picking it up, she saw that it was a photostat of his NYU record, the words *Student Copy* stamped on it. "If I had any lingering doubts," she said, "I wouldn't be here, would I?"

"True," Powell said, "true,"—and vanished from the stairwell.

Ellen took another look at the transcript and noted that his marks had indeed been pretty poor. Putting the paper on a table, she returned through the dining room to the kitchen. It was a depressing room with old-fashioned appliances and cream colored walls that were brown in the corners and behind the stove. There was, however, a pleasant breeze blowing through from the back.

She found cups and saucers and a can of Nescafé in the various cupboards, and while she was spooning the powder into the cups, she noticed a radio with a cracked plastic case on the counter next to the stove. She turned it on, and once it had warmed up, slowly twisted the selector knob until she found KBRI. She almost passed over it because the small celluloid-vibrating set made Gant's voice sound unfamiliarly thin. ". . . and a little too much about things political," he was saying, "so let's get back to music. We've just got time for one more record, and it's the late Buddy Clark singing *If This Isn't Love*."

Powell, having dropped the transcript down to Ellen, turned around and went back into his room. Squatting before the bed, he shot his hand underneath it—to bang his fingertips painfully against the suitcase, which had been pulled forward from its usual position flush against the wall. He jerked his hand out, waggling the fingers and blowing on them, and cursing his landlady's daughter-in-law who apparently had not been satisfied with only secreting his shoes beneath the bureau.

He reached under the bed again, more cautiously this time, and dragged the heavy-as-lead suitcase all the way out into the open. He took a bunch of keys from his pocket, found the right one and twisted it in the two locks springing them. Replacing the keys, he lifted the lid. The suitcase was filled with textbooks, a tennis racket, a bottle of Canadian Club, golf shoes . . . He took out the larger items and put them on the floor so that it would be easier to get at the notebooks underneath.

There were nine of them; pale green, spiral-bound notebooks. He gathered them into a bundle, stood up with the

114

bundle in his arm and began inspecting them one at a time; examining both covers, dropping the books one by one back into the suitcase.

It was on the seventh one, on the back cover. The penciled address was rubbed and smudged, but it was still legible. He dropped the other two notebooks into the suitcase and turned around, his mouth opening to form Ellen's name in a triumphant shout.

The shout didn't come through. The exultant expression clung to his face for a moment, like a stopped movie, and then it cracked and slid slowly away, like thick snow cracking and sliding from a canted roof.

The closet door was open and a man in a trenchcoat stood framed there. He was tall and blond, and a gun bulked large in his gloved right hand.

10

HE WAS SWEATING. Not cold sweat though; hot healthy sweat from standing in the sweatbox of an airless closet in the sweat-suit of an imporous trenchcoat. His hands too; the gloves were brown leather with a fuzzy lining and elastic cuffs that held in the heat even more; his hands were sweating so much that the fuzzy lining was sodden and caked.

But the automatic (weightless now like part of him after dragging heavily in his pocket all evening) was motionless; the inevitable trajectory of the bullet as palpable in the air as a dotted line in a diagram. Point A: the rock-steady muzzle; Point B: the heart under the lapel of the cheesy-looking prob-ably-bought-in-Iowa suit. He looked down at the Colt .45 as though to verify its blue steel existence, so light it was, and then he took a step forward from the mouth of the closet, re-ducing by a foot the length of dotted line AB.

Well say something, he thought, enjoying the slow stupid melting of Mister Dwight Powell's face. Start talking. Start pleading. Probably can't. Probably he's all talked out after the —what's that word?—the logorrhea of the cocktail lounge. Good word.

"I bet you don't know what logorrhea means," he said, standing there powerfully with the gun in his hand.

Powell stared at the gun. "You're the one . . . with Dorothy," he said.

"It means what you've got. Diarrhea of the mouth. Words keep running. I thought my ear would fall off in that cocktail lounge." He smiled at Powell's widening eyes. "I was respon-sible for poor Dorothy's death," he mimicked. "A pity. A real

115

pity." He stepped closer. "The notebook, *por favor*," he said, extending his left hand. "And don't try anything."

From downstairs, singing came softly:

> *If this isn't love,*
> *Then winter is summer . . .*

He took the notebook that Powell held out, dropped back a step and pressed it against his side, bending it in half lengthwise, cracking the cover, never taking his eyes or the gun off Powell. "I'm awfully sorry you found this. I was standing in there hoping you wouldn't." He stuck the folded notebook into his coat pocket.

"You really killed her . . ." Powell said.

"Let's keep the voices low." He moved the gun admonishingly. "We don't want to disturb the girl detective, do we?" It annoyed him the way Mister Dwight Powell was standing there so blankly. Maybe he was too stupid to realize . . . "Maybe you don't realize it, but this is a real gun, and it's loaded."

Powell didn't say anything. He just went on looking at the gun, not even staring now,—just looking at it with mildly distasteful interest, as though it were the first ladybug of the year.

"Look, I'm going to kill you."

Powell didn't say anything.

"You're such a great one for analyzing yourself—tell me, how do you feel now? I bet your knees are shaking, aren't they? Cold sweat all over you?"

Powell said, "She thought she was going there to get married . . ."

"Forget about her! You've got yourself to worry about." Why wasn't he trembling? Didn't he have brains enough . . .?

"Why did you kill her?" Powell's eyes finally lifted from the gun. "If you didn't want to marry her, you could have left her. That would have been better than killing her. "

"Shut up about her! What's the matter with you? You think I'm bluffing? Is that it? You think—"

Powell leaped forward.

Before he had gone six inches a loud explosion roared; dotted line AB was solidified and fulfilled by tearing lead.

Ellen had been standing in the kitchen looking out through the closed window and listening to the fading theme of Gordon Gant's program, when she suddenly realized that with the window closed, where was that pleasant breeze coming from?

There was a shadowed alcove in a rear corner of the room. She went to it and saw the back door, with the pane of glass nearest the knob smashed in and lying in fragments on the

116

floor. She wondered if Dwight knew about it. You'd think he would have swept up the—

That was when she heard the shot. It smacked loudly through the house, and as the sound died the ceiling light shivered as if something upstairs had fallen. Then there was silence.

The radio said, "At the sound of the chimes, ten PM, Central Standard Time," and a chime toned.

"Dwight?" Ellen said.

There was no answer.

She went into the dining room. She called the name louder: "Dwight?"

In the living room she moved hesitantly to the staircase. There was no sound from overhead. This time she spoke the name with dry throated apprehension: "Dwight?"

The silence held for another moment. Then a voice said, "It's all right, Ellen. Come on up."

She hurried up the stairs with her heart drumming. "In here," the voice said from the right. She pivoted around the newel post and swept to the lighted doorway.

The first thing she saw was Powell lying on his back in the middle of the room, limbs sprawled loosely. His jacket had fallen away from his chest. On his white shirt blood was flowering from a black core over his heart.

She steadied herself against the jamb. Then she raised her eyes to the man who stood beyond Powell, the man with the gun in his hand.

Her eyes dilated, her face went rigid with questions that couldn't work their way to her lips.

He shifted the gun from the firing position to a flat appraising weight on his gloved palm. "I was in the closet," he said, looking her straight in the eye, answering the unasked questions. "He opened that suitcase and took out this gun. He was going to kill you, I jumped him. The gun went off."

"No . . . Oh God . . ." She rubbed her forehead dizzily. "But how . . . how did you . . .?"

He put the gun in the pocket of his coat. "I was in the cocktail lounge," he said. "Right behind you. I heard him talking you into coming up here. I left while you were in the phone booth."

"He told me he . . ."

"I heard what he told you. He was a good liar."

"Oh God, I believed him . . . I believed him . . . "

"That's just your trouble," he said with an indulgent smile. "You believe everybody."

"Oh God . . ." she shivered.

He came to her, stepping between Powell's spraddled legs. She said, "But I still don't understand . . . How were you there, in the lounge . . . ?"

"I was waiting for you in the lobby. I missed you when you

went out with him. Got there too late. I kicked myself for that. But I waited around. What else could I do?"

"But how . . . how . . . ?"

He stood before her with his arms wide, like a soldier returning home. "Look, a heroine isn't supposed to question her nick-of-time rescuer. Just be glad you gave me his address. I may have thought you were being a fool, but I wasn't going to take any chances on having you get your head blown off."

She threw herself into his arms, sobbing with relief and retrospective fear. The leather-tight hands patted her back comfortingly. "It's all right, Ellen," he said softly. "Everything's all right now."

She buried her cheek against his shoulder. "Oh Bud," she sobbed, "thank God for you! Thank God for you, Bud!"

11

THE TELEPHONE RANG DOWNSTAIRS.

"Don't answer it," he said as she started to draw away.

There was a lifeless glaze in her voice: "I know who it is."

"No, don't answer it. Listen,"—his hands were solid and convincing on her shoulders—"someone is sure to have heard that shot. The police will probably be here in a few minutes. Reporters, too." He let that sink in. "You don't want the papers to make a big story out of this, do you? Dragging up everything about Dorothy, pictures of you . . ."

"There's no way to stop them . . ."

"There is. I have a car downstairs. I'll take you back to the hotel and then come right back here." He turned off the light. "If the police haven't shown up yet, I'll call them. Then you won't be here for the reporters to jump on, and I'll refuse to talk until I'm alone with the police. They'll question you later, but the papers won't know you're involved." He led her out into the hallway. "By that time you'll have called your father; he's got enough influence to keep the police from letting out anything about you or Dorothy. They can say Powell was drunk and started a fight with me, or something like that."

The telephone stopped ringing.

"I wouldn't feel right about leaving . . ." she said as they started down the stairs.

"Why not? I'm the one who did it, not you. It's not as if I'm going to lie about your being here; I'll need you to back up my story. All I want to do is prevent the papers from having a field day with this." He turned to her as they descended into the living room. "Trust me, Ellen," he said, touching her hand.

She sighed deeply, gratefully letting tension and responsibility drop from her shoulders. "All right," she said. "But you don't have to drive me. I can get a cab."

"Not at this hour, not without phoning. And I think the streetcars stop running at ten." He picked up her coat and held it for her.

"Where did you get a car?" she asked dully.

"I borrowed it."—he gave her her purse—"From a friend." Turning off the lights, he opened the door to the porch. "Come on," he said, "we haven't got too much time."

He had parked the car across the street and some fifty feet down the block. It was a black Buick sedan, two or three years old. He opened the door for Ellen, then went around to the other side and slipped in behind the wheel. He fumbled with the ignition key. Ellen sat silently, hands folded in her lap. "You feel all right?" he asked.

"Yes," she said, her voice thin and tired. "It's just that . . . he was going to kill me . . ." She sighed. "At least I was right about Dorothy. I *knew* she didn't commit suicide." She managed a reproachful smile. "And you tried to talk me out of making this trip . . ."

He got the motor started. "Yes," he said. "You were right."

She was silent for a moment. "Anyway, there's a sort of a silver lining to all this," she said.

"What's that?" He shifted gears and the car glided forward.

"Well, you saved my life," she said. "You really saved my life. That should cut short whatever objections my father might have, when you meet him and we speak to him about us."

After they had been driving down Washington Avenue for a few minutes, she moved closer to him and hesitantly took his arm, hoping it wouldn't interfere with his driving. She felt something hard pressing against her hip and realized that it was the gun in his pocket, but she didn't want to move away.

"Listen, Ellen," he said. "This is going to be a lousy business, you know."

"What do you mean?"

"Well, I'll be held for manslaughter."

"But you didn't mean to kill him! You were trying to get the gun away from him."

"I know, but they'll still have to hold me . . . all kinds of red tape . . ." He stole a quick glance at the downcast figure beside him and then returned his gaze to the traffic ahead. "Ellen . . . when we get to the hotel, you could just pick up your things and check out. We could be back in Caldwell in a couple of hours . . ."

"Bud!" Her voice was sharp with surprised reproach. "We couldn't do a thing like that!"

"Why not? He killed your sister, didn't he? He got what was coming to him. Why should we have to get mixed up—"

"We can't do it," she protested. "Aside from its being such a—a *wrong* thing to do, suppose they found out anyway that you . . . killed him. Then they'd never believe the truth, not if you ran away."

"I don't see how they could find out it was me," he said. "I'm wearing gloves, so there can't be any fingerprints. And nobody saw me there, except you and him."

"But suppose they *did* find out! Or suppose they blamed someone else for it! How would you feel then?" He was silent. "As soon as I get to the hotel, I'll call my father. Once he's heard the story, I know he'll take care of lawyers and everything. I guess it *will* be a terrible business. But to run away . . ."

"It was a foolish suggestion," he said. "I didn't really expect you to agree."

"No, Bud, you wouldn't want to do a thing like that, would you?"

"I only tried it as a lást resort," he said. Suddenly he swung the car in a wide left turn from the brightly lighted orbit of Washington Avenue to the darkness of a northbound road.

"Shouldn't you stay on Washington?" Ellen asked.

"Quicker this way. Avoid traffic."

"What I can't understand," she said, tapping her cigarette on the edge of the dashboard tray, "is why he didn't do anything to me there, on the roof." She was settled comfortably, turned towards Bud with her left leg drawn up under her, the cigarette suffusing her with sedative warmth.

"You must have been pretty conspicuous, going there at night," he said. "He was probably afraid that an elevator man or someone would remember his face."

"Yes, I suppose so. But wouldn't it have been less risky than taking me back to his house and . . . doing it there?"

"Maybe he didn't intend to do it there. Maybe he was going to force you into a car and drive you out into the country someplace."

"He didn't have a car."

"He could have stolen one. It's not such a hard thing to steal a car." A street light flashing by brushed his face with white, then dropped it back into the darkness where the cleanly-hewn features were touched only by the dashboard's nebulous green.

"The lies he told me! 'I loved her. I was in New York. I felt responsible.'" She mashed the cigarette into the ashtray, shaking her head bitterly. "Oh my God!" she gasped.

He flicked a glance at her. "What is it?"

Her voice had taken on the sick glaze again. "He showed me his transcript . . . from NYU. He *was* in New York . . ."

"That was probably a fake. He must have known someone in the registrar's office there. They could fake something like that."

"But suppose it wasn't . . . Suppose he was telling the truth!"

"He was coming after you with a gun. Isn't that proof enough he was lying?"

"Are you sure, Bud? Are you sure he didn't—maybe take the gun out to get at something else? The notebook he mentioned?"

"He was going to the door with the gun."

"Oh God, if he really didn't kill Dorothy . . ." She was silent for a moment. "The police will investigate," she said positively. "They'll prove he was right here in Blue River! They'll prove he killed Dorothy!"

"That's right," he said.

"But even if he didn't, Bud, even if it was a—a terrible mistake,—they wouldn't blame you for anything. You couldn't know; you saw him with the gun. They could never blame you for anything."

"That's right," he said.

Shifting uncomfortably, she drew her folded leg out from under her. She squinted at her watch in the dashboard's glow. "It's twenty-five after ten. Shouldn't we be there already?"

He didn't answer her.

She looked out the window. There were no more streetlights, no more buildings. There was only the pitch blackness of fields under the star-heightened blackness of the sky. "Bud, this isn't the way into town."

He didn't answer her.

Ahead of the car a white onrush of highway narrowed to implied infinity always beyond the headlights' reach.

"Bud, you're going the wrong way!"

12

"WHAT YOU WANT from *me*?" Chief of Police Eldon Chesser asked blandly. He lay supine, his long legs supported beneath the ankles by an arm of the chintz-covered sofa, his hands laced loosely across the front of his red flannel shirt, his large brown eyes vaguely contemplating the ceiling.

"Get after the car. That's what I want," Gordon Gant said, glaring at him from the middle of the living room.

"Ha," said Chesser. "Ha ha. A dark car is all the man next door knows; after he called about the shot he saw a man and a woman go down the block and get into a dark car. A dark car with a man and a woman. You know how many dark cars there is driving around town with a man and woman in them? We didn't even have a description of the girl until you come shooting in. By that time they could've been half-way to Cedar Rapids. Or parked in some garage two blocks from here, for all we know."

Gant paced malevolently. "So what are we supposed to do?"

"Wait, is all. I notified the highway boys, didn't I? Maybe this is bank night. Why don't you sit down?"

"Sure, sit down," Gant snapped. "She's liable to be murdered!" Chesser was silent. "Last year her sister,—now her."

"Here we go again," Chesser said. The brown eyes closed in weariness. "Her sister committed suicide," he articulated slowly. "I saw the note with my own two eyes. A handwriting expert—" Gant made a noise. "And who killed her?" Chesser demanded. "You said Powell was supposed to be the one, only now it couldnt've been him 'cause the girl left a message for you that he was all right, and you found this paper here from New York U. that makes it look like he wasn't even in these parts last spring. So if the only suspect didn't do it, who did? Answer: nobody."

His voice tight with the exasperation of repetition, Gant said, "Her message said that Powell had an idea who it was. The murderer must have known that Powell—"

"There *was* no murderer, until tonight," Chesser said flatly. "The sister committed suicide." His eyes blinked open and regarded the ceiling.

Gant glare at him and resumed his bitter pacing.

After a few minutes Chesser said, "Well, I guess I got it all reconstructed now."

"Yeah?" Gant said.

"Yeah. You didn't think I was laying here just to be lazy, did you? This is the way to think, with your feet higher'n your head. Blood goes to the brain." He cleared his throat. "The guy breaks in about a quarter to ten—man next door heard the glass break but didn't think anything of it. No sign of any of the other rooms having been gone through, so Powell's must have been the first one he hit. A couple minutes later Powell and the girl come in. The guy is stuck upstairs. He hides in Powell's closet—the clothes are all pushed to the side. Powell and the girl go into the kitchen. She starts making coffee, turns on the radio. Powell goes upstairs to hang up his coat, or maybe he heard a noise. The guy comes out. He's already tried to open the suitcase—we found glove smudges on it. He makes Powell unlock it and goes through it. Stuff all over the floor. Maybe he finds something, some money. Anyway, Powell jumps him. The guy shoots Powell. Probably panics, probably didn't intend to shoot him—they never do; they only carry guns to scare people. Always wind up shooting 'em. Forty-five shell. Most likely an Army Colt. Million of 'em floating around.

"Next thing the girl comes running upstairs—same prints on the door frame up there as on the cups and stuff in the kitchen'. The guy is panicky, no time to ... He forces her to leave with him."

"Why? Why wouldn't he have left her here ... the way he left Powell?"

"Don't ask me. Maybe he didn't have the nerve. Or maybe he got ideas. Sometimes they get ideas when they're holding a gun and there's a pretty girl on the other end of it."

"Thanks," Gant said. "That makes me feel a whole lot better. Thanks a lot."

Chesser sighed. "You might as well sit down," he said. "There ain't a damn thing we can do but wait."

Gant sat down. He began rubbing his forehead with the heel of his hand.

Chesser finally turned his face from the ceiling. He watched Gant sitting across the room. "What is she? Your girlfriend?" he asked.

"No," Gant said. He remembered the letter he had read in Ellen's room. "No, there's some guy in Wisconsin."

13

BEHIND THE RACING ISLAND of the headlights' reach, the car arrowed over the tight line of highway, tarred seams in concrete creating a regular rhythm under the tires. The speedometer's luminous green needle split the figure fifty. The foot on the accelerator was steady as the foot of a statue.

He drove with his left hand, occasionally giving the steering wheel an inappreciable right or left movement to relieve the hypnotic monotony of the highway. Ellen was huddled all the way over against the door, her body knotted tight, her eyes staring brokenly at the handkerchief-twisting hands in her lap. On the seat between them, snakelike, lay his gloved right hand with the gun in it, the muzzle riveted against her hip.

She had cried; long throat-dragging animal moans; more sound and shaking than actual tears.

He had told her everything, in a bitter voice, glancing frequently at her green-touched face in the darkness. There were moments of awkward hesitancy in his narration, as an on-leave soldier telling how he won his medals hesitates before describing to the gentle townsfolk how his bayonet ripped open an enemy's stomach, then goes on and describes it because they asked how he won his medals, didn't they?—describes it with irritation and mild contempt for the gentle townsfolk who never had had to rip open anyone's stomach. So he told Ellen about the pills and the roof and why it had been necessary to kill Dorothy, and why it had then been the most logical course to transfer to Caldwell and go after *her*, Ellen, knowing her likes and dislikes from conversations with Dorothy, knowing how to make himself the man she was waiting for—not only the most logical and inevitable course, going after the girl with whom he had such an advantage, but also the course most ironically satisfying, the course most compensatory for past bad luck—(the course most law-defying, black-slapping, ego-preening)—he told her these things with irritation and contempt; this girl with her hands over her mouth in horror had had everything given her on a silver platter; she didn't know what it was to live on a swaying catwalk over the chasm of failure, stealing perilously inch by inch towards the solid ground of success so many miles away.

She listened with the muzzle of his gun jabbing painfully into her hip; painfully only at first, then numbingly, as though that part of her were already dead, as though death came from the gun not in a swift bullet but in slow radiation from the point of contact. She listened, and then she cried, because she was so sickened and beaten and shocked that there was nothing else she could do to express it all. Her cries were long throat-dragging animal moans; more sound and shaking than actual tears.

And then she sat staring brokenly at the handkerchief-twisting hands in her lap.

"I *told* you not to come," he said querulously. "I *begged* you to stay in Caldwell, didn't I?" He glanced at her as though expecting an affirmation. "But *no*. No, you had to be the girl detective! Well this is what happens to girl detectives." His eyes returned to the highway. "If you only *knew* what I've gone through since Monday," he clenched, remembering how the world had dropped out from under him Monday morning when Ellen had phoned—"Dorothy didn't commit suicide! I'm leaving for Blue River!"—running down to the station, barely catching her, futilely desperately trying to keep her from leaving but she stepped onto the train—"I'll write you this minute! I'll explain the whole thing!"—leaving him standing there, watching her glide away, sweating, terrified. It made him sick just thinking about it.

Ellen said something faintly.

"What?"

"They'll catch you . . ."

After a moment's silence he said, "You know how many don't get caught? More than fifty per cent, that's how many. Maybe a *lot* more." After another moment he said, "How are they going to catch me? Fingerprints?—none. Witnesses?—none. Motive?—none that they know about. They won't even think of me. The gun?—I have to go over the Mississippi to get back to Caldwell; good-by gun. This car?—two or three in the morning I leave it a couple of blocks from where I took it; they think it was some crazy high school kids. Juvenile de-

124

linquents." He smiled. "I did it last night too. I was sitting two rows behind you and Powell in the theater and I was right around a bend in the hall when he kissed you goodnight." He glanced at her to see her reaction; none was visible. His gaze returned to the road and his face clouded again. "That letter of yours—how I sweated till it came! When I first started to read it I thought I was safe; you were looking for someone she'd met in her English class in the fall; I didn't meet her till January, and it was in Philosophy. But then I realized who that guy you were looking for actually was—Old Argyle-Socks, my predecessor. We'd had Math together, and he'd seen me with Dorrie. I thought he might know my name. I knew that if he ever convinced you he didn't have anything to do with Dorrie's murder . . . if he ever mentioned my name to you . . ."

Suddenly he jammed down on the brake pedal and the car screeched to a halt. Reaching left-handed around the steering column, he shifted gears. When he stepped on the gas again, the car rolled slowly backwards. On their right, the dark form of a house slid into view, low-crouching behind a broad expanse of empty parking lot. The headlights of the retreating car caught a large upright sign at the highway's edge: *Lillie and Doane's—The Streak Supreme*. A smaller sign hung swaying from the gallows of the larger one: *Reopening April 15th*.

He shifted back into first, spun the wheel to the right, and stepped on the gas. He drove across the parking lot and pulled up at the side of the low building, leaving the motor running. He pressed the horn ring; a loud blast banged through the night. He waited a minute, then sounded the horn again. Nothing happened. No window was raised, no light went on. "Looks like nobody's home," he said, turning off the headlights.

"Please . . ." she said, "please . . ."

In the darkness the car rolled forward, turned to the left, moved behind the house where the asphalt of the parking lot flowed into a smaller paved area. The car swung around in a wide curve, almost going off the edge of the asphalt into the dirt of a field that swept off to meet the blackness of the sky. It swung all the way around until it was facing the direction from which it had come.

He set the emergency brake and left the motor running.

"Please . . ." she said.

He looked at her. "You think I want to do this? You think I like the idea? We were almost engaged!" He opened the door on his left. "You had to be smart . . ." He stepped out onto the asphalt, keeping the gun aimed at her huddled figure. "Come here," he said. "Come out on this side."

"Please . . ."

"Well what am I supposed to do, Ellen? I can't let you go, can I? I asked you to go back to Caldwell without saying anything, didn't I?" The gun made an irritated gesture. "Come out."

She pulled herself across the seat, clutching her purse. She stepped out onto the asphalt.

The gun directed her in a semicircular path until she stood with the field at her back, the gun between her and the car.

"Please . . ." she said, holding up the purse in a futile shielding gesture, "please . . ."

14

From the Blue River Clarion-Ledger; *Thursday, March 15, 1951:*

DOUBLE SLAYING HERE

POLICE SEEK
MYSTERY GUNMAN

Within a period of two hours last night, an unknown gunman committed two brutal murders. His victims were Ellen Kingship, 21, of New York City, and Dwight Powell, 23, of Chicago, a junior at Stoddard University...

Powell's slaying occurred at 10:00 PM, in the home of Mrs. Elizabeth Honig, 1520 West 35th St., where Powell was a roomer. As police reconstruct the events, Powell, entering the house at 9:50 in the company of Miss Kingship, went to his second-floor room where he encountered an armed burglar who had earlier broken into the house through the back door...

...the medical examiner established the time of Miss Kingship's death as somewhere near midnight. Her body, however, was not discovered until 7:20 this morning, when Willard Herne, 11, of nearby Randalia, crossed through a field adjacent to the restaurant... Police learned from Gordon Gant, KBRI announcer and a friend of Miss Kingship, that she was the sister of Dorothy Kingship who last April committed suicide by jumping from the roof of the Blue River Municipal Building...

Leo Kingship, president of Kingship Copper, Inc., and father of the slain girl, is expected to arrive in Blue River this afternoon, accompanied by his daughter, Marion Kingship.

An Editorial from the Clarion-Ledger; *Thursday, April 19, 1951.*

DISMISSAL OF GORDON GANT

In dismissing Gordon Gant from their employ (story on p. 5) the management of KBRI points out that "despite frequent warnings, he has persisted in using (KBRI's) microphones to harass and malign the Police Department in a manner bordering on the slanderous." The matter involved was the month-old Kingship-Powell slayings, in which Mr. Gant has taken a personal and somewhat acrimonious interest. His public criticism of the police was, to say the least, indiscreet, but considering that no progress has been made towards reaching a solution of the case, we find ourselves forced to agree with the appropriateness of his remarks, if not with their propriety.

15

AT THE END OF THE SCHOOL YEAR he returned to Menasset and sat around the house in somber depression. His mother tried to combat his sullenness and then began to reflect it. They ar-

gued, like hot coals boosting each other in to flame. To get out
of the house and out of himself, he reclaimed his old job at
the haberdashery shop. From nine to five-thirty he stood behind a glass display counter not looking at the binding-strips
of gleaming burnished copper.

One day in July he took the small gray strongbox from his
closet. Unlocking it on his desk, he took out the newspaper
clippings about Dorothy's murder. He tore them into small
pieces and dropped them into the wastebasket. He did the
same with the clippings on Ellen and Powell. Then he took
out the Kingship Copper pamphlets; he had written away for
them a second time when he started to go with Ellen. As his
hands gripped them, ready to tear, he smiled ruefully. Dorothy,
Ellen . . .

It was like thinking "Faith, Hope . . ." "Charity" pops into
the mind to fulfill the sequence.

Dorothy, Ellen . . . Marion.

He smiled at himself and gripped the pamphlets again.

But he found that he couldn't tear them. Slowly he put
them down on the desk, mechanically smoothing the creases
his hands had made.

He pushed the strongbox and the pamphlets to the back of
the desk and sat down. He headed a sheet of paper *Marion* and
divided it into two columns with a vertical line. He headed one
column *Pro;* the other *Con.*

There were so many things to list under *Pro:* months of conversations with Dorothy, months of conversations with Ellen;
all studded with passing references to Marion; her likes, her
dislikes, her opinions, her past. He knew her like a book without even having met her; lonely, bitter, living alone . . . A
perfect set-up.

Emotion was on the *Pro* side too. Another chance. Hit a
home run and the two strikes that preceded it are washed away.
And three was the lucky number . . . third time lucky . . .
all the childhood fairy tales with the third try and the third
wish and the third suitor . . .

He couldn't think of a thing to list under *Con.*

That night he tore up the *Pro* and *Con* list and began another one, of Marion Kingship's characteristics, opinions, likes
and dislikes. He made several notations and, in the weeks that
followed, added regularly to the list. In every spare moment he
pushed his mind back to conversations with Dorothy and
Ellen; conversations in luncheonettes, between classes, while
walking, while dancing; dredging words, phrases and sentences
up from the pool of his memory. Sometimes he spent entire
evenings flat on his back, remembering, a small part of his

128

mind probing the larger, less conscious part like a Geiger counter that clicked on *Marion*.

As the list grew, his spirits swelled. Sometimes he would take the paper from the strongbox even when he had nothing to add,—just to admire it; the keenness, the planning, the potence displayed. It was almost as good as having the clippings on Dorothy and Ellen.

"You're crazy," he told himself aloud one day, looking at the list. "You're a crazy nut," he said affectionately. He didn't really think that; he thought he was daring, audacious, brilliant, intrepid and bold.

"I'm not going back to school," he told his mother one day in August.

"What?" She stood small and thin in the doorway of his room, one hand frozen in mid-passage over her straggly gray hair.

"I'm going to New York in a few weeks."

"You got to finish *school*," she said plaintively. He was silent. "What is it, you got a job in New York?"

"I don't but I'm going to get one. I've got an idea I want to work on. A—a project, sort of."

"But you got to finish school, Bud," she said hesitantly.

"I don't 'got to' do anything!" he snapped. There was silence. "If this idea flops, which I don't think it will, I can always finish school next year."

Her hands wiped the front of her housedress nervously. "But, you're past twenty-five. You got to—have to finish school and get yourself started someplace. You can't keep—"

"Look, will you just let me live my own life?"

She stared at him. "That's what your father used to give me," she said quietly, and went away.

He stood by his desk for a few moments, hearing the angry clanking of cutlery in the kitchen sink. He picked up a magazine and looked at it, pretending he didn't care.

A few minutes later he went into the kitchen. His mother was at the sink, her back towards him. "Mom," he said pleadingly, "you know I'm as anxious as you are to see myself get someplace." She didn't turn around. "You know I wouldn't quit school if this idea wasn't something important." He went over and sat down at the table, facing her back. "If it doesn't work, I'll finish school next year. I *promise* I will, Mom."

Reluctantly, she turned. "What kind of idea is it?" she asked slowly. "An invention?"

"No. I can't tell you," he said regretfully. "It's only in the— the planning stage. I'm sorry . . ."

She sighed and wiped her hands on a towel. "Can't it wait till next year? When you'd be through with school?"

"Next year might be too late, Mom."

She put down the towel. "Well I wish you could tell me what is is."

"I'm sorry, Mom. I wish I could too. But it's one of those things that you just can't explain."

She went around behind him and laid her hands on his shoulders. She stood there for a moment, looking down at his anxiously upturned face. "Well," she said, pressing his shoulders, "I guess it must be a *good* idea."

He smiled up at her happily.

1

WHEN MARION KINGSHIP was graduated from college (Columbia University, an institution demanding long hours of earnest study; unlike that Midwestern Twentieth Century-Fox playground that Ellen was entering), her father offhandedly mentioned the fact to the head of the advertising agency which handled the Kingship Copper account, and Marion was offered a job as a copy writer. Although she wanted very much to write advertising copy, she refused the offer. Eventually she managed to find a position with a small agency where Kingship was a name stamped in the washroom plumbing and where Marion was assured that in the not-too-distant future she would be permitted to submit copy for some of the smaller accounts, provided that the writing of the copy did not interfere with her secretarial duties.

A year later, when Dorothy inevitably followed Ellen's lead and went off to football cheers and campus kisses, Marion found herself alone in an eight-room apartment with her father, the two of them like charged metal pellets that drift and pass but never touch. She decided, against her father's obvious though unvoiced disapproval, to find a place of her own.

She rented a two-room apartment on the top floor of a converted brownstone in the East Fifties. She furnished it with a great deal of care. Because the two rooms were smaller than those she had occupied in her father's home, she could not take all her possessions with her. Those that she did take, therefore, were the fruit of a thoughtful selection. She told herself she was choosing the things she liked best, the things that meant the most to her, which was true; but as she hung each picture and placed each book upon the shelf, she saw it not only through her own eyes but also through the eyes of a visitor who would some day come to her apartment, a visitor as yet unidentified except as to his sex. Every article was invested with significance, an index to her self; the furniture and the lamps and the ashtrays (modern but not modernistic), the reproduction of her favorite painting (Charles Demuth's *My Egypt;* not quite realistic; its planes accentuated and enriched by the eye of the artist), the records (some of the jazz and some of the Stravinsky and Bartók, but mostly the melodic listen-in-the-dark themes of Grieg and Brahms and Rachmaninoff), and the books—especially the books, for what better index of the personality is there?—(the novels and plays, the non-fiction and verse, all chosen in proportion and representation of her tastes). It was like the concentrated abbreviation of a Help

132

Wanted ad. The egocentricity which motivated it was not that of the spoiled, but of the too little spoiled; the lonely. Had she been an arist she would have painted a self-portrait; instead she decorated two rooms, charging them with objects which some visitor, some day, would recognize and understand. And through that understanding he would divine all the ·capacities and longings she had found in herself and was unable to communicate.

The map of her week was centered about two landmarks; on Wednesday evenings she had dinner with her father, and on Saturdays she thorough-cleaned her two rooms. The first was a labor of duty; the second, of love. She waxed wood and polished glass, and dusted and replaced objects with sacramental care.

There were visitors. Dorothy and Ellen came when they were home on vacation, unconvincingly envying Marion as a woman of the world. Her father came, puffing from the three flights of stairs, looking dubiously at the small living-bedroom and smaller kitchen and shaking his head. Some girls from the office came, playing Canasta as though life and honor were at stake. And a man came once; the bright young junior account executive; very nice, very intelligent. His interest in the apartment manifested itself in sidelong glances at the studio couch.

When Dorothy committed suicide, Marion returned to her father's apartment for two weeks, and when Ellen died, she stayed with him for a month. They could no more get close to each other than could charged metal pellets, no matter how they tried. At the end of the month, he suggested with a diffidence unusual in him that she move back permanently. She couldn't; the thought of relinquishing her own apartment was unimaginable, as though she had locked too much of herself into it. After that though, she had dinner at her father's three evenings a week instead of only one.

On Saturday she cleaned the rooms, and once each month she opened all the books to prevent their bindings from growing stiff.

One Saturday morning in September, the telephone rang. Marion, on her knees in the act of polishing the underside of a plate glass coffee table, froze at the sound of the bell. She gazed down through the blue-toned glass at the flattened dustcloth, hoping that it was a mistake, that someone had dialed the wrong number, had realized it at the last moment and hung up. The phone rang again. Reluctantly she rose to her feet and went over to the table beside the studio couch, still holding the dustcloth in her hand.

"Hello," she said flatly.

"Hello." It was a man's voice, unfamiliar. "Is this Marion Kingship?"

"Yes."

"You don't know me. I was . . . a friend of El
Marion felt suddenly awkward; a friend of Ellen's; so
handsome and clever and fast-talking . . . Someone d
derneath, someone *she* wouldn't care for anyway. The
wardness retreated. "My name," the man continued, "is F
Corliss . . . Bud Corliss."

". . . Oh, yes. Ellen told me about you . . ." ('I lov
so much.' Ellen had said during the visit that had proved
her last, 'and he loves me too,'—and Marion, though
for her, had for some reason been somber the rest of th
ning.)

"I wonder if I could see you," he said. "I have som
that belonged to Ellen. One of her books. She lent it
just before . . . before she went to Blue River, and I th
you might like to have it."

Probably some Book-of-the-Month novel, Marion th
and then, hating herself for her smallness, said, "Yes, I"
very much to have it. Yes, I would."

For a moment there was silence from the other end
wire. "I could bring it over now," he said. "I'm in the neig
hood."

"No," she said quickly, "I'm going out."

"Well then, sometime tomorrow . . ."

"I . . . I won't be in tomorrow either." She shifted u
fortably, ashamed of her lying, ashamed that she didn't
him in her apartment. He was probably likeable enough
he'd loved Ellen and Ellen was dead, and he was going
his way to give her Ellen's book . . . "We could meet
place this afternoon," she offered.

"Fine," he said. "That would be fine."

"I'm going to be . . . around Fifth Avenue."

"Then suppose we meet, say, in front of the statue at R
feller Center, the one of Atlas holding up the world."

"All right."

"At three o'clock?"

"Yes. Three o'clock. Thank you very much for callin
very nice of you."

"Don't mention it," he said. "Good-by, Marion." Ther
a pause. "I'd feel funny calling you Miss Kingship. Ellen
about you so much."

"That's all right . . ." She felt awkward again, and self
scious. "Good-by . . ." she said, unable to decide whetl
call him Bud or Mr. Corliss.

"Good-by," he repeated.

She replaced the receiver and stood looking at the telep
for a moment. Then she turned and went to the coffee
Kneeling, she resumed her work, sweeping the dustclo
unaccustomedly hurried arcs, because now the whole
noon was broken up.

134

2

IN THE SHADOW OF THE TOWERING BRONZE STATUE, he stood with his back to the pedestal, immaculate in gray flannel, a paper-wrapped package under his arm. Before him passed intermeshing streams of oppositely-bound people, slow-moving against a backdrop of roaring busses and impatient taxis. He watched their faces carefully. The Fifth Avenue set; men with unpadded shoulders and narrowly knotted ties; women self-consciously smart in tailored suits, kerchiefs crisp at their throats, their beautiful heads lifted high, as though photographers might be waiting farther down the street. And, like transient sparrows tolerated in an aviary, the pink rural faces gawking at the statue and the sun-sharpened spires of Saint Patrick's across the street. He watched them all carefully, trying to recall the snapshot Dorothy had shown him so long ago. "Marion could be very pretty, only she wears her hair like this." He smiled, remembered Dorrie's fierce frown as she pulled her hair back primly. His fingers toyed with a fold in the wrapping of the package.

She came from the north, and he recognized her when she was still a hundred feet away. She was tall and thin, a bit too thin, and dressed much like the women around her; a brown suit, a gold kerchief, a small Vogue-looking felt hat, a shoulder-strap handbag. She seemed stiff and uncomfortable in the outfit, though, as if it had been made to someone else's measure. Her pulled-back hair was brown. She had Dorothy's large brown eyes, but in her drawn face they were too large, and the high cheekbones that had been so beautiful in her sisters were, in Marion, too sharply defined. As she came nearer, she saw him. With an uncertain, questioning smile, she approached, appearing ill at ease in the spotlight of his gaze. Her lipstick, he noticed, was the pale rose he associated with timorously experimenting adolescents.

"Marion?"

"Yes." She offered her hand hesitantly. "How do you do," she said, directing a too quick smile at a point somewhere below his eyes.

Her hand in his was long-fingered and cold. "Hello," he said. "I've been looking forward to meeting you."

They went to a determinedly Early American cocktail lounge around the corner. Marion, after some indecision, ordered a Daquiri.

"I . . . I can't stay long, I'm afraid," she said, sitting erect on

135

the edge of her chair, her fingers stiff around the cocktail glass.

"Where are they always running, these beautiful women?" he inquired smilingly—and immediately saw that it was the wrong approach; she smiled tensely and seemed to grow more uncomfortable. He looked at her curiously, allowing the echo of his words to fade. After a moment he began again. "You're with an advertising agency, aren't you?"

"Camden and Galbraith," she said. "Are you still at Caldwell?"

"No."

"I thought Ellen said you were a junior."

"I was, but I had to quit school." He sipped his Martini. "My father is dead. I didn't want my mother to work any more."

"Oh, I'm sorry . . ."

"Maybe I'll be able to finish up next year. Or I may go to night school. Where did you go to school?"

"Columbia. Are you from New York?"

"Massachusetts."

Every time he tried to steer the conversation around to her, she turned it back towards him. Or to the weather. Or to a waiter who bore a startling resemblance to Claude Raines.

Eventually she asked, "Is that the book?"

"Yes. *Dinner at Antoine's.* Ellen wanted me to read it. There are some personal notes she scribbled on the flyleaf, so I thought you might like to have it." He passed the package to her.

"Personally," he said, "I go for books that have a little more meaning."

Marion stood up. "I'll have to be leaving now," she said apologetically.

"But you haven't finished your drink yet."

"I'm sorry," she said quickly, looking down at the package in her hands, "I have an appointment. A business appointment. I couldn't possibly be late."

He rose. "But . . ."

"I'm sorry." She looked at him uncomfortably.

He put money on the table.

They walked back to Fifth Avenue. At the corner she offered her hand again. It was still cold. "It's been very nice meeting you, Mr. Corliss," she said. "Thank you for the drink. And the book. I appreciate it . . . very thoughtful . . ." She turned and melted into the stream of people.

Emptily, he stood on the corner for a moment. Then his lips clenched and he started walking.

He followed her. The brown felt hat had a gold ornament that glittered brightly. He stayed some thirty feet behind it.

She walked up to Fifty-Fourth Street, where she crossed the avenue, heading east towards Madison. He knew where she was going; he remembered the address from the telephone

136

book. She crossed Madison and Park. He stopped on the corner and watched her climb the steps of the brownstone house.

"Business appointment," he muttered. He waited around for a few minutes, not knowing exactly why he waited, and then he turned and walked slowly back towards Fifth Avenue.

3

SUNDAY AFTERNOON Marion went to the Museum of Modern Art. The main floor was still occupied by an automobile exhibit which she had seen before and found uninteresting, and the second floor was unusually crowded, so she continued up the turning stairway to the third floor, there to wander among the pleasantly familiar paintings and sculptures; the arched white smoothness of the *Girl Washing Her Hair*, the perfect spear of *Bird In Space*.

Two men were in the room that held the Lehmbruck sculptures, but they went out soon after Marion entered, leaving her alone in the cool gray cube with the two statues, the male and female, he standing and she kneeling in opposite quarters of the room, their bodies elongated and gauntly beautiful. The attenuation of the statues gave them an unearthly air, almost like religious art, so that Marion had always been able to look at them with none of the slight embarrassment she usually felt on viewing nude sculptures. She moved slowly around the figure of the young man.

"Hello." The voice was behind her, pleasantly surprised.

It must be for me, she thought, there's no one else here. She turned around.

Bud Corliss smiled in the doorway.

"Hello," Marion said confusedly.

"It really *is* a small world," he said, coming to her. "I came in right behind you downstairs, only I wasn't sure it was you. How are you?"

"Fine, thank you." There was an uncomfortable pause. "How are you?" she added.

"Fine, thanks."

They turned to the statue. Why did she feel so clumsy? Because he was handsome? Because he had been part of Ellen's circle?— had shared football cheers and campus kisses and love . . .

"Do you come here often?" he asked.

"Yes."

"So do I."

The statue embarrassed her now, because Bud Corliss was standing beside her. She turned away and moved towards the

137

figure of the kneeling woman. He followed at her side. "Did you make that appointment on time?"

"Yes," she said. What brought him here? You'd think he'd be strolling in Central Park with some poised flawless Ellen on his arm . . .

They looked at the statue. After a moment, he said, "I really didn't think it was you downstairs."

"Why not?"

"Well, Ellen wasn't the museum type . . ."

"Sisters aren't exactly alike," she said.

"No, I guess not." He began to circle around the kneeling figure.

"The Fine Arts department at Caldwell had a small museum," he said. "Mostly reproductions and copies. I dragged Ellen there once or twice. Thought I'd indoctrinate her." He shook his head. "No luck."

"She wasn't interested in art."

"No," he said. "It's funny the way we try to push our tastes on people we like."

Marion looked at him, facing her on the other side of the statue. "I once took Ellen and Dorothy—Dorothy was our youngest sister—"

"I know . . ."

"I took them here once when they were just going into their teens. They were bored, though. I guess it was too young."

"I don't know," he said, retracing his semicircular path towards her. "If there'd been a museum in my home town when I was that age . . . Did *you* come here when you were twelve or thirteen?"

"Yes."

"See?" he said. His smile made them fellow members of a group to which Ellen and Dorothy had never belonged.

A man and woman with two children in tow came bursting into the room.

"Let's move on," he suggested, at her side again.

"I . . ."

"It's Sunday," he said. "No business appointments to run to." He smiled at her; a very nice smile, soft and lenitive. "I'm alone; you're alone . . ." He took her elbow gently. "Come on," he said, with the persuasive smile.

They went through the third floor and half of the second, commenting on the works they saw, and then they went down to the main floor, past the gleaming automobiles incongruous within a building, and out through the glass doors to the garden behind the museum. They strolled from statue to statue, pausing before each. They came to the Maillol woman, full-bodied, strident.

"The last of the red-hot mammas," Bud said.

Marion smiled. "I'll tell you something," she said. "I always get a little embarrassed looking at . . . statues like this."

138

"This one embarrasses *me* a little," he said, smiling. "It's not a nude; it's a naked." They both laughed.

When they had looked at all the statues, they sat down on one of the benches at the back of the garden and lighted cigarettes.

"You and Ellen were going steady, weren't you?"

"Not exactly."

"I thought . . ."

"Not officially, I mean. Anyway, going steady in college doesn't always mean as much as going steady outside of college."

Marion smoked in silence.

"We had a great many things in common, but they were mainly surface things; having the same classes, knowing the same people . . . things having to do with Caldwell. Once we were through with college though, I don't think we would've . . . I don't think we would've gotten married." He stared at his cigarette. "I was fond of Ellen. I liked her better than any girl I've ever known. I was miserable when she died. But . . . I don't know . . . she wasn't a very *deep* person." He paused. "I hope I'm not offending you."

Marion shook her head watching him.

"Everything was like that museum business. I thought I could at least get her interested in some of the uncomplicated artists, like Hopper or Wood. But it didn't work. She wasn't interested at all. And it was the same thing with books or politics—anything serious. She always wanted to be *doing* something."

"She'd led a restricted life at home. I guess she was making up for it."

"Yes," he said. "And then, she was four year younger than I." He put out his cigarette. "But she was the sweetest girl I've ever known."

There was a pause.

"Didn't they ever find out *anything* about who did it?" he asked incredulously.

"Nothing. Isn't it awful . . ."

They sat in silence for a moment. Then they began to talk again; about how many interesting things there were to do in New York, what a pleasant place the museum was, about the Matisse exhibit that was coming soon.

"Do you know who I like?" he asked.

"Who?"

"I don't know if you're familiar with his work," he said. "Charles Demuth."

4

LEO KINGSHIP SAT WITH HIS ELBOWS PROPPED on the table, his fingers interlocked around a cold-frosted glass of milk which he studied as though it were a beautifully colored wine. "You've been seeing him frequently, haven't you," he said, trying to sound casual.

With elaborate care, Marion placed her coffee cup in the indentation of the blue and gold Aynsley saucer, and then looked across the crystal and silver and damask at her father. His full red face was bland. Reflected light blanked the lenses of his eyeglasses, masking his eyes. "Bud?" she said, knowing it was Bud he meant.

Kingship nodded.

"Yes," Marion said squarely, "I've been seeing him frequently." She paused. "He's calling for me tonight, in about fifteen minutes." She watched her father's expressionless face with waiting eyes, hoping that there would not be an argument because it would tarnish the entire evening, and hoping that there *would* be one because it would try the strength of what she felt for Bud.

"This job of his," Kingship said, setting down the milk. "What are its prospects?"

After a cold moment Marion said, "He's on the executive training squad. He should be a section manager in a few months. Why all the questions?" She smiled with her lips only.

Kingship removed his glasses. His blue eyes wrestled uncomfortably with Marion's cool stare. "You brought him here to dinner, Marion," he said. "You never brought anyone to dinner before. Doesn't that entitle me to ask a few questions?"

"He lives in a rooming house," Marion said. "When he doesn't eat with me, he eats alone. So I brought him to dinner one night."

"The nights you don't dine here, you dine with him?"

"Yes, most of them. Why should we both eat alone? We work only five blocks from each other." She wondered why she was being evasive; she hadn't been caught doing something wrong. "We eat together because we enjoy each other's company," she said firmly. "We like each other very much."

"Then I do have a right to ask some questions, don't I," Kingship pointed out quietly.

"He's someone I like. Not someone applying for a job with Kingship Copper."

"Marion . . ."

140

She plucked a cigarette from a silver cup and lighted it with a silver table lighter. "You don't like him, do you?"

"I didn't say that."

"Because he's poor," she said.

"That's not true, Marion, and you know it."

There was silence for a moment.

"Oh yes," Kingship said, "he's poor all right. He took pains to mention it exactly three times the other night. And that anecdote he dragged in, about the woman his mother did sewing for."

"What's wrong with his mother taking in sewing?"

"Nothing, Marion, nothing. It's the way he alluded to it so casually, so very casually. Do you know who he reminded me of? There's a man at the club who has a bad leg, limps a little. Every time we play golf he says, 'You boys go on ahead. Old Peg-leg'll catch up with you.' So everyone walks extra slowly and you feel like a heel if you beat him."

"I'm afraid the similarity escapes me," Marion said. She rose from the table and went out towards the living room, leaving Kingship to rub a hand despairingly over the few yellow-white hairs that thinly crossed his scalp.

In the living room there was a large window that looked out over the East River. Marion stood before it, one hand on the thick cloth of the draperies. She heard her father come into the room behind her.

"Marion, believe me, I only want to see you happy." He spoke awkwardly. "I know I haven't always been so . . . concerned, but haven't I . . . done better since Dorothy and Ellen . . ."

"I know," she admitted reluctantly. She fingered the drapes. "But I'm practically twenty-five . . . a grown woman. You don't have to treat me as if—"

"I just don't want you rushing into anything, Marion."

"I'm not," she said softly.

"That's all I want."

Marion stared out the window. "Why do you dislike him?" she asked.

"I don't dislike him. He—I don't know, I . . ."

"Is it that you're afraid I'll go away from you?" She spoke the question slowly, as though the idea surprised her.

"You're already away from me, aren't you? In that apartment."

She turned from the window and faced Kingship at the side of the room. "You know, you really should be grateful to Bud," she said. "I'll tell you something. I didn't want him to have dinner here. As soon as I suggested it, I was sorry. But he insisted. 'He's your father,' he said. 'Think of his feelings.' You see, Bud is strong on family ties, even if I'm not. So you should be grateful to him, not antagonistic. Because if he does

141

anything, it will be to bring us closer together." She faced the window again.

"All right," Kingship said. "He's probably a wonderful boy. I just want to make sure you don't make any mistakes."

"What do you mean?" She turned from the window again, this time more slowly, her body stiffening.

"I just don't want you to make any mistakes, that all," Kingship said uncertainly.

"Are you asking other questions about him?" Marion demanded. "Asking other people? Do you have someone checking on him?"

"No!"

"Like you did with Ellen?"

"Ellen was seventeen at the time! And I was right, wasn't I? Was that boy any good?"

"Well I'm twenty-five and I know my own mind! If you have anyone checking on Bud—"

"The idea never entered my mind!"

Marion's eyes stung him. "I like Bud," she said slowly, her voice tight. "I like him very much. Do you know what that means, to finally find someone you like?"

"Marion, I—"

"So if you do *anything*, anything at all, to make him feel unwelcome or unwanted, to make him feel that he's not good enough for me . . . I'll never forgive you. I swear to God I'll never speak to you again as long as I live."

She turned back to the window.

"The idea never entered my mind. Marion, I swear . . ." He looked futilely at her rigid back and then sank into a chair with a weary sigh.

A few minutes later the chimes of the front door sounded. Marion left the window and crossed the room towards the double door that led the foyer.

"Marion." Kingship stood up.

She paused and looked back at him. From the foyer came the sound of the front door opening and the murmur of voices in conversation.

"Ask him to stay a few minutes . . . have a drink."

A moment passed. "All right," she said. At the doorway she hesitated for a second. "I'm sorry I spoke the way I did." She went out.

Kingship watched her go. Then he turned and faced the fireplace. He took a step back and regarded himself in the mirror tilted over the mantel. He looked at the well-fed man in the three hundred and forty dollar suit in the seven hundred dollar a month living-room.

Then he straightened up, put a smile on his face, turned and walked towards the doorway, extending his right hand. "Good evening, Bud," he said.

MARION'S BIRTHDAY FELL ON A SATURDAY early in November. In the morning she cleaned her apartment hastily. At one o'clock she went to a small building in a quiet tributary of Park Avenue, where a discreet silver plaque beside a white door confided that the premises were occupied, not by a psychiatrist nor an interior decorator, but by a restaurant. Leo Kingship was waiting within the white door, sitting gingerly on a Louis Quinze sofa and scanning a management-owned copy of *Gourmet*. He put down the magazine, rose, kissed Marion on the cheek and wished her a happy birthday. A maître d'hôtel with fluttering fingers and neon teeth ushered them to their table, swooped away a Reserved placard and seated them with Gallic effusion. There was a centerpiece of roses on the table, and, at Marion's place, a small box wrapped in white paper and clouds of gold ribbon. Kingship pretended not to be aware of it. While he was occupied with the wine card and "If I may suggest, Monsieur," Marion freed the box of its gold entanglement, excitement coloring her cheeks and shining her eyes. Nested between layers of cotton was a golden disc, its surface constellated with tiny pearls. Marion exclaimed over the brooch, and when the maître d' had gone, thanked her father happily, squeezing his hand, which lay as if by chance near hers on the table.

The brooch was not one which she would have chosen herself; its design was too elaborate for her taste. Her happiness, however, was genuine, inspired by the giving, if not by the gift. In the past, Leo Kingship's standard birthday present to his daughters had been a one hundred dollar gift certificate redeemable at a Fifth Avenue department store, a matter automatically attended to by his secretary.

After leaving her father, Marion spent some time at a beauty salon and then returned to her apartment. Late in the afternoon the buzzer sounded. She pressed the button that released the door downstairs. A few minutes later a messenger appeared at her door, panting dramatically, as though he had been carrying something much heavier than a florist's box. The receipt of a quarter soothed his respiration.

In the box, under green waxed paper, was a white orchid arranged in a corsage. The card with it said simply, "—Bud." Standing before a mirror, Marion held the bloom experimentally to her hair, her wrist, and her shoulder. Then she went

143

into the kitchen and placed the flower in its box and in the waist-high refrigerator, first sprinkling a few drops of water on its thick-veined tropical petals.

He arrived promptly at six. He gave the button next to Marion's nameplate two quick jabs and stood waiting in the stuffy hallway, removing a gray suede glove to pick a speck of lint from, the lapel of his navy blue coat. Soon footsteps sounded on the stairs. The dingily curtained door opened and Marion appeared, radiant, the orchid bursting whitely on her black coat. They clasped each other's hands. Wishing her the happiest of birthdays, he kissed her on the cheek so as not to smudge her lipstick, which he noticed was of a deeper shade than she had worn when first he met her.

They went to a steak house on Fifty-Second Street. The prices on the menu, although considerably lower than those on the one from which she had selected her lunch, seemed exorbitant to Marion, because she was seeing them through Bud's eyes. She suggested that he order for both of them. They had black onion soup and sirloin steaks, preceded by champagne cocktails—"To you, Marion." At the end of the meal, placing eighteen dollars on the waiter's salver, Bud caught Marion's faint frown. "Well, it's your birthday, isn't it?" he said, smiling.

From the restaurant they took a taxi to the theater where *Saint Joan* was playing. They sat in the orchestra, sixth row center. During the intermission Marion was unusually voluble, her doelike eyes glittering brightly as she talked of Shaw and the acting and a celebrity who was seated in the row in front of them. During the play their hands were warm in each other's.

Afterwards—because, she told herself, Bud had already spent so much money that evening—Marion suggested that they go to her apartment.

"I feel like a pilgrim who's finally being permitted to enter the shrine," he said as he slipped the key into the slit of the lock. He turned the key and doorknob simultaneously.

"It's nothing fancy," Marion said, her voice quick. "Really. They call it two rooms but it's more like one, the kitchen is so tiny."

He pushed the door open, withdrawing the key which he handed to Marion. She stepped into the apartment and reached for a wall switch beside the door. Lamps filled the room with diffused light. He entered, closing the door behind him. Marion turned to watch his face. His eyes were ranging over the deep gray walls, the blue and white striped drapes, the limed oak furniture. He gave an appreciative murmur.

"It's very small," Marion said.

144

"But nice," he said. *"Very* nice."

"Thank you." She turned away from him, unpinning the orchid from her coat, suddenly as ill at ease as when they first met. She put the corsage on a sideboard and started to remove her coat. His hands helped her. "Beautiful furniture," he said over her shoulder.

She hung their coats in the closet mechanically, and then turned to the mirror over the sideboard. With fumbling fingers, she pinned the orchid to the shoulder of her russet dress, her eyes focused beyond her own reflection, on Bud's image. He had walked down to the center of the room. Standing before the coffee table, he picked up a square copper plate. His face, in profile, was expressionless, giving no indication whether he liked or disliked the piece. Marion found herself motionless. "Mmmm," he said at last, liking it. "A present from your father, I bet."

"No," Marion said into the mirror. "Ellen gave it to me."

"Oh." He looked at it for a moment and then put it down.

Fingering the collar of her dress, Marion turned from the mirror and watched as he crossed the room with three easy strides. He stood before the low bookcase and looked at the picture on the wall above it. Marion watched him. "Our old friend Demuth," he said. He glanced at her, smiling. She smiled back. He looked at the picture again.

After a moment, Marion moved forward and went to his side.

"I never could figure out why he called a picture of a grain elevator 'My Egypt,' " Bud said.

"Is that what it is? I was never sure."

"It's a beautiful picture, though." He turned to Marion. "What's the matter? Have I got some dirt on my nose or something?"

"What?"

"You were looking—"

"Oh. No. Would you like something to drink?"

"Mmm-hmm."

"There's nothing but wine."

"Perfect."

Marion turned towards the kitchen.

"Before you go . . ." He took a small tissue-wrapped box from his pocket. "Happy Birthday."

"Oh, Bud, you shouldn't have!" "I shouldn't have," he mimicked simultaneously. "But aren't you glad I did?"

There were silver earrings in the box, simple polished triangles. "Oh, thank you! They're lovely!" Marion exclaimed, and kissed him.

She hurried to the sideboard to try them on. He came up behind her, looking at her in the mirror. When she had fastened both earrings, he turned her around. "Lovely is right," he said.

When the kiss ended he said, "Now where's that wine we were talking about?"

Marion came out of the kitchen with a raffia-covered bottle of Bardolino and two glasses on a tray. Bud, his jacket off, was sitting crosslegged on the floor in front of the bookcase, a book opened on his lap. "I didn't know you liked Proust," he said.

"Oh, I do!" She set the tray on the coffee table.

"Here," he said, pointing to the bookcase. Marion transferred the tray to the bookcase. She filled the two glasses and handed one to Bud. Holding the other, she worked her feet out of her shoes and lowered herself to the floor beside him. He leafed through the pages of the book. "I'll show you the part I'm crazy about," he said.

He pressed the switch. The tone arm swung slowly and dipped down to touch with its serpent's head the rim of the spinning record. Closing the cover of the phonograph, he crossed the room and sat beside Marion on the blue-covered studio couch. The first deep piano notes of the Rachmaninoff Second Concerto sounded. "Just the right record," Marion said.

Leaning back against the thick bolster that ran along the wall, Bud scanned the room, now softly lighted by a single lamp. "Everything's so perfect here," he said. "Why haven't you asked me up before?"

She picked at a filament of raffia that had got caught on one of the buttons on the front of her dress. "I don't know . . ." she said. "I . . . I thought maybe you wouldn't like it."

"How could I not like it?" he asked.

His fingers worked dexterously down the row of buttons. Her hands, warm, closed over his, restraining them between her breasts.

"Bud, I've never . . . done anything before."

"I know that, darling. You don't have to tell me that."

"I've never loved anyone before."

"Neither have I. I've never loved anyone. Not until you."

"Do you mean that? Do you?"

"Only you."

"Not even Ellen?"

"Only you. I swear it."

He kissed her again.

Her hands freed his and rose to find his cheeks.

6

From The New York Times; *Monday, December 24, 1951:*

MARION J. KINGSHIP
TO BE WED SATURDAY

Miss Marion Joyce Kingship, daughter of Mr. Leo Kingship of Manhattan and the late Phyllis Hatcher, will be married to Mr. Burton Corliss, son of Mrs. Joseph Corliss of Menasset, Mass., and the late Mr. Corliss, on the afternoon of Saturday, December 29, in the home of her father.

Miss Kingship was graduated from the Spence School in New York and is an alumna of Columbia University. Until last week she was with the advertising agency of Camden and Galbraith.

The prospective bridegroom, who served with the Army during the second World War and attended Caldwell College in Caldwell, Wis., has recently joined the domestic sales division of the Kingship Copper Corporation.

7

SEATED AT HER DESK, Miss Richardson stretched out her right hand in a gesture she considered quite graceful and squinted at the gold bracelet that constricted the plumpness of her wrist. It was definitely too young looking for her mother, she decided. She would get something else for mother and keep the bracelet for herself.

Beyond her hand the background suddenly turned blue. With white pin-stripes. She looked up, starting to smile, but stopped when she saw that it was the pest again.

"Hello," he said cheerfully.

Miss Richardson opened a drawer and busily ruffled the edges of some blank typing paper. "Mr. Kingship is still at lunch," she said frigidly.

"Dear lady, he was at lunch at twelve o'clock. It is now three o'clock. What is he, a rhinoceros?"

"If you wish to make an appointment for later in the week . . ."

"I would like an audience with His Eminence this afternoon."

Miss Richardson closed the drawer grimly. "Tomorrow is Christmas," she said. "Mr. Kingship is interrupting a four day weekend by coming in today. He wouldn't do that unless he were very busy. He gave me strict orders not to disturb him on any account. On no account whatsoever."

"Then he isn't at lunch."

"He gave me strict orders . . ."

The man sighed. Slinging his folded coat over one shoulder, he drew a slip of paper from the rack next to Miss Richardson's telephone. "May I?" he asked, already having taken the paper. Placing it on a large blue book which he held in the crook of his arm, he removed Miss Richardson's pen from its onyx holder and began to write.

"Well I never!" said Miss Richardson. "Honestly!" she said.

Finished writing, the man replaced the pen and blew on the paper. He folded it carefully into quarters and handed it to Miss Richardson. "Give him this," he said. "Slip it under the door, if need be."

Miss Richardson glared at him. Then she calmly unfolded the paper and read it.

Uncomfortably, she looked up. "Dorothy and Ellen—?" His face was expressionless.

She hoisted herself from the chair. "He told me not to disturb him on any account," she repeated softly, as though seeking guidance in the incantation. "What's your name?"

"Just give him that, please, like the angel you are."

"Now look . . ."

He was doing just that; looking at her quite seriously, despite the lightness of his voice. Miss Richardson frowned, glanced again at the paper, and refolded it. She moved to a heavily paneled door. "All right," she said darkly, "but you'll see. He gave me strict orders." Gingerly she tapped on the door. Opening it, she slipped in with the paper held appeasingly before her.

She reappeared a minute later with a betrayed expression on her face. "Go ahead," she said sharply, holding the door open.

148

The man breezed past her, his coat over his shoulder, the book under his arm. "Keep smiling," he whispered.

At the faint sound of the door closing, Leo Kingship looked up from the slip of paper in his hand. He was standing behind his desk in his shirtsleeves, his jacket draped on the back of the chair behind him. His eyeglasses were pushed up on his pink forehead. Sunlight, sliced by a Venetian blind, striped his stocky figure. He squinted anxiously at the man approaching him across the paneled and carpeted room.

"Oh," he said, when the man came close enough to block the sunlight, enabling Kingship to recognize his face. "You." He looked down at the slip of paper and crumpled it, his expression of anxiety turning to relief and then to annoyance.

"Hello, Mr. Kingship," the man said, offering his hand.

Kingship took it halfheartedly. "No wonder you wouldn't give your name to Miss Richardson."

Smiling, the man dropped into the visitor's chair. He settled his coat and the book in his lap.

"But I'm afraid I've forgotten it," Kingship said. "Grant?" he ventured.

"Gant." The long legs crossed comfortably. "Gordon Gant."

Kingship remained standing. "I'm extremely busy, Mr. Gant," he said firmly, indicating the paper-strewn desk. "So if this 'information about Dorothy and Ellen' "—he held up the crumpled slip of paper—"consists of the same 'theories' you were expounding back in Blue River . . ."

"Partially," Gant said.

"Well, I'm sorry. I don't want to listen."

"I gathered that I wasn't number one on your Hit Parade."

"You mean I didn't like you? That isn't so. Not at all. I realized your motives were of the best; you had taken a liking to Ellen; you showed a—a youthful enthusiasm . . . But it was misdirected, misdirected in a way that was extremely painful to me. Barging into my hotel room so soon after Ellen's death . . . bringing up the past at such a moment . . ." He looked at Gant appealingly. "Do you think I wouldn't have liked to believe that Dorothy didn't take her own life?"

"She didn't."

"The note," he said wearily, "the note . . ."

"A couple of ambiguously worded sentences that could have referred to a dozen things beside suicide. Or that she could have been tricked into writing." Gant leaned forward. "Dorothy went to the Municipal Building to get married. Ellen's theory was right; the fact that she was killed proves it."

"It does no such thing," Kingship snapped. "There was no connection. You heard the police—"

"A housebreaker!"

"Why not? Why not a housebreaker?"

"Because I *don't* believe in coincidences. Not that kind."

149

"A sign of immaturity, Mr. Gant."

After a moment Gant said flatly, "It was the same person both times."

Kingship braced his hands tiredly on the desk, looking down at the papers there. "Why do you have to revive all this?" he sighed. "Intruding in other people's business. How do you think I feel . . . ?" He pushed his eyeglasses down into place and fingered the pages of a ledger. "Would you please go now."

Gant made no move to rise. "I'm home on vacation," he said. "Home is White Plains. I didn't spend an hour on the New York Central just to rehash what was already said last March."

"What then?" Kingship looked warily at the long-jawed face.

"There was an article in the morning's *Times* . . . the society page."

"My daughter?"

Gant nodded. He took a pack of cigarettes from his breast pocket. "What do you know about Bud Corliss?" he asked.

Kingship eyed him in silence. "Know about him?" he said slowly. "He's going to be my son-in-law. What do you mean, know about him?"

"Do you know that he and Ellen were going together?"

"Of course." Kingship straightened up. "What are you driving at?"

"It's a long story," Gant said. The blue eyes were sharp and steady under the thick blond brows. He gestured towards Kingship's chair. "And my delivery is bound to suffer if you stand towering over me."

Kingship sat down. He kept his hands on the edge of the desk before him, as though ready to rise again in an instant.

Gant lit his cigarette. He sat silently for a moment, regarding it thoughtfully and working his lower lip with his teeth, as though awaiting a time signal. Then he began to speak in the easy, fluid, announcer's voice.

"When she left Caldwell," he said, "Ellen wrote a letter to Bud Corliss. I happened to read that letter soon after Ellen arrived in Blue River. It made quite an impression on me, since it described a murder suspect whom I resembled much too closely for comfort." He smiled. "I read the letter twice, and carefully, as you can imagine.

"On the night Ellen was killed, Eldon Chesser, that lover of prima-facie evidence, asked me if Ellen were my girlfriend. It was probably the only constructive thing he ever did during his entire detective career, because it set me thinking of friend Corliss. Partly to take my mind off Ellen, who was God-knows-where with an armed killer, and partly because I liked her and wondered what kind of a man she liked, I thought about that letter which was still fresh in my mind and which was my only source of information about my 'rival,' Bud Corliss."

Gant paused for a second, and then continued. "At first it

150

seemed to contain nothing; a name—Dear Bud—and an address on the envelope—Burton Corliss, something-or-other Roosevelt Street, Caldwell, Wisconsin. No other clues. But on further reflection I found several bits of information in Ellen's letter, and I was able to fit them together into an even bigger piece of information about Bud Corliss; it seemed insignificant at the time; a purely external fact about him rather than an indication of his personality, which was what I was really looking for. But that fact stayed with me, and today it seems significant indeed."

"Go ahead," Kingship said as Gant drew on his cigarette.

Gant leaned back comfortably. "First of all: Ellen wrote Bud that she wouldn't fall behind in her work while away from Caldwell because she would be able to get all the notes from him. Now, Ellen was a senior, which meant that she was taking advanced courses. In every college senior courses are closed to freshmen and often to sophomores. If Bud shared *all* Ellen's classes—they probably made out their programs together—it meant that he was conceivably a sophomore, but in all probability a junior or a senior.

"Secondly: at one point in the letter Ellen described her behavior during her first three years at Caldwell, which apparently differed from her behavior after Dorothy's death. She described how she had been 'the rah-rah girl,' and then she said, and I think I remember the exact words, 'You wouldn't recognize me.' Which meant, as clearly as could possibly be, that Bud had not seen her during those first three years. This would be highly conceivable at a good-sized university like Stoddard, but we come to thirdly.

"Thirdly: Caldwell is a very small college; one tenth the size of Stoddard, Ellen wrote, and she was giving it the benefit of doubt. I checked in the Almanac this morning; Stoddard has over twelve thousand students; Caldwell, barely eight hundred. Furthermore, Ellen mentioned in the letter that she hadn't wanted Dorothy to come to Caldwell precisely because it was the kind of place where everyone knew everybody else and knew what they were doing.

"So, we add one, two, and three: Bud Corliss, who is at least in his third year of college, was a stranger to Ellen at the beginning of her fourth year, despite the fact that they both attended a very small school where, I understand, the social side of life plays hob with the scholastic. All of which can be explained in only one way and can be condensed to a simple statement of fact; the fact which seemed insignificant last March, but today seems like the most important fact in Ellen's letter. *Bud Corliss was a transfer student, and he transferred to Caldwell in September of 1950, at the beginning of Ellen's fourth year and after Dorothy's death.*"

Kingship frowned. "I don't see what—"

"We come now to today, December 24, 1951," Gant said,

crushing his cigarette in an ashtray, "when my mother, bless her, brings the prodigal son breakfast in bed, along with *The New York Times*. And there, on the society page, is the name of Kingship. Miss Marion Kingship to wed Mr. Burton Corliss. Imagine my surprise. Now, my mind, in addition to being insatiably curious and highly analytical, is also very dirty. It looks to me, says I, as though the new member of the domestic sales division was determined not be be disqualified from the Kingship Copper sweepstakes."

"Now look here, Mr. Gant—"

"I considered," Gant went on, "how when one sister was killed he proceeded directly to the next one. Beloved of two of the Kingship daughters. Two out of three. Not a bad score.

"And then the analytical side and the dirty side of my brain blended, and I thought: three out of three would have been an even better score for Mr. Burton Corliss who transferred to Caldwell College in September of 1950."

Kingship stood up, staring at Gant.

"A random thought," Gant said. "Wildly improbable. But easily removed from the realm of doubt. A simple matter of sliding out from under the breakfast tray, going to the bookcase, and taking therefrom *The Stoddard Flame*, yearbook for 1950." He displayed the large blue leatherette book with its white-lettered cover. "In the sophomore section," he said, "there are several interesting photographs. One of Dorothy Kingship and one of Dwight Powell, both of whom are now dead. None of Gordon Gant; didn't have five spare bucks to have my face recorded for posterity. But many sophomores did, among them—" He opened the book to a page marked by a strip of newsprint, turned the volume around and put it down on the desk, his fingers stabbing one of the checkerboard photographs. He recited the inscription beside it from memory: "Corliss, Burton quote Bud unquote, Menasset, Mass., Liberal Arts."

Kingship sat down again. He looked at the photograph, hardly larger than a postage stamp. Then he looked at Gant. Gant reached forward, turned a few pages, and pointed to another picture. It was Dorothy. Kingship looked at that, too. Then he looked up again.

Gant said, "It struck me as awfully odd. I thought you should know."

"Why?" Kingship asked stolidly. "What is this supposed to be leading up to?"

"May I ask you one question, Mr. Kingship, before I answer that?"

"Go ahead."

"He never told you he went to Stoddard, did he?"

"No. But we've never discussed things like that," he explained quickly. "He must have told Marion. Marion must know."

"I don't think she does."

"Why not?" Kingship demanded.

"*The Times*. Marion gave them the information for that article, didn't she? The bride-to-be usually does."

"Well?"

"Well there's no mention of Stoddard. And in the other wedding and engagement articles, it's mentioned when someone's attended more than one school."

"Maybe she just didn't bother to tell them."

"Maybe. Or maybe she doesn't know. Maybe Ellen didn't know either."

"All right, now what are you saying, mister?"

"Don't be sore at *me*, Mr. Kingship. The facts speak for themselves; I didn't invent them." Gant closed the year book and put it in his lap. "There are two possibilities," he said. "Either Corliss told Marion that he attended Stoddard, in which case it might conceivably be a coincidence; he went to Stoddard and he transferred to Caldwell; he might not have known Dorothy any more than he knew me." He paused. "Or else, he *didn't* tell Marion he went there."

"Which means?" Kingship challenged.

"Which means that he must have been involved with Dorothy in some way. Why else would he conceal it?" Gant looked down at the book in his lap. "There was a man who wanted Dorothy out of the way because he had gotten her pregnant . . ."

Kingship stared at him. "You're back to the same thing! Someone killed Dorothy, then killed Ellen . . . You've got this —this cockeyed moving picture theory and you don't want to admit . . ." Gant was silent. "Bud?" Kingship asked incredulously. He sat back. He shook his head, smiling pityingly. "Come on, now," he said. "That's crazy. Just crazy." He kept shaking his head—"What do you think that boy is, a maniac?" —and smiling—"You've got this crazy idea . . ."

"All right," Gant said, "it's crazy. For the time being. But if he didn't tell Marion he went to Stoddard, then in some way he must have been involved with Dorothy. And if he was involved with Dorothy, and then Ellen, and now with Marion,— then he was goddamned good and determined to marry one of your daughters! Any one!"

The smile left Kingship's face slowly, draining it of expression. His hands were motionless on the edge of the desk.

"That *isn't* so crazy, I take it."

Kingship removed his glasses. He blinked a couple of times and then straightened up. "I have to speak to Marion," he said.

Gant looked at the telephone.

"No," Kingship said emptily. "She's had her phone disconnected. She's giving up her apartment, staying with me until the wedding." His voice faltered. "After the honeymoon they're moving into an apartment I'm furnishing for them . . . Sutton Terrace . . . Marion didn't want to accept it at first, but he convinced her. He's been so good with her . . . made the two of us get along so much better . . ." They looked at each other for a moment; Gant's eyes steady and challenging, Kingship's apprehensive.

Kingship stood up.

"Do you know where she is?" Gant asked.

"At her place . . . packing things." He put on his jacket. "He *must* have told her about Stoddard . . ."

When they came out of the office Miss Richardson looked up from a magazine.

"That's all for today, Miss Richardson. If you'll just clear my desk."

She frowned with frustrated curiosity. "Yes, Mr. Kingship. Merry Christmas."

"Merry Christmas, Miss Richardson."

They walked down a long corridor, on the walls of which were black and white photographs, matted and mounted between plates of glass held together by copper brackets at top and bottom. There were photographs of underground and open-pit mines, smelters, refineries, furnaces, rolling mills, and artistic close-ups of tubing and copper wire.

Waiting for the elevator Kingship said, "I'm sure he told her."

8

"GORDON GANT?" Marion said, exploring the name, when they had shaken hands. "Don't I know that name?" She backed into the room, smiling, one hand finding Kingship's and drawing him with her, the other rising to the collar of her blouse and fingering the golden pearl-starred brooch.

"Blue River." Kingship's voice was wooden as when he had performed the introduction, and his eyes were not quite on Marion's. "I think I told you about him."

"Oh, yes. You knew Ellen, wasn't that it?"

"That's right," Gant said. He shifted his hand farther down the spine of the book at his side, to a spot where the leatherette wasn't damp, wishing he hadn't been so damned eager when Kingship had asked him to come up; the *Times* photo of Marion had offered no hint in its dotted grays of the lucency of her eyes, the radiance of her cheeks, the halo of I'm-getting-married-Saturday that glowed all over her.

She gestured at the room despairingly. "I'm afraid there
154

isn't even a place to sit down." She moved towards a chair on which some shoe boxes were piled.

"Don't bother," Kingship said. "We just stopped by. Only for a minute. A lot of work waiting for me at the office."

"You haven't forgotten tonight, have you?" Marion asked. "You can expect us a seven or so. She's arriving at five, and I guess she'll want to stop at her hotel first." She turned to Gant. "My prospective mother-in-law," she said significantly.

Oh Lord, Gant thought, I'm supposed to say 'You're getting married?'—'Yes, Saturday.'—'Congratulations, good luck, best wishes!' He smiled wanly and didn't say anything. Nobody said anything.

"To what do I owe the pleasure of this visit?" Marion inquired, a curtsey in her voice.

Gant looked at Kingship, waiting for him to speak.

Marion looked at both of them. "Anything special?"

After a moment, Gant said, "I knew Dorothy, too. Very slightly."

"Oh," Marion said. She looked down at her hands.

"She was in one of my classes. I go to Stoddard." He paused. "I don't think Bud was ever in any of my classes though."

She looked up. "Bud?"

"Bud Corliss. Your . . ."

She shook her head, smiling. "Bud was never at Stoddard," she corrected him.

"He was, Miss Kingship."

"No," she insisted amusedly, "he went to Caldwell."

"He went to Stoddard, *then* to Caldwell."

Marion smiled quizzically at Kingship, as though expecting him to offer some explanation for the obstinacy of the caller he had brought.

"He was at Stoddard, Marion," Kingship said heavily. "Show her the book."

Gant opened the yearbook and handed it to Marion, pointing to the picture.

"Well for goodness' sake," she said. "I have to apologize. I never knew . . ." She glanced at the cover of the book. "Nineteen-fifty."

"He's in the forty-nine yearbook too," Gant said. "He went to Stoddard for two years and then transferred to Caldwell."

"For goodness' sake," she said. "Isn't that funny? Maybe he knew Dorothy." She sounded pleased, as though this were yet another bond between her and her fiancé. Her eyes slipped back to his picture.

"He never mentioned it to you at all?" Gant asked, despite Kingship's prohibitive headshakings.

"Why, no, he never said a . . ."

Slowly she looked up from the book, becoming aware for the first time of the strain and discomfort of the two men. "What's the matter?" she asked curiously.

"Nothing," Kingship said. He glanced at Gant, seeking corroboration.

"Then why are the two of you standing there as if . . ." She looked at the book again, and then at her father. There was a tightening movement in her throat. "Is this why you came up here, to tell me this?" she asked.

"We . . . we only wondered if you knew, that's all."

"Why?" she asked.

"We just wondered, that's all."

Her eyes cut to Gant. "Why?"

"Why should Bud conceal it," Gant asked, "unless—"

Kingship said, "Gant!"

"*Conceal* it?" Marion said. "What kind of a word is that? He didn't *conceal* it; we never talk about school much, because of Ellen; it just didn't come up."

"Why should the girl he's marrying not know he spent two years at Stoddard," Gant rephrased implacably, "unless he was involved with Dorothy?"

"*Involved*? With *Dorothy*?" Her eyes, wide with incredulity, probed into Gant's, and then swung slowly, narrowing, to Kingship. "What is this?"

Kingship's face flickered with small uneasy movements, as though dust were blowing at it.

"How much are you paying him?" Marion asked coldly. "Paying him?"

"For snooping!" she flared. "For digging up dirt! For *inventing* dirt!"

"He came to me of his own accord, Marion!"

"Oh yes, he just *happened* to pop up!"

Gant said, "I saw the article in *The Times*."

Marion glared at her father. "You swore you wouldn't do this," she said bitterly. "Swore! It would *never* enter your mind to ask *ques*tions to *in*vestigate, treat him like a *crim*inal. Oh no, not much!"

"I *haven't* been asking questions," Kingship protested.

Marion turned her back. "I thought you changed," she said. "I really did. I thought you liked Bud. I thought you liked *me*. But you can't . . ."

"Marion . . ."

"No, not if you're doing this. The apartment, the job . . . and all along *this* has been going on."

"*Nothing* is going on, Marion. I swear. . . ."

"Nothing? I'll tell you *exactly* what's going on." She faced him again. "You think I don't know you? He was 'involved' with Dorothy—is he supposed to be the one who got her in trouble?—and he was 'involved' with Ellen, and now he's 'involved' with me—all for the money, all for your precious money. That's what's going on—*in your mind!*" She thrust the yearbook into his hands.

156

"You've got it wrong, Miss Kingship," Gant said. "That's what's going on in *my* mind, not your father's."

"See?" Kingship said. "He came to me of his own accord."

Marion stared at Gant. "Just who are you? What makes this your business?"

"I knew Ellen."

"So I understand," she snapped. "Do you know Bud?"

"I've never had the pleasure."

"Then will you please explain to me what you're doing here, making accusations against him behind his back!"

"It's quite a story—"

"You've said enough, Gant," Kingship interrupted.

Marion said, "Are you jealous of Bud? Is that it? Because Ellen preferred him to you?"

"That's right," Gant said drily. "I'm consumed with jealousy."

"And have you heard of the slander laws?" she demanded.

Kingship edged towards the door, signaling Gant with his eyes. "Yes," Marion said, "you'd better go."

"Wait a minute," she said as Gant opened the door. "Is this going to stop?"

Kingship said, "There's nothing *to* stop, Marion."

"Whoever's behind it,"—she looked at Gant—"it's got to stop. We never talked about school. Why should we, with Ellen? It just never came up."

"All right, Marion," Kingship said, "all right." He followed Gant into the hall and turned to pull the door closed.

"It's got to stop," she said.

"All right." He hesitated, and his voice dropped. "You're still coming tonight, aren't you, Marion?"

Her lips clenched. She thought for a moment. "Because I don't want to hurt Bud's mother's feelings," she said finally.

Kingship closed the door.

They went to a drugstore on Lexington Avenue, where Gant ordered coffee and cherry pie, and Kingship, a glass of milk.

"So far, so good," Gant said.

Kingship was gazing at a paper napkin he held. "What do you mean?"

"At least we know where we stand. He didn't tell her about Stoddard. That makes it practically certain that—"

"You heard Marion," Kingship said. "They don't talk about school because of Ellen."

Gant regarded him with slightly lifted eyebrows. "Come on," he said slowly, "that may satisfy *her;* she's in love with him. But for a man not to tell his fiancée where he went to college . . ."

"It isn't as if he lied to her," Kingship protested.

Sardonically Gant said, "They just didn't talk about school."

"Considering the circumstances, I think that's understandable."

"Sure. The circumstances being that he was mixed up with Dorothy."

"That's an assumption you have no right to make."

Gant stirred his coffee slowly and sipped it. He added more cream and stirred it again. "You're afraid of her, aren't you," he said.

"Of Marion? Don't be ridiculous." Kingship set his glass of milk down firmly. "A man is innocent until he's proved guilty."

"Then we've got to find proof, don't we?"

"You see? You're assuming he's a fortune hunter before you've started."

"I'm assuming a hell of a lot more than that," Gant said, lifting a forkful of pie to his mouth. When he had swallowed it he said, "What are you going to do?"

Kingship was looking at the napkin again. "Nothing."

"You're going to let them get married?"

"I couldn't stop them even if I wanted to. They're both over twenty-one, aren't they?"

"You could hire detectives. There are four days yet. They might find something."

"Might," Kingship said. "If there's anything to find. Or Bud might get wind of it and tell Marion."

Gant smiled. "I thought I was being ridiculous about you and Marion."

Kingship sighed. "Let me tell you something," he said, not looking at Gant. "I had a wife and three daughters. Two daughters were taken from me. My wife I pushed away myself. Maybe I pushed one of the daughters too. So now I have only one daughter. I'm fifty-seven years old and I have one daughter and some men I play golf and talk business with. That's all."

After a moment Kingship turned to Gant, his face set rigidly. "What about you?" he demanded. "What *is* your real interest in this affair? Maybe you just enjoy chattering about your analytical brain and showing people what a clever fellow you are. You didn't have to go through that whole rigamarole, you know. In my office, about Ellen's letter. You could have just put the book on my desk and said 'Bud Corliss went to Stoddard.' Maybe you just like to show off."

"Maybe," Gant said lightly. "Also maybe I think he might have killed your daughters and I've got this quixotic notion that murderers should be punished."

Kingship finished his milk. "I think you'd better just go back to Yonkers and enjoy your vacation."

"White Plains." Gant scraped together the syrupy remains of the pie with the side of his fork. "Do you have ulcers?" he asked, glancing at the empty milk glass.

Kingship nodded.

Gant leaned back on his stool and surveyed the man beside
158

him. "And about thirty pounds overweight, I'd say." He put the red-clotted fork in his mouth and drew it out clean. "I should estimate that Bud has you figured for ten more years, tops. Or maybe he'll get impatient in three or four years and try to hurry you on."

Kingship got off his stool. He pulled a dollar from a money-clipped roll and put it on the counter. "Good-by, Mr. Gant," he said, and strode away.

The counterman came over and took the dollar. "Anything else?" he asked.

Gant shook his head.

He caught the 5:19 for White Plains.

9

IN WRITING TO HIS MOTHER, Bud had made only the most vague allusions to Kingship's money. Once or twice he had mentioned *Kingship Copper*, but never with any clarifying phrases, and he was certain that she, whose poverty-formed conception of wealth was as hazy and inexact as a pubert's visions of orgies, had not the slightest real comprehension of the luxuriance of living into which the presidency of such a corporation could be translated. He had looked forward eagerly, therefore, to the moment when he could introduce her to Marion and her father, and to the surrounding magnificence of Kingship's duplex apartment, knowing that in light of the coming marriage her awe-widened eyes would regard each inlaid table and glittering chandelier as evidence, not of Kingship's capabilities, but of his own.

The evening, however, was a disappointment.

Not that his mother's reaction was anything less than he had anticipated; with mouth partially opened and teeth lightly touching her lower lip, she drew in her breath with soft sibilance, as though seeing not one but a series of miracles; the formally attired servant—a butler!—the velvety depth of the carpets, the wallpaper that wasn't paper at all but intricately textured cloth, the leather-bound books, the golden clock, the silver tray from which the butler served champagne—champagne!—in crystal goblets . . . Vocally, she restrained her admiration to a gently smiling "Lovely, lovely," accompanied by a slight nodding of the stiff newly-waved gray hair, giving the impression that such surroundings were by no means completely alien to her,—but when her eyes met Bud's as the toast was drunk, the bursting pride she felt leaped out to him like a thrown kiss, while one work-roughened hand surreptitiously marveled at the cloth of the couch on which she sat.

159

No, his mother's reaction was warming and wonderful. What made the evening a disappointment was the fact that Marion and Leo had apparently had an argument; Marion spoke to her father only when appearances made it inescapable. And furthermore, the argument must have been about him, since Leo addressed him with hesitant unfocused eyes, while Marion was determinedly, defiantly effusive, clinging to him and calling him 'dear' and 'darling,' which she had never done before when others were present. The first faint worry began to sting him like a pebble in his shoe.

Dinner, then, was dismal. With Leo and Marion at the ends of the table and his mother and he at the sides, conversation passed only around the edges; father and daughter would not talk; mother and son could not talk, for anything they had to say would be personal and exclusive-sounding before these people who were still in a sense outsiders. So Marion called him 'darling' and told his mother about the Sutton Terrace apartment, and his mother spoke to Leo about 'the children,' and Leo asked him to pass the bread please, not quite looking at him.

And he was silent, lifting each fork and spoon slowly as he selected it, so that his mother could see and do likewise; an affectionate conspiracy fallen into without word or signal, dramatizing the bond between them and forming the one enjoyable aspect of the meal—that and the smiles that passed across the table when Marion and Leo were looking down at their food, smiles prideful and loving and all the more pleasing to him because of the unsuspecting heads whose path they slipped across.

At the end of the meal, although there was a silver lighter on the table, he lit Marion's and his own cigarette with his matches, afterwards tapping the folder absentmindedly on the cloth until his mother had noticed the white cover on which *Bud Corliss* was stamped in copper leaf.

But all along there was the pebble in his shoe.

Later, it being Christmas Eve, they went to church, and after church Bud expected to take his mother back to her hotel while Marion returned home with Leo. But Marion, to his annoyance, assumed an unfamiliar coquetry and insisted on accompanying them to the hotel, so Leo went off by himself as Bud squired the two women into a taxi. He sat between them, reciting to his mother the names of what landmarks they passed. The cab, at his direction, departed from its course so that Mrs. Corliss, who had never been to New York before, might see Times Square at night.

He left her in the lobby of her hotel, outside the elevator. "Are you very tired?" he asked, and when she said she was, he seemed disappointed. "Don't go to sleep right away," he said. "I'll call you later." They kissed goodnight and, still holding

160

Bud's hand, Mrs. Corliss kissed Marion happily on the cheek.

During the taxi ride back to Leo's, Marion was silent.

"What's the matter, darling?"

"Nothing," she said, smiling unconvincingly. "Why?"

He shrugged.

He had intended to leave her at the door of the apartment, but the pebble of worry was assuming the proportions of a sharp stone; he went in with her. Kingship had already retired. They went into the living room where Bud lighted cigarettes while Marion turned on the radio. They sat on the couch.

She told him that she liked his mother very much. He said he was glad, and he could tell that his mother liked her too. They began to speak of the future, and he sensed from the stiff casualness of her voice that she was working up to something. He leaned back with his eyes half closed, one arm around her shoulders, listening as he had never listened before, weighing every pause and inflection, fearful all the while of what it was leading up to. It couldn't be anything important! It couldn't be! He had slighted her somehow, forgotten something he'd promised to do, that was all. What could it be? . . . He paused before each reply, examining his words before he spoke them, trying to determine what response they would bring, like a chess player touching pieces before making his move.

She worked the conversation around to children. "Two," she said.

His left hand, on his knee, pinched the crease of his trousers. He smiled. "Or three," he said. "Or four."

"Two," she said. "Then one can go to Columbia and one to Caldwell."

Caldwell. Something about Caldwell. Ellen? "They'll probably both wind up at Michigan or someplace," he said.

"Or if we only have one," Marion went on, "he can go to Columbia and then transfer to Caldwell. Or vice-versa." She leaned forward, smiling, and pressed her cigarette into an ashtray. Much more carefully than she usually put out her cigarettes, he observed. Transfer to Caldwell. Transfer to Caldwell . . . He waited in silence. "No," she said, "I really wouldn't want him to do that,"—following up her statement with a tenacity she never would have applied to mere idle chatter—"because he would lose credits. Transferring must be very involved."

They sat side by side, silently for a moment.

"No it isn't," he said.

"Isn't it?" she asked.

"No," he said. "I didn't lose any credits."

"You didn't transfer, did you?" She sounded surprised.

"Of course," he said. "I told you."

"No you didn't. You never said—"

"I did, honey. I'm sure I told you. I went to Stoddard University, and then to Caldwell."

"Why, that's where my sister Dorothy went, Stoddard!"

"I know. Ellen told me."

"Don't tell me you *knew* her."

"No. Ellen showed me her picture though, and I think I remember seeing her around. I'm sure I told you, that first day, in the museum."

"No, you didn't. I'm positive."

"Well sure, I was at Stoddard two years. And you mean to say you didn't—" Marion's lips stopped the rest of the sentence, kissing him fervidly, atoning for doubt.

A few minutes later he looked at his watch. "I'd better be leaving," he said. "I want to get as much sleep as I can this week, because I have an idea I won't be getting much sleep at all next week."

It only meant that Leo had somehow learned he'd been at Stoddard. There was no real danger. There wasn't! Trouble maybe; the wedding plans might be blown up—oh Jesus!—but there was no *danger,* no police danger. There's no law against going after a rich girl, is there?

But why so late? If Leo wanted to check on him, why hadn't he done it sooner? Why today? . . . The announcement in *The Times* . . . of course! Someone had seen it, someone who'd been at Stoddard. The son of one of Leo's friends or someone like that. "My son and your future son-in-law were at Stoddard together." So Leo puts two and two together; Dorothy, Ellen, Marion—gold-digger. He tells Marion, and that was their argument.

God damn, if only it had been possible to mention Stoddard at the beginning! That would have been crazy though; Leo would have suspected right off, and Marion would have listened to him then. But why did it have to come up now!

Still, what could Leo do, with only suspicions? They must be only suspicions; the old man couldn't know for sure that he'd known Dorothy, or else Marion wouldn't have been so happy when he himself told her he hadn't known her. Or could Leo have withheld part of his information from Marion? No, he would have tried to convince her, given her all the evidence he had. So Leo wasn't certain. Could he *make* certain? How? The kids at Stoddard, mostly seniors now, would they remember who Dorothy had gone with? They might. But it's Christmas! Vacation. They're scattered all over the country. Only four days to the wedding. Leo could never talk Marion into postponing.

All he had to do was sit tight and keep his fingers crossed. Tuesday, Wednesday, Thursday, Friday . . . *Saturday*. If worst came to worst, so he was after the money; that was all

Leo could ever prove. He couldn't prove that Dorothy didn't commit suicide. He couldn't drag the Mississippi for a gun that was probably buried under twenty feet of mud.

And if best came to best, the wedding would go off as per schedule. Then what could Leo do even if the kids at Stoddard did remember? Divorce? Annulment? Not nearly enough grounds for either, even if Marion could be persuaded to seek one, which she probably couldn't. What then? Maybe Leo would try to buy him off . . .

Now *there* was a thought . . . How much would Leo be willing to pay to free his daughter from the big bad gold-digger? Quite a lot, probably.

But not nearly as much as Marion would have some day. Bread now or cake later?

When he got back to his rooming house, he telephoned his mother.

"I hope I didn't wake you. I walked back from Marion's."

"That's all right, darling. Oh Bud, she's a lovely girl! Lovely! So sweet . . . I'm so happy for you!"

"Thanks, Mom."

"And Mr. Kingship, such a fine man! Did you notice his hands?"

"What about them?"

"So clean!" He laughed. "Bud," her voice lowered, "they must be rich, very rich . . ."

"I guess they are, Mom."

"That apartment . . . like a movie! My goodness. . . . !"

He told her about the Sutton Terrace apartment—"Wait till you see it, Mom!"—and about the visit to the smelter—"He's taking me there Thursday. He wants me to be familiar with the whole set-up!"—and towards the end of the conversation, she said:

"Bud, what ever happened to that idea of yours?"

"What idea?"

"The one why you didn't go back to school."

"Oh, that," he said. "It didn't pan out."

"Oh . . ." She was disappointed.

"You know that shaving cream?" he said. "Where you press the button and it comes out of the can like whipped cream?"

"Yes?"

"Well that was it. Only they beat me to it."

She breathed a drawn-out "Oh" of commiseration. "If that isn't a shame . . . You didn't talk to anyone about it, did you?"

"No. They just beat me to it."

"Well," she said with a sigh, "things like that happen. It certainly is a shame though. An idea like that . . ."

When he had finished talking to her, he went into his room

and stretched out on the bed, feeling good all over. Leo and his suspicions, nuts to him! Everything was going to be perfect.

Jesus, that was one thing he was going to do—see that she got some of the money.

10

THE TRAIN, HAVING PASSED THROUGH STAMFORD, Bridgeport, New Haven and New London, continued grinding eastward along the southern border of Connecticut, passing between flat snow on the left and flat water on the right; a segmented serpent 'from whose body trapped people vapidly gazed. Inside, aisles and vestibules were clogged with the Christmas Day overflow.

In one of the vestibules, facing a dirt-smeared window, Gordon Gant occupied himself by counting codfish-cake billboards. It was, he reflected, a hell of a way to spend Christmas Day.

Shortly after six o'clock the train reached Providence.

In the station, Gant addressed several questions to the bored oracle of the information booth. Then, regarding his watch, he left the building. It was already dark outside. Crossing a wide and slushy thoroughfare, he entered an establishment which called itself a 'spa,' where he made quick work of a steak sandwich, mincemeat pie and coffee. Christmas dinner. He left the spa and went to a drugstore two doors away, where he purchased an inch-wide roll of Scotch Tape. He returned to the station. He sat on an uncomfortable bench and read a Boston tabloid. At ten minutes of seven he left the station again, proceeding to a nearby place where three busses stood waiting. He boarded a blue and yellow one marked *Menasset—Somerset—Fall River*.

At twenty minutes past seven the bus paused midway down Menasset's four block Main Street, discharging several passengers, Gant among them. After a brief acclimatizing glance, he entered a 1910-looking pharmacy where he consulted a thin directory, from which he copied an address and telephone number. He tried the number in the phone booth and, when the phone on the other end of the line had rung ten times without answer, hung up.

The house was a shabby gray box, one story, the sills of its darkened windows furred with snow. Gant looked at it closely as he passed. It was set back only a few yards from the sidewalk; the snow between door and sidewalk was undisturbed.

He walked to the end of the deserted block, turned and came

back, passing the gray house again, this time paying more attention to the houses on either side of it. In one, framed in the window's homemade Christmas wreath, a Spanish-looking family was dining in an atmosphere of magazine cover warmth. In the house on the other side of the gray one, a solitary man was holding a globe of the world in his lap, spinning it in its frame and then stopping it with his finger and looking to see which country his finger had chosen. Gant passed, walked to the other end of the block, turned and came back. This time, as he passed the gray house, he turned sharply, cutting between it and the Spanish-family house. He went around to the back.

There was a small porch. Facing it, across a little yard laced with stiff clotheslines, was a high board fence. Gant went up on the porch. There were a door and a window, a garbage can and a basket of clothespins. He tried the door; it was locked. The window was locked also. Propped on the sill within was an ice company sign, a square placard with 5, 10, 25, and X printed around the four sides. The X side was uppermost. Gant took the roll of Scotch Tape from his pocket. Tearing off a ten inch length, he pressed it across one of the window's dozen panes, the one below the central latch. He fitted the ends of the tape over the pane's molding and tore off another ten inch strip.

In a few minutes he had crosshatched the rectangular pane with cellophane strips. He struck it with his gloved fist. There was a cracking sound; the broken glass sagged, held in place by the tape. Gant began to pull the tape ends from the molding. When that was done he drew the rectangle of cellophane and broken glass from the window and lowered it noiselessly to the bottom of the garbage can. Reaching through the window, he unfastened the latch and raised the lower section. The ice placard fell back into the darkness.

He took a pencil flashlight from his pocket and leaned through the open window. There was a chair piled with folded newspapers before it. He pushed the chair aside and climbed in, closing the window after him.

The flashlight's disc of pallid light glided swiftly over a cramped and shabby kitchen. Gant moved forward, treading softly on worn-through linoleum.

He came to a living room. The chairs were fat and velvet, rubbed bald at the arms. Cream colored shades were drawn down over the windows, flanked by floral-patterned paper drapes. There were pictures of Bud all over; Bud as a child in short pants, Bud at high school graduation, Bud in a private's uniform, Bud in a dark suit, smiling. Snapshots were tucked in the frames of the portraits, surrounding the large smiling faces with smaller faces also smiling.

Gant went through the living room to a hallway. The first room off the hallway was a bedroom; a bottle of lotion on the

165

dresser, an empty dress box and tissue paper on the bed, a wedding picture and a picture of Bud on the night table. The second room was the bathroom; the flashlight caught decals of swans on moisture-faded walls.

The third room was Bud's. It might have been a room in a second class hotel; aside from the high school diploma over the bed, it was barren of anything suggesting the occupant's individuality. Gant went in.

He inspected the titles of some books on a shelf; they were mainly college texts and a few classic novels. No diaries, no engagement books. He sat behind the desk and went through the drawers one at a time. There were stationery and blank scratch pads, back issues of *Life* and the *New Yorker,* term papers from college, road maps of New England. No letters, no calendars with appointments written in, no address books with names crossed out. He rose from the desk and went to the dresser. Half the drawers were empty. The others contained summer shirts and swimming trunks, a couple of pairs of argyle socks, underwear, tarnished cufflinks, celluloid collar stays, bow ties with broken clips. No papers lost in corners, no forgotten pictures.

Perfunctorily he opened the closet. On the floor in the corner there was a small gray strongbox.

He took it out and put it on the desk. It was locked. He lifted and shook it. Its contents shifted, sounding like packets of paper. He put the box down again and picked at its lock with the blade of a small knife he carried on his keychain. Then he took it into the kitchen. He found a screwdriver in one of the drawers and tried that. Finally he wrapped the box in newspaper, hoping that it didn't contain Mrs. Corliss' life's savings.

He opened the window, took the ice placard from the floor, and climbed out onto the porch. When he had closed and locked the window, he tore the placard to size and fitted it in the open pane, blank side out. With the strongbox under his arm, he moved quietly between the houses to the sidewalk.

11

LEO KINGSHIP RETURNED TO HIS APARTMENT at ten o'clock on Wednesday night, having worked late in order to compensate for some of the lost hours Christmas had entailed. "Is Marion in?" he asked the butler, giving him his coat.

"Out with Mr. Corliss. She said she'd be in early though. There's a Mr. Dettweiler waiting in the living room."

"Dettweiler?"

166

"He said Miss Richardson sent him about the securities. He has a little strongbox with him."

"Dettweiler?" Kingship frowned.

He went into the living room.

Gordon Gant rose from a comfortable chair adjacent to the fireplace. "Hello," he said pleasantly.

Kingship looked at him for a moment. "Didn't Miss Richardson make it clear this afternoon that I don't want—" His hands fisted at his sides. "Get out of here," he said. "If Marion comes in . . ."

"Exhibit A," Gant pronounced, raising a pamphlet in each hand, "in the case against Bud Corliss."

"I don't want to—" The sentence hung unfinished. Apprehensively, Kingship came forward. He took the pamphlets from Gant's hands. "Our publications . . ."

"In the possession of Bud Corliss," Gant said. "Kept in a strongbox which until last night resided in a closet in Menasset, Massachusetts." He gave a light kick to the strongbox on the floor beside him. The open lid was bent out of shape. There were four oblong Manila envelopes inside. "I stole it," Gant said.

"*Stole* it?"

He smiled. "Fight fire with fire. I don't know where he's staying in New York, so I decided to sally forth to Menasset."

"You crazy . . ." Kingship sat heavily on a couch that faced the fireplace. He stared at the pamphlets. "Oh God," he said.

Gant resumed his seat next to the couch. "Observe the condition of Exhibit A, if you will. Frayed around the edges, soiled by many fingermarks, center pages worked loose from the staples. I would say he had them for quite some time. I would say he drooled over them considerably."

"That . . . that son of a bitch . . ." Kingship spoke the phrase distinctly, as though not accustomed to using it.

Gant prodded the strongbox with his toe. "The History of Bud Corliss, a drama in four envelopes," he said. "Envelope one: newspaper clippings of the high school hero; class president, chairman of the prom committee, Most Likely To Succeed and so on and forth. Envelope two: honorable discharge from the Army, Bronze Star, Purple Heart, several interesting though obscene photographs and a pawn ticket which I have discovered may be exchanged for a wristwatch if you have a couple of hundred dollars you don't need. Envelope three: college days; transcripts from Stoddard and Caldwell. Envelope four: two well-read brochures describing the magnitude of Kingship Copper Incorporated, and this . . ."—he drew a folded sheet of blue-lined yellow paper from his pocket and passed it to Kingship—"which I can't make head or tail of."

Kingship unfolded the paper. He read halfway down it. "What is it?"

"I'm asking you."

He shook his head.

"It must have some bearing on this," Gant said. "It was in with the pamphlets."

Kingship shook his head and handed the paper back to Gant, who returned it to his pocket. Kingship's gaze dropped to the pamphlets. The grip of his hands crackled the thick paper. "How am I going to tell Marion?" he said. "She *loves* him . . ." He looked at Gant dismally. Then slowly his face smoothed out. He glanced at the pamphlets and back at Gant, his eyes narrowing. "How do I know these were in the strongbox? How do I know that you didn't put them there yourself?"

Gant's jaw dropped. "Oh, for . . ."

Kingship went around the end of the couch and across the room. There was a telephone on a carved table. He dialed a number.

"Come on now," Gant chided.

In the silence of the room the buzzing and the clicks of the phone were audible. "Hello? Miss Richardson? This is Mr. Kingship. I'd like to ask a favor of you. A big favor, I'm afraid. And absolutely confidential." An unintelligble twittering emanated from the phone. "Would you please go down to the office—yes, now. I wouldn't ask you, only it's terribly important, and I—" There was more twittering. "Go to the public relations department," Kingship said. "Go through the files and see whether we've ever sent any promotional publications to . . . Bud Corliss."

"Burton Corliss," Gant said.

"Or Burton Corliss. Yes, that's right—Mr. Corliss. I'm at my home, Miss Richardson. Call me as soon as you find out. Thank you. Thank you very much, Miss Richardson. I appreciate this . . ." He hung up.

Gant shook his head wryly. "We're really grasping at straws, aren't we."

"I have to be sure," Kingship said. "You have to be sure of your evidence in a thing like this." He came back across the room and stood behind the couch.

"You're sure already, and you know damn well you are," Gant said.

Kingship braced his hands on the couch, looking down at the pamphlets in the hollow of the cushion where he had been sitting.

"You know damn well you are," Gant repeated.

After a moment Kingship's breath sighed out tiredly. He came around the couch, picked up the pamphlets, and sat down. "How am I supposed to tell Marion?" he asked. He rubbed his knee. "That son of a bitch . . . that God-damned son of a bitch . . ."

Gant leaned towards him, his elbows on his knees. "Mr. Kingship, I was right about this much. Will you admit I might be right all the way?"

"What 'all the way'?"

"About Dorothy and Ellen." Kingship drew an irritated breath. Gant spoke quickly: "He didn't tell Marion he went to Stoddard. He *must* have been mixed up with Dorothy. He *must* be the one who got her pregnant. He killed her, and Powell and Ellen somehow found out it was him he had to kill them too."

"The note . . ."

"He could have tricked her into writing it! It's been done before—there was a case in the papers just last month about a guy who did it, and for the same reason; the girl was pregnant."

Kingship shook his head. "I'd believe it of him," he said. "After what he's done to Marion, I'd believe anything of him. But there's a flaw in your theory, a big flaw."

"What?" Gant demanded.

"He's after the money, isn't he?" Gant nodded. "And you 'know' Dorothy was murdered because she was wearing something old, something new, something borrowed, something blue?" Gant nodded again. "Well," Kingship said, "if he were the one who'd gotten her into trouble, and if she were ready to marry him that day, then why would he have killed her? He would have gone ahead and married her, wouldn't he? He would have married her and gotten in on the money."

Gant looked at him wordlessly.

"You were right about this," Kingship said, lifting the pamphlets, "but you're wrong about Dorothy. All wrong."

After a moment Gant rose. He turned and paced up to the window. He looked through it dully, gnawing his lower lip. "I may jump," he announced.

When the door chimes toned, Gant turned from the window. Kingship had risen and was standing before the fiireplace, gazing at the birch logs neatly pyramided there. He turned reluctantly, holding the rolled pamphlets at his side, his face averted from Gant's watching eyes.

They heard the front door open, and then voices: ". . . Come in for a while?"

"I don't think so, Marion. We'll have to get up early tomorrow." There was a long silence. "I'll be in front of my place at seven-thirty."

"You'd better wear a dark suit. A smelter must be a filthy place." Another silence. "Good night, Bud . . ."

"Good night."

The door closed.

Kingship wound the pamphlets into a tighter cylinder.

"Marion," he called, but it came out too low. "Marion," he called again, louder.

"Coming," her voice answered cheerfully.

The two men waited, suddenly conscious of a clock's ticking.

She appeared in the wide doorway, perking up the collar of her crisp white full-sleeved blouse. Her cheeks were luminous from the cold outside. "Hi," she said. "We had a——"

She saw Gant. Her hands froze, dropped.

"Marion, we . . ."

She whirled and was gone.

"Marion!" Kingship hurried to the doorway and into the foyer. "Marion!" She was halfway up the curving white staircase, her legs driving furiously. "Marion!" he shouted grimly, commanding.

She stopped, facing rigidly up the stairs, one hand on the bannister. "Well?"

"Come down here," he said. "I have to speak to you. This is extremely important." A moment passed. "Come down here," he said.

"All right." She turned and descended the stairs with regal coldness. "You can speak to me. Before I go upstairs and pack and get out of here."

Kingship returned to the living room. Gant was standing uncomfortably in the middle of the room, his hand on the back of the couch. Kingship, shaking his head dolefully, went to his side.

She came into the room. Their eyes followed her as, without looking at them, she came up to the chair across from the one in which Gant had sat, at the end of the couch nearer the door. She sat down. She crossed her legs carefully, smoothing the red wool of her skirt. She put her hands on the arms of the chair. She looked up at them, standing behind the couch to her left. "Well?" she said.

Kingship shifted uneasily, withering under her gaze. "Mr. Gant went to . . . Yesterday he . . ."

"Yes?"

Kingship turned to Gant helplessly.

Gant said: "Yesterday afternoon, absolutely without your father's knowledge, I went to Menasset. I broke into your fiancé's home——"

"No!"

"——and I took from it a strongbox I found in the closet in his room——"

She pressed back into the chair, her knuckles gripping white, her mouth clamped to a lipless line, her eyes shut.

"I brought it home and jimmied the cover——"

Her eyes shot open, flashing. "What did you find? The plans of the atom bomb?"

They were silent.

170

"What did you find?" she repeated, her voice lowering, growing wary.

Kingship moved down to the end of the couch and handed her the pamphlets, awkwardly unrolling them.

She took them slowly and looked at them.

"They're old," Gant said. "He's had them for some time."

Kingship said, "He hasn't been back to Menasset since you started going with him. He had them before he met you."

She smoothed the pamphlets carefully in her lap. Some of the corners were folded over. She bent them straight. "Ellen must have given them to him."

"Ellen never had any of our publications, Marion. You know that. She was as little interested as you are."

She turned the pamphlets over and examined their backs. "Were you there when he broke open the box? Do you know for certain they were in the box?"

"I'm checking on that," Kingship said. "But what reason would Mr. Gant have for . . ."

She began turning the pages of one of the pamphlets; casually, as though it were a magazine in a waiting room. "All right," she said stiffly, after a moment, "maybe it *was* the money that attracted him at first." Her lips formed a strained smile. "For once in my life I'm grateful for your money." She turned a page. "What is it they say?—it's as easy to fall in love with a rich girl as with a poor."—and another page—"You really can't blame him too much, coming from such a poor family. Environmental influence . . ." She stood up and tossed the pamphlets on the couch. "Is there anything else you wanted?" Her hands were trembling slightly.

"Anything else?" Kingship stared. "Isn't that enough?"

"Enough?" she inquired. "Enough for what? Enough for me to call off the wedding? No."—she shook her head—"No, it isn't enough."

"You *still* want to—"

"He *loves* me," she said. "Maybe it was the money that attracted him at first, but—well, suppose I were a very pretty girl; I wouldn't call off the wedding if I found out it was my looks that attracted him, would I?"

"At first?" Kingship said. "The money is still what attracts him."

"You have no right to say that!"

"Marion, you *can't* marry him now . . ."

"No? Come down to City Hall Saturday morning!"

"He's a no-good scheming—"

"Oh yes! You always know just who's good and who's bad, don't you! You knew Mom was bad and you got rid of her, and you knew Dorothy was bad and that's why she killed herself because you brought us up with your good and bad, your right and wrong! Haven't you done enough with your good and bad?"

"You're *not* going to marry a man who's only after you for your money!"

"He *loves* me! Don't you understand English? He loves me! I love him! I don't care *what* brought us together! We think alike! Feel alike! We like the same books, the same plays, the same music, the same—"

"The same food?" Gant cut in. "Would you both be fond of Italian and Armenian food?" She turned to him, her mouth ajar. He was unfolding a sheet of blue-lined yellow paper he had taken from his pocket. "And those books," he said, looking at the paper, "would they include the works of Proust, Thomas Wolfe, Carson McCullers?"

Her eyes widened. "How did you . . .? What is that?"

He came around the end of the couch. She turned to face him. "Sit down," he said.

"What are you . . .?" She moved back. The edge of the couch pressed against the back of her knees.

"Sit down, please," he said.

She sat down. "What is that?"

"This was in the strongbox with the pamphlets," he said. "In the same envelope. The printing is his, I presume." He handed her the yellow paper. "I'm sorry," he said.

She looked at him confusedly, and then looked down at the paper.

> *Proust, T. Wolfe, C. McCullers, "Madame Bovary," Alice in Wonderland," Eliz. B. Browning—READ!*
> *ART (Mostly modern)—Hopley or Hopper, DeMeuth (sp?) READ general books on mod. art*
> *Pink phase in high school.*
> *Jealous of E.?*
> *Renoir, VanGogh*
> *Italian & Armenian food—LOOK UP restaurants in NYC.*
> *Theater: Shaw, T. Williams,—serious stuff . . .*

She read barely a quarter of the closely printed page, her cheeks draining of color. Then she folded the paper with trembling care. "Well," she said, folding it again, not looking up, "haven't I been the . . . trusting soul . . ." She smiled crazily at her father coming gently around the end of the couch to stand helplessly beside her. "I should have known, shouldn't I?" The blood rushed back to her cheeks, burning red. Her eyes were swimming and her fingers were suddenly mashing and twisting the paper with steel strength. "Too good to be true," she smiled, tears starting down her cheeks, her fingers plucking at the paper. "I really should have known . . ." Her hands released the yellow fragments and flew to her face. She began to cry.

Kingship sat beside her, his arm about her bended shoul-

172

ders. "Marion . . . Marion . . . Be glad you didn't find out too late . . ."

Her back was shaking under his arm. "You don't understand," she sobbed through her hands, "you can't understand . . ."

When the tears had stopped she sat numbly, her fingers knotted around the handkerchief Kingship had given her, her eyes on the pieces of yellow paper on the carpet.

"Do you want me to take you upstairs?" Kingship asked.

"No. Please . . . just . . . just let me sit here . . ."

He rose and joined Gant at the window. They were silent for a while, looking at the lights beyond the river. Finally Kingship said, I'll do *something* to him. I swear to God, I'll do *something*."

A minute passed. Gant said, "She referred to your 'good and bad.' Were you very strict with your daughters?"

Kingship thought for a moment. "Not very," he said.

"I thought you were, the way she spoke."

"She was angry," Kingship said.

Gant stared across the river at a Pepsi-Cola sign. "In the drugstore the other day, after we left Marion's apartment, you said something about maybe having pushed one of your daughters away. What did you mean?"

"Dorothy," Kingship said. "Maybe if I hadn't been . . ."

"So strict?" Gant suggested.

"No. I *wasn't* very strict. I taught them right from wrong. Maybe I . . . overemphasized a little, because of their mother . . ." He sighed. "Dorothy shouldn't have felt that suicide was the only way out," he said.

Gant took out a pack of cigarettes and removed one. He turned it between his fingers. "Mr. Kingship, what would you have done if Dorothy had married without first consulting you, and then had had a baby . . . too soon?"

After a moment Kingship said, "I don't know."

"He would have thrown her out," Marion said quietly. The two men turned. She was sitting motionlessly on the couch, as she had been before. They could see her face in the canted mirror over the mantel. She was still looking at the papers on the floor.

"Well?" Gant said to Kingship.

"I don't think I would have thrown her out," he protested.

"You would have," Marion said tonelessly.

Kingship turned back to the window. "Well," he said finally, "under those circumstances, shouldn't a couple be expected to assume the responsibilities of marriage, as well as the . . ." He left the sentence unfinished.

Gant lit his cigarette. "There you are," he said. "That's why he killed her. She must have told him about you. He knew he wouldn't get near the money even of he did marry her, and if he didn't marry her he would get into trouble, so . . . Then he decides to have a second try, with Ellen, but she starts to investigate Dorothy's death and gets too close to the truth. So close that he has to kill her and Powell. And then he tries a third time."

"Bud?" Marion said. She spoke the name blankly, her face in the morror showing the barest flicker of surprise, as though her fiancé had been accused of having imperfect table manners.

Kingship stared narrow-eyed out the window. "I'd believe it," he said intently. "I'd believe it . . ." But as he turned to Gant the resolution faded from his eyes. "You're basing it all on his not telling Marion he went to Stoddard. We're not even sure he *knew* Dorothy, let alone he was the one she was . . . seeing. We have to be *sure*."

"The girls at the dorm," Gant said. "Some of them must have known who she was going with."

Kingship nodded. "I could hire someone to go out there, speak to them . . ."

Gant pondered and shook his head. "It's no good. It's vacation; by the time you managed to find one of the girls who knew, it would be too late."

"Too late?"

"Once he knows the wedding is off,"—he glanced at Marion; she was silent—"he's not going to wait around to find out why, is he?"

"We'd find him," Kingship said.

"Maybe. And maybe not. People disappear." Gant smoked thoughtfully. "Didn't Dorothy keep a diary or anything?"

The telephone rang.

Kingship went to the carved table and lifted the receiver. "Hello?" There was a long pause. Gant looked at Marion; she was leaning forward, picking up the pieces of paper from the floor. "When?" Kingship asked. She put the pieces of paper in her left hand and squeezed them together. She looked at them, not knowing what to do with them. She put them on the couch beside her, on top of the two pamphlets. "Thank you," Kingship said. "Thank you very much." There was the sound of the receiver being replaced, and then silence. Gant turned to look at Kingship.

He was standing beside the table, his pink face rigid. "Miss Richardson," he said. "Promotional literature was sent to Burton Corliss in Caldwell, Wisconsin, on October 16, 1950."

"Just when he must have started his campaign with Ellen," Gant said.

Kingship nodded. "But that was the second time," he said slowly. "Promotional literature was also sent to Burton Corliss on February 6, 1950, in Blue River, Iowa."

Gant said, "Dorothy . . ."

Marion moaned.

174

Gant remained after Marion had gone upstairs. "We're still in the same boat Ellen was in," he said. "The police have Dorothy's 'suicide note' and all we have are suspicions and a flock of circumstantial evidence."

Kingship held one of the pamphlets. "I'll make sure," he said.

"Didn't they find *anything* at Powell's place? A fingerprint, a thread of cloth . . .?"

"Nothing," Kingship said. "Nothing at Powell's place, nothing at that restaurant where Ellen . . ."

Gant sighed. "Even if you could get the police to arrest him, a first year law student could get him released in five minutes."

"I'll get him somehow," Kingship said. "I'll make sure, and I'll get him."

Gant said, "We've either got to find out how he got her to write that note, or else find the gun he used on Powell and Ellen. And before Saturday."

Kingship looked at the photograph on the pamphlet's cover. "The smelter . . ." Sorrowfully he said, "We're supposed to fly out there tomorrow. I wanted to show him around. Marion too. She was never interested before."

"You'd better see that she doesn't let him know the wedding is off until the last possible moment."

Kingship smoothed the pamphlet on his knee. He looked up. "What?"

"I said you should see that she doesn't let him know the wedding is off until the last possible moment."

"Oh," Kingship said. His eyes returned to the pamphlet. A moment passed. "He picked the wrong man," he said softly, still looking at the photograph of the smelter. "He should have picked on somebody else's daughters."

12

WAS THERE EVER SUCH A PERFECT DAY? That was all he wanted to know,—was there? He grinned at the plane; it looked as impatient as he; it craned forward at the runway, its compact body gleaming, the coppered KINGSHIP and the crown trademark on its side emblazoned by the early morning sun. He grinned at the busy scene further down the field, where *commercial* planes stood, their waiting passengers herded behind wire fences like dumb animals. Well, we all can't have private planes at our disposal! He grinned at the ceramic blue of the sky, then stretched and pounded his chest happily, watching his breath plume upwards. No, he decided judicially, there

175

really never was such a perfect day. What, never? No, never! What, *never*? Well . . . hardly ever! He turned and strode back to the hangar, humming Gilbert and Sullivan.

Marion and Leo were standing in the shade, having one of their tight-lipped arguments. "I'm going!" Marion insisted.

"What's the dif*few*culty?" he smiled, coming up to them. Leo turned and walked away.

"What's the matter?" he asked Marion.

"Nothing's the matter. I don't feel well, so he doesn't want me to go." Her eyes were on the plane beyond him.

"Bridal nerves?"

"No. I just don't feel well, that's all."

"Oh," he said knowingly.

They stood in silence for a minute, watching a pair of mechanics fuss with the plane's fuel tank, and then he moved towards Leo. Leave it to Marion to be off on a day like this. Well, it was probably all for the good; maybe she'd keep quiet for a change. "All set to go?"

"A few minutes," Leo said. "We're waiting for Mr. Dettweiler."

"Who?"

"Mr. Dettweiler. His father is on the board of directors."

A few minutes later a blond man in a gray overcoat approached from the direction of the commercial hangars. He had a long jaw and heavy eyebrows. He nodded at Marion and came up to Leo. "Good morning, Mr. Kingship."

"Good morning, Mr. Dettweiler." They shook hands. "I'd like you to meet my prospective son-in-law, Bud Corliss. Bud, this is Gordon Dettweiler."

"How do you do."

"Well," Dettweiler said—he had a handshake like a mangle —"I've certainly been looking forward to meeting you. Yes sir, I certainly have." A character, Bud thought, or maybe he was trying to get in good with Leo.

"Ready, sir?" a man asked from within the plane.

"Ready," Leo said. Marion came forward. "Marion, I honestly wish you wouldn't . . ."—but she marched right past Leo, up the three-step platform and into the plane. Leo shrugged and shook his head. Dettweiler followed Marion in. Leo said, "After you, Bud."

He jogged up the three steps and entered the plane. It was a six-seater, its interior done in pale blue. He took the last seat on the right, behind the wing. Marion was across the aisle. Leo took the front seat, across from Dettweiler.

When the engine coughed and roared to life, Bud fastened his seatbelt. Son of a gun, if it didn't have a copper buckle! He shook his head, smiling. He looked out the window at the people waiting behind fences, and wondered if they could see him . . .

The plane began to roll forward. On the way . . . Would

Leo be taking him to the smelter if he were still suspicious? Never! What, never? No, never! He leaned over, tapped Marion's elbow and grinned at her. She smiled back, looking ill all right and returned to her window. Leo and Dettweiler were talking softly to each other over the aisle. "How long will it take, Leo?" he asked cheerfully. Leo turned—"Three hours. Less if the wind's good."—and turned back to Dettweiler.

Well, he hadn't wanted to talk to anyone anyway. He returned to his window and watched the ground slide past.

At the edge of the field the plane turned slowly around. The engine whined higher, building up power . . .

He stared out the window, fingering the copper buckle. On the way to the smelter . . . The smelter! The grail! The fountainhead of wealth!

Why the hell did his mother have to be afraid of flying? Christ, it would have been *terrific* having her along!

The plane roared forward.

He was the first to spot it; far ahead and below, a small black geometric cluster on the bedsheet of snow; a small black cluster like a twig on the end of a curving stem of railroad tracks. "There it is," he heard Leo saying, and he was faintly conscious of Marion crossing the aisle and taking the seat in front of him. His breath fogged the window; he wiped it clean.

The twig vanished under the wing. He waited. He swallowed and his ears popped as the plane soared lower.

The smelter reappeared directly below him, sliding out from under the wing. There were half a dozen rectilinear brown roofs with thick tails of smoke dragging from their centers. They crowded together, huge and shadowless in the overhead sun, beside the glittering chainmail patch of a filled parking lot. Railroad tracks looped and encircled them, merging below into a multi-veined stem, down which a freight train crawled, its smudge of smoke dwarfed by the giant black plumes behind it, its chain of cars scintillating with salmon-colored glints.

His head turned slowly, his eyes locked to the smelter that slid towards the tail of the plane. Fields of snow followed it. Scattered houses appeared. The smelter was gone. There were more houses, then roads separating them into blocks. Still more houses, closer now, and stores and signs and creeping cars and dot-like people, a park, the cubist pattern of a housing development . . .

The plane banked, circling. The ground tilted away, then leveled, swept closer, and finally came slicing up under the wing of the plane. A jolt; the seatbelt's buckle bit his stomach. Then the plane rolled smoothly. He drew the pale blue webbing from the copper clamp.

There was a limousine waiting when they descended from the plane; a custom-built Packard, black and polished. He sat on a jump-seat next to Dettweiler. He leaned forward, looking

177

over the driver's shoulder. He peered down the long perspective of the town's main street to a white hill far away on the horizon. At its summit, from the far side, columns of smoke arose. They were curving and black against the sky, like the cloud-fingers of a genie's hand.

The main street became a two lane highway that speared between fields of snow, and the highway became an asphalt road that embraced the curve of the hill's base, and the asphalt road became a gravel one that jounced over the serried ribs of railroad tracks and turned to the left, rising up the hillside parallel to the tracks. First one slowly climbing train was overtaken, and then another. Sparks of hidden metal winked from ore-heaped gondola cars.

Ahead, the smelter rose up. Brown structures merged into a crude pyramid, their belching smokestacks ranked around the largest one. Nearer, the buildings swelled and clarified; their clifflike walls were streaky brown metal, laced in spots with girdered fretwork and irregularly patched with soot-stained glass; the shapes of the buildings were hard, geometric; they were bound together by chutes and catwalks. Still nearer, the buildings merged again, the sky space between them lost behind projecting angles. They became a single massive form, large hulks buttressing larger ones into an immense smoke-spired industrial cathedral. It loomed up mountainously, and then suddenly swept off to the side as the limousine veered away.

The car pulled up before a low brick building, at the door of which waited a lean, white-haired, unctuously smiling man in a dark gray suit.

He forgot what he was eating, that's how interested he was in lunch. He pulled his eyes from the window across the room, the window through which could be seen the buildings wherein heaps of gray-brown dirt were purified to gleaming copper, and looked down at his plate. Creamed chicken. He started eating more quickly, hoping the others would follow suit.

The carefully dressed white-haired man had turned out to be a Mr. Otto, the manager of the smelter. Leo having introduced him, Mr. Otto had led them into a conference room and begun apologizing for things. He apologized smilingly for the tablecloth that left bare one end of the long table—"We're not in the New York office, you know"—and he apologized suavely for cool food and warm wine—"I'm afraid we lack the facilities of our big city brethren." Mr. Otto longed transparently for the New York office. Over the soup he spoke of the copper shortage and disparaged the suggestions of the National Production Authority for its mitigation. Occasionally he referred to copper as "the red metal."

"Mr. Corliss." He looked up. Dettweiler was smiling at him

178

across the table. "You'd better be careful," Dettweiler said. "I found a bone in mine."

Bud glanced at his nearly empty plate and smiled back at Dettweiler. "I'm anxious to see the smelter," he said.

"Aren't we all," Dettweiler remarked, still smiling.

"You found a bone in yours?" Mr. Otto inquired. "That woman! I told her to take care. These people can't even cut up a chicken properly."

Now that they had at long last left the brick building and were crossing the asphalt yard to the buildings of the smelter itself, he walked slowly. The others, coatless, hurried ahead, but he drifted behind, savoring the climactic sweetness of the moment. He watched an ore-laden train disappear behind a steel wall at the left of the buildings. At the right, a train was being loaded; cranes swung copper into the cars; great square slabs like solidified flame that must have weighed five or six hundred pounds each. A heart! he thought, gazing up at the monstrous brown form that filled more and more of the sky,— a giant heart of American industry, drawing in bad blood, pumping out good! Standing so close to it, about to enter it, it was impossible not to share the surging of its power!

The others had vanished into a doorway at the base of the towering steel mass. Now Mr. Otto smiled within the doorway, beckoning.

He moved forward less slowly, like a lover going to a long awaited tryst. Success rewarded! Promise fulfilled! There should be a fanfare! he thought. There should be a fanfare!

A whistle screamed.

Thank you. *Muchas gracias.*

He went into the darkness of the doorway. The door closed after him.

The whistle screamed again, piercingly, like a bird in a jungle.

13

HE STOOD ON A CHAIN-RAILED CATWALK staring fascinatedly at an army of huge cylindrical furnaces ranked before him in diminishing perspective like an ordered forest of giant redwood trunks. At their bases men moved methodically, regulating incomprehensible controls. The air was hot and sulphurous.

"There are six hearths, one above the other, in each furnace," Mr. Otto lectured. "The ore is introduced at the top. It's moved steadily downward from hearth to hearth by rotating arms attached to a central shaft. The roasting removes excess sulphur from the ore."

He listened intently, nodding. He turned to the others to express his awe, but only Marion stood on his right, wooden-faced as she had been all day. Leo and that Dettweiler were gone. "Where'd your father and Dettweiler go?" he asked her.

"I don't know. Dad said he wanted to show him something."

"Oh." He turned back to the furnaces. What would Leo want to show Dettweiler? Well . . . "How many are there?"

"Furnaces?" Mr. Otto dabbed perspiration from his upper lip with a folded handkerchief. "Fifty-four."

Fifty-four! Jesus! "How much ore goes through them in a day?" he asked.

It was wonderful! He'd never been so interested in anything in his whole life! He asked a thousand questions and Mr. Otto, visibly reacting to his fascination, answered them in detail, speaking only to him, while Marion trailed unseeingly behind.

In another building there were more furnaces; brick walled, flat, and over a hundred feet long. "The reverberatory furnaces," Mr. Otto said. "The ore that comes from the roasting furnaces is about ten per cent copper. Here it's melted down. The lighter minerals flow off as slag. What's left is iron and copper—we call it 'matte'—forty per cent copper."

"What do you use for fuel?"

"Pulverized coal. The waste heat is used to generate steam for making power."

He shook his head, whistling between his teeth.

Mr. Otto smiled. "Impressed?"

"It's wonderful," Bud said. "Wonderful." He gazed down the endless stretch of furnaces. "It makes you realize what a great country this is."

"This," Mr. Otto said, pushing his voice over a roaring tide of sound, "is probably the most spectacular part of the entire smelting process."

"Jesus!"

"The converters," Mr. Otto said loudly.

The building was a vast steel shell, percussant with the sustained thunder of machines and men. A greenish haze obscured its far reaches, swimming around shafts of yellow-green sunlight that pillared down through crane tracks and catwalks from windows in the peaked roof dim and high above.

At the near end of the building, on either side, lay six massive dark cylindroid vessels, end to end, like giant steel barrels on their sides, dwarfing the workmen on railed platforms between them. Each vessel had an opening in its uppermost surface. Flames burst forth from these mouths; yellow, orange, red, blue; roaring up into funnel-like hoods overhead that swallowed and bore them away.

One of the converters was turned forward on the cogged rollers that supported it, so that its round mouth, scabrous with

180

coagulated metal, was at the side; liquid fire rushed from the radiant throat, pouring down into an immense crucible on the floor. The molten flow, heavy and smoking, filled the steel container. The converter rolled back groaningly, its mouth dripping. The yoke of the crucible lifted, caught by a great blunt hook from whose block a dozen cables rose in unwavering ascension, rose higher than the converters, higher than the central spine of catwalk, up to the underbelly of a grimy cab that hung from a single-railed track below the dimness of the roof. The cables contracted; the crucible lifted in slow, weightless levitation. It rose until it was higher than the converters, some twenty-five feet above the ground, and then cab, cables and crucible began to draw away, retreating towards the cuprous haze at the northern end of the building.

The center of it all! The heart of the heart! With rapt eyes Bud followed the heat-shimmering column of air over the departing crucible.

"Slag," Mr. Otto said. They stood on an island of railed platform against the south wall, a few feet above the floor and midway between the two banks of converters. Mr. Otto touched his handkerchief to his forehead. "The molten matte from the reverberatory furnaces is poured into these converters. Silica is added, and then compressed air is blown in through pipes at the back. The impurities are oxidized; slag forms and is poured off, as you just saw. More matte is added, more slag forms, and so on. The copper keeps getting richer and richer until, after about five hours, it's ninety-nine per cent pure. Then it's poured out in the same way as the slag."

"Will they be pouring copper soon?"

Mr. Otto nodded. "The converters are operated on a stagger system, so that there's a continuous output."

"I'd like to see them pour the copper," Bud said. He watched one of the converters on the right pouring off slag. "Why are the flames different colors?" he asked.

"The color changes as the process advances. That's how the operators tell what's going on inside."

Behind them a door closed. Bud turned. Leo was standing beside Marion, Dettweiler leaned against a ladder that climbed the wall beside the door. "Are you enjoying the tour?" Leo asked over the thunder.

"It's wonderful, Leo! Overpowering!"

"They're going to pour copper over there," Mr. Otto said loudly.

Before one of the converters on the left, a crane had lowered a steel vat, larger than the crucible into which the slag had been poured. Its steep sides were a three inch thickness of dull gray metal, as high as a man. Its rim was seven feet across.

The mammoth cylinder of the converter began to turn, rumbling, rolling forward in its place. A wraith of blue flame flickered over its clotted mouth. It turned further; a volcanic

181

radiance blasted from its interior, veils of white smoke arose, and then a flood of racing incandescence came bursting out. It spilled forward and fell gleamingly into the giant bowl. The steady molten flow seemed motionless, a solid, shining shaft between the converter and the depths of the vat. The converter turned further; new ribs twisted fluidly down the shaft, and again it was motionless. Within the vat the surface of the liquid appeared, slowly rising, clouded by whorls of smoke. The bitter smell of copper singed the air. The streaming shaft thinned, twisting, as the converter began rolling back. The thin stream petered out, its last few drops rolling over the swell of the cylinder and sparkling to the cement floor.

The smoke above the vat dissolved to vaporous wisps. The surface of the molten copper, a few inches below the vessel's rim, was an oblique disc of glistening oceanic green.

"It's green," Bud said, surprised.

"When it cools it regains its usual color," Mr. Otto said.

Bud stared at the restless pool. Blisters formed, swelled, and popped glutinously on its surface. "What's the matter, Marion?" he heard Leo ask. The heated air above the vat trembled as though sheets of cellophane were being shaken. "Matter?" Marion said. Leo said, "You look pale."

Bud turned around. Marion seemed no paler than usual. "I'm all right," she was saying.

"But you're pale," Leo insisted, and Dettweiler nodded agreement.

"It must be the heat or something," Marion said.

"The fumes," Leo said. "Some people can't stand the fumes. Mr. Otto, why don't you take my daughter back to the administration building. We'll be along in a few minutes."

"Honestly, Dad," she said tiredly, "I feel—"

"No nonsense," Leo smiled stiffly. "We'll be with you in a few minutes."

"But . . ." She hesitated a moment, looking annoyed, and then shrugged and turned to the door. Dettweiler opened it for her.

Mr. Otto followed after Marion. He paused in the doorway and turned back to Leo. " I hope you're going to show Mr. Corliss how we mold the anodes." He turned to Bud. "Very impressive," he said, and went out. Dettweiler closed the door.

"Anodes?" Bud said.

"The slabs they were loading on the train outside," Leo said. Bud noticed an odd mechanical quality in his voice, as though he were thinking of something else. "They're shipped to the refinery in New Jersey. Electrolytic refining."

"My God," Bud said, "it's some involved process." He turned back to the converters on the left. The vat of copper, its angular handle hooked by the crane overhead, was about to be raised. The dozen cables tensed, vibrating, and then rigidified sharply. The vat lifted from the floor.

Behind him Leo said, "Did Mr. Otto take you up on the catwalk?"

"No," Bud said.

"You get a much better view," Leo said. "Would you like to go up?"

Bud turned. "Do we have the time?"

"Yes," Leo said.

Dettweiler, his back against the ladder, stepped aside. "After you," he smiled.

Bud went to the ladder. He grasped one of the metal rungs and looked upwards. The rungs, like oversize staples, ran narrowingly up the brown wall. They focused at a trap in the floor of the catwalk, which projected perpendicularly from the wall some fifty feet above.

"Bottleneck," Dettweiler murmured beside him.

He began to climb. The rungs were warm, their upper surfaces polished smooth. He climbed in a steady rhythm, keeping his eyes on the descending wall before him. He heard Dettweiler and Leo following after him. He tried to visualize the sight the catwalk would offer. To look down on that scene of industrial power . . .

He climbed the ladder up through the trap and stepped off onto the ridged metal floor of the catwalk. The thunder of the machines was diminished up here, but the air was hotter and the smell of copper stronger. The narrow runway, railed by heavy chain between iron stanchions, extended in a straight line down the spine of the building. It ended halfway down the building's length, where it was cut off by a broad strip of steel partition wall that hung from roof to floor, some twelve feet wider than the catwalk. Overhead, on either side, crane tracks paralleled the runway. They passed clear of the partition that ended the catwalk and continued into the northern half of the building.

He peered over the left side of the catwalk, his hands folded over the top of one of the waist-high stanchions. He looked down upon the six converters, the men scurrying between them . . .

His eyes shifted. To his right, twenty feet below and ten feet out from the catwalk, hung the vat of copper, a steel rimmed pool of green on its slow procession towards the far end of the building. Ghosts of smoke rose from the liquid sheen of its surface.

He followed it, walking slowly, his left hand tracing over the dipping curves of the chain railing. He stayed far enough behind the vat so that he could just feel the fringe of its radiant heat. He heard Leo and Dettweiler following. His eyes climbed the vat's cables, six and six on either side of the block, up to the cab a dozen feet above him. He could see the shoulder of the operator inside. His eyes dropped back to the copper.

183

How much is in there? How many tons? What was it worth? One thousand? Two thousand? Three? Four? Five? . . .

He was nearing the steel partition, and now he saw that the catwalk didn't end there after all; instead it branched six feet to right and left, following the partition to its edges like the head of a long-stemmed T. The vat of copper vanished beyond the partition. He turned onto the left wing of the T. A three foot chain swung across the catwalk's end. He put his left hand on the corner stanchion and his right on the edge of the partition, which was quite warm. He leaned forward a bit and peered around the partition at the receding vat. "Where does it go now?" he called out.

Behind him Leo said, "Refining furnaces. Then it's poured into molds."

He turned around, Leo and Dettweiler faced him shoulder to shoulder, blocking the stem of the T. Their faces were oddly inflexible. He patted the partition on his left. "What's behind here?" he asked.

"The refining furnaces," Leo said. "Any more questions?"

He shook his head, puzzled by the grimness of the two men.

"Then I've got one for you," Leo said. His eyes were like blue marbles behind his glasses. "How did you get Dorothy to write that suicide note?"

14

EVERYTHING FELL AWAY; the catwalk, the smelter, the whole world; everything melted away like sand castles sucked into the sea, leaving him suspended in emptiness with two blue marbles staring at him and the sound of Leo's question swelling and reverberating like being inside an iron bell.

Then Leo and Dettweiler confronted him again; the smelter's rumble welled up; the plates of the partition materialized slippery against his left hand, the knob of the stanchion damp under his right, the floor of the catwalk . . . but the floor didn't come back completely; it swayed anchorless and undulant beneath his feet, because his knees—Oh God!—were jelly, trembling and shaking. "What're you—" he started to say, but nothing came out. He swallowed air. "What're you . . . talking about . . ."

"Dorothy," Dettweiler told him. Slowly he said, "You wanted to marry her. For the money. But then she was pregnant. You knew you wouldn't get the money. You killed her."

He shook his head in confused protest. "No," he said, "No! She committed suicide! She sent a note to Ellen! You know that, Leo!"

184

"You tricked her into writing it," Leo said.

"How . . . Leo, how could I do that? How the hell could I do *that?*"

"That's what you're going to tell us," Dettweiler said.

"I hardly knew her!"

"You didn't know her at all," Leo said. "That's what you told Marion."

"That's right! I didn't know her at all!"

"You just said you *hardly* knew her."

"I didn't know her *at all!*"

Leo's fists clenched. "You sent for our publications in February nineteen hundred and fifty!"

Bud stared, his hand bracing tightly against the partition. "What publications?" It was a whisper; he had to say it again: "What publications?"

Dettweiler said, "The pamphlets I found in the strongbox in your room in Menasset."

The catwalk dipped crazily. The strongbox! Oh, Jesus Christ! The pamphlets and what else? The clippings?—he'd thrown them out, thank God! The pamphlets . . . *and the list on Marion!* Oh, Jesus! "Who are you?" he exploded. "Where the hell do you come off breaking into a person's—"

"Stay back!" Dettweiler warned.

Withdrawing the single step he had advanced, Bud gripped the stanchion again. "Who are you?" he shouted.

"Gordon Gant," Dettweiler said.

Gant! The one on the radio, the one who'd kept needling the police! How the hell did he—

"I knew Ellen," Gant said. "I met her a few days before you killed her."

"I—" He felt the sweat running. "Crazy!" he shouted. "You're crazy! Who else did I kill?" To Leo—"You listen to him? Then you're crazy too! I never killed anybody!"

Gant said, "You killed Dorothy and Ellen and Dwight Powell!"

"And almost killed Marion," Leo said. "When she saw that list . . ."

She saw the list! Oh God almighty! "I never killed anybody! Dorrie committed suicide and Ellen and Powell were killed by a burglar!"

"Dorrie?" Gant snapped.

"I— Everybody called her Dorrie! I . . . I never killed anybody! Only a Jap, and that was in the Army!"

"Then why are your legs shaking?" Gant asked. "Why is the sweat dripping down your cheek?"

He swiped at his cheek. Control! Self-control! He dragged a deep breath into his chest . . . Slow up, slow up . . . They can't prove a thing, not a goddamn thing! They know about the list, about Marion, about the pamphlets—okay—but they can't prove a thing about . . . He drew another breath . . .

185

"You can't prove a thing," he said. "Because there isn't anything to prove. You're crazy, both of you." His hands wiped against his thighs. "Okay," he said, "I knew Dorrie. So did a dozen other guys. And I've had my eyes on the money all along the way. Where's the law against that? So there's no wedding Saturday. Okay." He straightened his jacket with stiff fingers. "I'm probably better off poor than having a bastard like you for a father-in-law. Now get out of the way and let me pass. I don't feel like standing around talking to a couple of crazy lunatics."

They didn't move. They stood shoulder to shoulder six feet away.

"Move," he said.

"Touch the chain behind you," Leo said.

"Get out of the way and let me pass!"

"Touch the chain behind you!"

He looked at Leo's stonelike face for a moment and then turned slowly.

He didn't have to touch the chain; he just had to look at it; the metal eye of the stanchion had been bent open into a loose C that barely engaged the first of the heavy links.

"We were up here when Otto was showing you around," Leo said. "Touch it."

His hand came forward, brushed the chain. It collapsed. The free end clanked to the floor; it slid rattlingly off and swung down, striking noisily against the partition.

Fifty feet below cement floor yawned, seemed to sway . . .

"Not as much as Dorothy got," Gant was saying, "but enough."

He turned to face them, clutching the stanchion and the edge of the partition, trying not to think of the void behind his heels. "You wouldn't . . . dare . . ." he heard himself saying.

"Don't I have reason enough?" Leo asked. "You killed my daughters!"

"I didn't, Leo! I swear to God I didn't!"

"Is that why you were sweating and shaking the minute I mentioned Dorothy's name? Is that why you didn't think it was a bad joke, react the way an innocent person would have reacted?"

"Leo, I swear on the soul of my dead father . . ."

Leo stared at him coldly.

He shifted his grip on the stanchion. It was slick with sweat. "You wouldn't do it . . ." he said. "You'd never get away with it . . ."

"Wouldn't I?" Leo said. "Do you think you're the only one who can plan something like this?" He pointed to the stanchion. "The jaws of the wrench were wrapped in cloth; there are no marks on that ring. An accident, a terrible accident; a piece of iron, old, continually subjected to intense heat, weakens and bends when a six foot man stumbles against the chain attached to it. A terrible accident. And how can you prevent it?

186

Yell? no one will hear you over the noise. Wave your arms?; the men down there have jobs to attend to, and even if they should look up, there's the haze and the distance. Attack us?; one push and you're finished." He paused. "So tell me, why won't I get away with it? Why?

"Of course," he continued after a moment, "I would rather not do it. I would rather hand you over to the police." He looked at his watch. "So I'll give you three minutes. From now. I want something that will convince a jury, a jury that won't be able to take you by surprise and see the guilt written all over you."

"Tell us where the gun is," Gant said.

The two of them stood side by side; Leo with his left wrist lifted and his right hand holding back the cuff to expose his watch; Gant with his hands at his sides.

"How did you get Dorothy to write the note?" Gant asked.

His own hands were so tight against the partition and the stanchion that they throbbed with a leaden numbness. "You're bluffing," he said. They leaned forward to hear him. "You're trying to scare me into admitting—to something I never did."

Leo shook his head slowly. He looked at the watch. A moment passed. "Two minutes and thirty seconds," he said.

Bud whirled to the right, catching the stanchion with his left hand and shouting to the men over at the converters. "Help!" he cried, "Help! Help!"—bellowing as loud as he could, waving his right arm furiously, clutching the stanchion. "Help!"

The men far off and below might as well have been painted figures; their attention was centered on a converter pouring copper.

He turned back to Leo and Gant.

"You see?" Leo said.

"You'll be killing an innocent man, that's what you'll be doing!"

"Where's the gun?" Gant asked.

"There is no gun! I never had a gun!"

Leo said, "Two minutes."

They were bluffing! They must be! He looked around desperately; the main shaft of the catwalk, the roof, the crane tracks, the few windows, the . . . The crane tracks!

Slowly, trying not to make it too obvious, he glanced to the right again. The converter had rolled back. The vat before it was full and smoking, cables trailing slackly up to the cab above. The vat would be lifted; the cab, now over two hundred feet away, would bear the vat forward, approaching along the track that passed behind and above him; and the man in the cab—a dozen feet up? four feet out?—would be able to hear! To see!

If only they could be stalled! If only they could be stalled until the cab was near enough!

The vat lifted . . .

"One minute, thirty seconds," Leo said.

Bud's eyes flicked back to the two men. He met their stares for a few seconds, and then risked another glance to the right, cautiously, so that they should not guess his plan. (Yes, a plan! Even now, at this moment, a plan!) The distant vat hung between floor and catwalk, its skein of cables seeming to shudder in the heat-vibrant air. The boxlike cab was motionless under the track—and then it began to come forward, bearing the vat, growing imperceptibly larger. So slowly! Oh God, make it come faster!

He turned back to them.

"We aren't bluffing, Bud," Leo said. And after a moment: "One minute."

He looked again; the cab was nearer—a hundred and fifty feet? One thirty? He could distinguish a pale shape behind the black square of its window.

"Thirty seconds."

How could time race by so fast? "Listen," he said frantically, "listen. I want to tell you something—something about Dorrie. She . . ." He groped for something to say—and then stopped wide-eyed; there had been a flicker of movement in the dimness at the far end of the catwalk. Someone else was up here! Salvation!

"Help!" he cried, his arm semaphoring. "You! Come here! Help!"

The flicker of movement became a figure hurrying along the catwalk, speeding towards them.

Leo and Gant looked over their shoulders in confusion.

Oh dear God, thank you!

Then he saw that it was a woman.

Marion.

Leo cried out, "What are you— Get out of here! For God's sake, Marion, go back down!"

She seemed not to hear him. She came up behind them, her face flushed and large-eyed above their compacted shoulders.

Bud felt her gaze rake his face and then descend to his legs. Legs that were trembling again . . . If he only had a gun . . . "Marion," he pleaded, "stop them! They're crazy! They're trying to kill me! Stop them! They'll listen to you! I can explain about that list, I can explain everything! I swear I wasn't lying—"

She kept looking at him. Finally she said, "The way you explained why you didn't tell me about Stoddard?"

"I love you! I swear to God I do! I started out thinking about the money, I admit that, but I love you! You know I wasn't lying about that!"

"*How* do I know?" she asked.

188

"I swear it!"

"You swore so many things . . ." Her fingers appeared curving over the men's shoulders; long, white, pink-nailed fingers; they seemed to be pushing.

"Marion! You wouldn't! Not when we . . . after we . . ." Her fingers pressed forward into the cloth of the shoulders, pushing . . .

"Marion," he begged futilely.

Suddenly he became aware of a swelling in the smelter's thunder, an added rumble. A wave of heat was spreading up his right side. The cab! He wheeled, catching the stanchion with both hands. There it was!—not twenty feet away, grinding closer on the overhead track with the cables shooting down from its belly. Through the opening in its front end he could see a bent head in a visored gray cap. "You!" he bellowed, his jaw muscles cording. "You in the cab! Help! You!" Heat from the oncoming vat pressed heavily against his chest. "Help! You! In the cab!" The gray cap, coming closer, never lifted. *Deaf?* Was the stupid bastard *deaf?* Help!" he roared chokingly again and again, but it was no use.

He turned from the swelling heat, wanting to cry in despair.

Leo said, "The noisiest place in the smelter, up there in those cabs." As he said it, he took a step forward. Gant moved up beside him. Marion followed behind.

"Look," Bud said placatingly, clutching the partition in his left hand again. "Please . . ." He stared at their faces, masklike except for burning eyes.

They came another step closer.

The catwalk dipped and bucked like a shaken blanket. The baking heat on his right began extending itself across his back. They meant it! They weren't bluffing! They were going to kill him! Moisture trickled all over him.

"All right!" he cried. "All right! She thought she was doing a Spanish translation! I wrote out the note in Spanish! I asked her to translate—" His voice faded and stopped.

What was the matter with them? Their faces . . . the masklike blankness was gone, warped into—into embarrassment and sick contempt, and they were looking down at . . .

He looked down. The front of his pants was dark with a spreading stain that ran in a series of island blotches down his right trouser leg. Oh God! The Jap . . . the Jap he had killed—that wretched trembling, chattering, pants-wetting caricature of a man—was that *him?* Was that *himself?*

The answer was in their faces.

"No!" he cried. He clapped his hands over his eyes, but their faces were still there. "No! I'm not like him!" he wheeled away from them. His foot slipped on wetness and kicked out from under him. His hands flew from his face and flailed the air. Heat blasted up at him. Falling, he saw a giant disc of

189

glistening green sliding into space below; gaseous, restless, shimmering—

Hardness in his hands! The cables! The weight of his body swung down and around, pulling at his armpits and tearing his hands on protruding steel threads. He hung with his legs swinging against the taut cables and his eyes staring at one of them, seeing the frayed fibers that were stabbing like needles into his hands above. A chaos of sound; a whistle shrieking, a woman screaming, voices above, voices below . . . He squinted up at his hands—blood was starting to trickle down the insides of his wrists—the ovenlike heat was smothering, dizzying, engulfing him with the noxious stench of copper—voices shouted to him—he saw his hands starting to open—he was letting go because he wanted to, it wasn't the burning suffocation or the needles in his hands, he was letting go because he wanted to, just as he had jumped from the catwalk but instinct had made him grab the cables and now he was overcoming instinct—his left hand opened and fell—he hung by his right, turning slightly in the furnace heat—there was oil on the back of his hand from the stanchion or the chain or something—and they wouldn't have pushed him either—you think *anyone* can kill?—he had jumped and now he was letting go because he wanted to, that's all, and everything was all right and his knees weren't shaking any more, not that they had been shaking so much anyway, his knees weren't shaking any more because he was in command again—he hadn't noticed his right hand open but it must have opened because he was dropping into the heat, cables were shooting up, someone was screaming like Dorrie going into the shaft and Ellen when the first bullet wasn't enough—this person was screaming this godawful scream and suddenly it was himself and he couldn't stop! Why was he screaming? Why? Why on earth should he be—

The scream, which had knifed through the sudden stillness of the smelter, ended in a viscous splash. From the other side of the vat a sheet of green leaped up. Arcing, it sheared down to the floor where it splattered upon a million pools and droplets. They hissed softly on the cement and slowly dawned from green to copper.

15

KINGSHIP REMAINDED AT THE SMELTER. Gant accompanied Marion back to New York. In the plane they sat silent and immobile with the aisle between them.

After a while Marion took out a handkerchief and pressed it to her eyes. Gant turned to her, his face pale. "We only wanted

190

him to confess," he said defensively. "We weren't going to *do* it. And he *did* confess. What did he have to turn away like that for?"

The words took a long time to reach her. Almost inaudibly she said, "Don't . . ."

He looked at her downcast face. "You're crying," he told her gently.

She gazed at the handkerchief in her hands, saw the damp places in it. She folded it and turned to the window at her side. Quietly she said, "Not for him."

They went to the Kingship apartment. When the butler took Marion's coat—Gant kept his—he said, "Mrs. Corliss is in the living room."

"Oh God," Marion said.

They went into the living room. In the late afternoon sunlight, Mrs. Corliss was standing by a curio cabinet looking at the underside of a porcelain figurine. She put it down and turned to them. "So soon?" she smiled. "Did you enjoy—" She squinted through the light at Gant. "Oh, I thought you were . . ." She came across the room, peering beyond them into the empty hallway.

Her eyes returned to Marion. Her eyebrows lifted and she smiled.

"Where's Bud?" she asked.